THE 3 A.M. SHATTERED MUMS' CLUB

NINA MANNING

LON D1492849 NET

First published in Great Britain in 2022 by Boldwood Books Ltd.

Copyright © Nina Manning, 2022

Cover Design by Alice Moore Design

Cover Photography: Shutterstock

The moral right of Nina Manning to be identified as the author of this work has been asserted in accordance with the Copyright, Designs and Patents Act 1988.

All rights reserved. No part of this book may be reproduced in any form or by any electronic or mechanical means, including information storage and retrieval systems, without written permission from the author, except for the use of brief quotations in a book review.

This book is a work of fiction and, except in the case of historical fact, any resemblance to actual persons, living or dead, is purely coincidental.

Every effort has been made to obtain the necessary permissions with reference to copyright material, both illustrative and quoted. We apologise for any omissions in this respect and will be pleased to make the appropriate acknowledgements in any future edition.

A CIP catalogue record for this book is available from the British Library.

Paperback ISBN 978-1-80426-564-2

Large Print ISBN 978-1-80426-560-4

Hardback ISBN 978-1-80426-559-8

Ebook ISBN 978-1-80426-557-4

Kindle ISBN 978-1-80426-558-1

Audio CD ISBN 978-1-80426-565-9

MP3 CD ISBN 978-1-80426-562-8

Digital audio download ISBN 978-1-80426-556-7

Boldwood Books Ltd
23 Bowerdean Street
London SW6 3TN
www.boldwoodbooks.com

For all the shattered mums. I see you.

1

SOPHY

It was precisely seventeen minutes past midnight on Friday, 15 February when Sophy finally lost all control of her bowels. It was less of a loosening – as she had been quietly advised by elder relatives who had been through labour before – and more of an anus explosion. The second of the two cheery-but-firm midwives who had arrived in Sophy's sitting room a few minutes before began the evacuation of the birthing pool, supporting Sophy as she hauled her leg over the side. Jeff, Sophy's boyfriend – who had been laid out with his neck against the lip of the birthing pool, his head flopped back, eyes shut and mouth slightly open, arms over the side as though he were in a hot tub in a Cotswold's holiday cottage – shot out of the water at lightning speed. The water changed to a muddy brown just as Sophy was lifted out and onto the sofa.

Baby Max was delivered half an hour later, along with what the midwife referred to as 'a teeny wee tear'. As Sophy lay still and somewhat shocked on the sofa the midwife tacking her perineum back together, she was certain she heard Jeff whisper,

'Make sure to get it all nice and tight,' but Sophy had inhaled a whole tank of gas and air and had probably imagined it.

Finally, thirteen hours after her first contraction, Sophy was propped up in bed wearing the biggest knickers she had ever owned, stuffed to the breaches with a pad the size of a toddler's mattress, and holding her brand-new son.

Yesterday, she was Sophy West, a thirty-three-year-old social-media influencer and health guru.

Today, she was a mother.

* * *

'Hey there, healthy bods! It's Sophy, still here with loads of fab tips for you on staying fit and healthy, even though I just pushed a whopper out of my nether regions just over two weeks ago. Yes, it wasn't glamorous, and it hurt more than I believed any of you said it would. We have had a gorgeous couple of weeks cosied up in the house, just me, Max and Jeff, and now I'm ready to start whipping your butts back into shape.

'You might think that as soon as you give birth to that beautiful doe-eyed replica of yourself, all the healthy-eating regime must go out of the window, but believe me, there is a way to keep it up. It's called stamina. Think of those shiny abs and bulging biceps you worked so hard to achieve, you must KEEP. IT. UP.

'Listen, I know how hard it is and my life has just got a whole lot harder, as I now have a tiny baby that is literally sucking the life out of me and so I am going to have to work extra hard. But I'm doing it for you guys because I love you and you have totally been there for me all through this pregnancy with your tips and just general bump love. I'm not going to be one of those mums who post endless pics of their baby either. Max may make a cameo appearance from time to time in these vlogs, but basically, it's just me and you guys. And you know what? After what I have just been through, I know we are stronger than we ever consider ourselves to be, so put that bread-bin lid back on and push the cookies to the back of the cupboard. Seek out your quinoa, fresh veg, nut butter and bags of almonds, cos I'm back and I'm ready to give you all the help you need to maintain that perfect bod. Mwwaaahh!'

Sophy blew a kiss at the camera, then let out a huge sigh. She rubbed at her face where she had applied flawless make-up just an hour earlier and pulled off the pink sports leggings that were digging into her sides. She looked at the red marks they had left behind around her waist and hips – two areas of her body she barely recognised any more – and walked away from the corner of the bedroom she had transformed into a vlogging area. The bedroom was her space, and as much as Jeff constantly griped at how cluttered it felt, he only occupied it to pass out at the end of the day and had never participated in any of the decor and certainly none of the cleaning, so she felt he didn't have any right to comment.

Sophy flopped onto the bed in her huge knickers which were still stuffed with a heavy flow maternity pad. The healing process was taking much longer than she had anticipated. She had imagined she would be back to her old self by now, going for long walks with Max wrapped up in his pram, then returning pink-cheeked and glowing with maternal vitality. Not still be wincing every time she coughed, or better still, not having to pee in the bath with the shower head spraying between her legs to stop the burning sting.

She remembered an image she had seen on Facebook a few months back of an old school friend posing in front of a Silver Cross grey pram with the beach in the background. The picture had been captured by her husband and below it he had written: 'Just three days after giving birth – what a woman!'

'That will be me!' Sophy had announced to Jeff as she had shown him the picture and caption. And she had truly believed it.

'One hundred per cent, babes,' Jeff had said back to her.

Surely, Sophy thought, she should be up and about by now, fourteen days after having Max? But she was still finding it hard to move around the bedroom, let alone lug a pram up and down a promenade and pose for photos. Why weren't things turning out as she had imagined? This was not how it was supposed to be.

Sophy looked back over at the camera and realised she hadn't turned it off and the back light was still glaring at her. She used it to highlight the expensive flamboyant wallpaper she had chosen to decorate that one wall; her wall. The one wall that made it look as though she were in a separate room – an office maybe – and not in one of only two bedrooms in this tiny, terraced house in Clapham. She hauled herself up again, flicked the photography lamp off and put the camera on the bed – two pieces of equipment that had set her back a fair bit and had spurred Jeff to mention the price once or twice. Funny how he never complained about the holiday to Barbados they went on last year that was gifted to them by a nutrition company in exchange for a week's worth of stories and posts as part of a promotion. That was when Max was conceived. Up until then, Sophy had been struggling. She had been off the pill since her thirty-first birthday, but to no avail. She was just on the verge of going to get herself checked out when the holiday happened and boom, she was pregnant.

'I knew the bloody swimmers weren't dud! Get in!' were Jeff's congratulatory words when she had shown him the test that read 'two–three weeks pregnant'.

Sophy pulled off her vest, slipped into a cosy white cotton T-shirt and crawled onto the bed. It was just after 7 p.m. and Max had been asleep for over an hour. Who knew when he would wake up again for a feed? She was exclusively breastfeeding. She hated using that term, but so many people had asked her if she would be bottle-feeding soon. Well, she said *people*, but it was mainly Wendy, Jeff's mother who wanted to 'have a go' and had begun extolling her grandmotherly powers of getting a baby to take a whole bottle in one go. Sophy knew that if there was one thing she would be doing, it was going to be breastfeeding Max until he could hold a spoon in his hand and feed himself.

Sophy began editing the video in a sleep-blurred haze, expertly snipping out the *um*s and *err*s and pauses until it was flawless and the perfect length for her fans to engage with. She had only posted a couple of pictures of Max since he had been born, and already she had begun to feel the panic at what might happen to her account if she didn't keep up with content. She had made a huge effort to make herself look good for the video, even though she was practically shaking with tiredness. She would use the Insta stories, because she knew all the other influencers were using them, but she was still so nervous on social media that she felt better when she had edited a video. That way she had total control.

Sophy packed the camera and laptop and stowed it away in the corner of the room, took a peep in the baby bedside crib at a still-sleeping Max, then climbed into bed, pulled herself under the duvet and closed her eyes. Just as she was about to fall off the ledge of consciousness into the land of sleep, Max let out a tiny mewl that grew rapidly into a fully fledged wail. Sophy sat up and pulled Max from his SnuzPod – a device that had prompted Wendy to ask Sophy what exactly 'co-sleeping' was. In her day, babies were put in their beds and expected to sleep, and it didn't do them any harm. At which point, Sophy had looked over towards Jeff, who had been pointing his camera phone at his face in one hand, stroking his hair back with the other, whilst walking backwards towards the best light and nearly tripped over the laundry basket.

Sophy felt melancholy flood her body as she lifted her T-shirt and pulled a heavy, swollen breast from her maternity bra. She felt her whole body go tense as she looked down at Max, his tiny mouth in an O-shape ready to receive his meal. He had no idea the amount of pain he inflicted on her for those few short minutes until he latched on properly and they both fell into a flow. And she was so tired. She jolted as the tiny slithers of panic jabbed at her. How would she function again tomorrow? She took a deep breath and winced at the pain as Max greedily attached himself to her nipple. She thought this right one had started to heal, but judging by the needle-like shots that pulsated through her body and made her toes curl, causing a small yelp to escape her lips, she realised it was not the case. How on earth was she supposed to get used to this level of abuse? And would it ever stop hurting?

Eventually, Max latched on properly and the pain began to subside. Sophy felt her toes uncurling and her stomach muscles relax. This was the part she enjoyed, one of the little parts of the process of motherhood that she looked forward to. She wouldn't tell that to Jeff, though. For some unfathomable reason, Sophy felt she needed to make Jeff feel that breastfeeding was a massive inconvenience and that he had not helped out once with a feed. Jeff's response was of complete bewilderment.

'What do you want me to do, babes? Grow a pair of knockers?' So, a couple of days after Max had been born, which had felt like a year, Sophy decided to give her brand-new super turbo-powered breast pump a go. But nothing would bring the milk on like Max's latch, and so all Sophy had been left with was a sore breast and a dribble of milk. Jeff had given her a wide-eyed look, trying to offer up sympathy, but it came across more as 'I told you so.' Once Sophy had hurled the turbo breast pump with all its wires and bits still attached towards Jeff's head – where it missed and hit the bedroom wall – she decided to focus on breastfeeding Max by herself. Everything else in her world felt so out of control, and this was the one thing she could take ownership of. No one else could do it and Max needed her.

* * *

A few hours later, Sophy woke to Max trying to latch on again, she pulled him closer and relaxed into the feed. Or at least she tried to relax through the tornado of sound that was abusing her ears. She turned her head and looked at Jeff, who was lying flat on his back, snoring. She hadn't heard him come to bed, but now Max had woken her – maybe it was Jeff's snoring that had woken Max – she was sure she wouldn't be able to get back to sleep.

After he had finished feeding, Sophy lay there for what felt like ages, trying to get back to sleep, occasionally nudging Jeff so he would quieten for a few moments, only for him only to begin his incessant snoring again seconds later.

Eventually, she began to feel sick from tiredness and weak from lack of nourishment. She had done two big feeds in four hours, which was the equivalent to a massive workout, surely? Sophy tucked Max safely into his pod, slipped her feet into her fluffy slippers and padded downstairs. The clock on the digital oven blinked *03.02*. Sophy felt a surge of panic – she'd experienced it a lot lately. Why was she up at this time? Max would be awake again in a few hours and then she had all the housework to do, washing, shopping, and the endless sitting with Max as he stayed awake during the day for what felt like hours sometimes. He would only ever catnap throughout the day, leaving her very little time to do anything for herself, let alone more content for her social media.

Jeff would leave at seven thirty in the morning as usual to go to work at the estate agent's he had owned for over a decade now, Haddon's – aptly named after himself – then he wouldn't be back until gone 6 p.m. Over ten hours by herself. She was always desperately grateful when he returned, armed with pad Thai takeaway or curry. Then she hated herself for how she followed him around the house, Max in her arms, whilst he unwound, removing layers, setting the food out, pouring himself his nightly gin and tonic that might or might not turn into three or four, which would bring on immediate comatose. He would then wake in the early hours, drag himself to bed and proceed to snore for the rest of the night. There was only one other room in the house, which was Max's nursery, so there was nowhere else she could sleep, unless she bunked down on the floor there. It was a beautiful room and very inviting, with a big white cot and light grey walls. There were splashes of colour in the form of a rainbow-shaped rug, a few colourful prints of animals and a blue blanket draped along the back of the cot. Max had yet to lie in this one – Sophy couldn't bring herself to put him in it. Besides, Max only wanted to be close to her, rarely anyone else. Jeff would take Max off Sophy's hands for an hour each night whilst she went off and had a bath and painted her nails. No matter how tired she was, she had to keep up some level of maintenance. And she knew it wasn't just for her own benefit. Jeff had made a passing comment just before Max was born about mums who lost a bit of themselves after having their babies. 'Although I'm sure that isn't going to be you, babes. You'll always look hot,' he had added afterwards.

But the only 'hot' Sophy felt, was the hormonal kind: hot flushes through the night and any time she was trying to get Max ready, herself dressed or pack a bag. Last week, she had broken out in a full-body sweat trying to get into a bag of Kettle chips, followed by both of her breasts soaking her top with milk that was due for Max, who had slept for three hours straight. Much to Jeff's amusement and her mortification. It had set her back for the rest of the day.

Sophy had begun to feel as if it wasn't just Max who had been extracted from her on the day she'd given birth, but a huge part of herself had slipped out too, and she felt daily as if she were looking around and searching for it. She had heard of mothers missing their bumps after the baby was born, but Sophy missed who she had been. She had this constant overbearing sense that she had forgotten to do something, and even though she had hours each day to sit and just be with Max, she struggled to do that. In order to push away that feeling, she tried to achieve something unrelated to motherhood every day, which was why she was back uploading content, even though Max was only a couple of weeks old. She felt as though she was missing out; if she didn't keep going, she would get left behind. It wasn't that she had itchy feet to be back to work – her mind was already full with everything that Max needed from her – but she would get moments of panic. What if everyone forgot about her and all her followers left? She knew that being Max's mum was supposed to be enough for now. But she was thirty-three, if she stopped and let the world pass her by, she could become a has-been before she knew it. She had to crack on and be the mum that managed it all. Everyone would look up to her and say how amazing she looked, how well her business was doing. She already had 135,000 followers on Instagram – she couldn't lose them because she felt a bit tired or a bit vacant that day.

As she pottered about the kitchen, she thought about making some toast and marmalade, and then she thought of the calories that she would put on as a result and decided to forget about the snack for now. She would make some healthy porridge with fruit and seeds for breakfast. She could style it up and a take a photo of it for feed, give her followers a little boost in the right direction; after all, they followed her for a reason. Then she would get Max dressed up in that gorgeous snow suit that her mum had sent and do a flat lay of him in it, then post that. She knew that would bring in a few thousand likes. If she could achieve those two things tomorrow, it would give her a sense of accomplishment. A warm feeling unfurled inside her stomach at the prospect, but it didn't evolve into the full wave of happiness she had expected.

Although she had forgone the toast, she was still craving it, so decided to curb her pangs with a cuppa. She flicked the kettle on and pulled out a Pukka teabag. She imagined Jeff would still be snoring his head off, and although she could just move her and Max into the nursery, she knew it would be a slippery slope to a relationship counsellor. They weren't married as it was, but now Max was here, surely that was all the glue they needed to bind them together as a family.

The kettle finished boiling, and Sophy stood next to the island in the immaculate white and grey kitchen. *Jeff's* immaculate white and grey kitchen. Sophy was now the mother of his son, and although they had been together for four years and were a couple living together, she wondered at times if she wasn't much more than a housemate with added benefits. But she knew that thinking those thoughts wasn't helpful, because it was three o'clock in the morning, and that was never the time to start analysing your life. She dunked her teabag, staring at the clock on the oven, which now read *03.10*, but she wished it was later as she was struck by an overwhelming sense of loneliness. She wished more than anything there was someone she could call or text at this time of the morning, but it was just her, and that made Sophy feel sadder than she had ever felt.

2

AISHA

Why did she always feel in a rush when there was nothing to do except sit around and feed the twins all day? Over the last few weeks, there had been a rash of visitors all day long, so maybe that was it. Having given birth to twins six weeks ago, meant Aisha had seen every member of her family, including her two older sisters, Carmel and Laila, her cousins, Ruben and Marcel. Even her best friend from school, who now lived up north, had made the effort to come down and visit, but Claire's reaction to the mass of dirty nappies, piles of bottles and alarming tones of dual cries from the two tiny helpless infants – and the way she had hurried out of the door after just one hour – made Aisha realise that Claire would not be making the trip back down from Hebden Bridge any time soon. One regular visitor, however, was Aisha's mother, Martina, who had been coming over almost every day with Tupperwares loaded with her grandmother's recipe of jerk chicken, rice and peas, plus extra treats and bags of fruit and nuts. Aisha had been eating spicy food since she could first put a fork to her mouth, and because of her mum's Jamaican roots, she had craved it by the bucketload when she got pregnant, and it hadn't let up since.

Aisha heard the familiar three-rap knock on the front door, and even though her mum had a key 'for emergencies', she never used it. Aisha was completely at ease with her own mother letting herself in, especially now she was trying to juggle twin babies – in fact, it was often quite an inconvenience to have to get up mid-feeds, or when she was trying to rest – but Aisha understood why her mum insisted on knocking. Although she was fully supportive of Aisha's choice to settle and live with a woman and always included Charley, Aisha wasn't sure she was as comfortable with it as she made out. She referred to Aisha and Charley's life as 'the set-up', which to Aisha made it sound temporary; like Charley was a pop-up lesbian, only here for a short while, then she would be gone. But Charley was the other mother to the twins: Otis and Jude. Of course, they had come from Aisha's egg – artificially inseminated – so there was nothing biological linking Charley to the boys. Therefore, she could see her mother's anxieties about the lack of a conventional, genetic bond in the relationship. But then there was nothing simple about Aisha's whole life, and so Aisha wondered if that was why somewhat traditional Martina was still not entirely comfortable talking about Aisha's loving and long-term relationship, only referring to Charley as her daughter's girlfriend every once in a while. The knocking was because Martina was terrified of walking in on something. What exactly that 'something' was at this stage in the 'set-up' with twin babies, Aisha really couldn't fathom.

Both boys were lying on their backs in the Moses baskets they kept in the sitting room. Their olive-toned skin and dark eyes captivated visiting midwives, who always asked about their heritage. With a pure Jamaican mother and a white British father, and now a white British girlfriend, Aisha knew she would have to be answering such questions for the foreseeable future.

Martina's repeated three-rap knock brought Aisha out of her daydream, as she had been lying on the sofa and had almost nodded off completely again. Martina never rang the doorbell, which was another consideration on Aisha's mother's part, this time for the babies, who, despite being more than used to the noise that went on in the house day and night, Martina believed would awaken at the loud trill. Charley wrote jingles in the converted basement, so there was always music playing and plenty of people arriving day and night. Charley's home-based work also meant that Aisha had an extra pair of hands, should she need to ask. Although she rarely did. Charley had taken a couple of weeks off in the beginning, but now, six weeks in, it was just Aisha, and these regular visits from her mum. Aisha was trying to get used to doing things on her own, but in these recent weeks, she had never been more grateful that Martina lived just over a mile away.

'So, girl, what's happening?' All five foot eleven inches of Martina stepped into the hallway as her daughter opened the door. She wiped her feet, took her coat off and hung it neatly on the coat stand. She patted the tight curls that she liked to wear short these days. A few beads of sweat were glistening around Martina's forehead, and for some reason, Aisha thought of a halo of an angel.

Aisha realised she was staring at her mum when Martina asked again what was happening... Maybe a few months ago, Aisha would have some bit of news or gossip that she could have shared with her mum, and they could have gnawed over it together for half an hour, but the fact that Aisha had barely even walked down the street in the last six weeks meant that she had nothing of value to bring to her mother's attention. Well, nothing that she felt she wanted to share with her right now, knowing it would only worry her.

Martina had her bag by her feet. It was always packed with goodies for Aisha's house that Martina had picked up at the Jamaican store in town – those shops were one of the reasons Aisha was glad her mum had remained in Brixton and not followed her to Clapham. Martina was part of a strong community back in Brixton, and Aisha would hate for her mother to be without it. Aisha looked longingly at the bag, which she knew Martina would unpack later in the kitchen, giving Aisha a full inventory as she did so, but for now, she would want to see the twins.

'Oh, Mum. Nothing is happening. We're in the fourth trimester – I told you, we're just chilling.'

Martina, who was almost as broad as she was tall, also had a large chest, which had nursed three babies of her own, Aisha included, and two nephews. Aisha felt her mother's ample bosom brush against her shoulder as she squeezed past her in the tiny hallway, and it only served to remind her of her own failures as a mother because she had not been able to breastfeed the twins. Martina squeezed Aisha's shoulder on her way past into the lounge, as though she could read her thoughts. She left behind her the strong smell of her vanilla perfume, and it took Aisha back to a memory of years before when her mum was standing at the stove stirring vanilla custard at their small house in Brixton when she was about ten years old. It was a bittersweet memory, because it had also been only a few hours before that her father had left, on the premise of going out to grab the morning paper. Martina had looked at the clock all day, wringing a tea towel between her hands. Eventually, she had pulled out a huge pot, filled it with two pints of milk and Bird's custard powder and began stirring.

With the smell of vanilla custard lingering in the hallway whenever Martina arrived, Aisha was perpetually reminded of her father leaving. A strange dichotomy she had yet to overcome.

Martina strode boldly into the lounge. Aisha's house was such a contrast to the squashed, busy Brixton house that had smelled constantly of cinnamon, sugar and chips – the sort of smell you got at a fairground. There had been a lot of frying in their kitchen when Aisha was young. Growing up around so much food and then working in restaurants her whole life, it was a wonder she wasn't as big as a house. Aisha's three-bedroom home was also a terrace – she had still wanted to feel the intimacy of neighbours on either side – but without the busy feel of her cousins and neighbours' kids trawling in and out all day. Aisha had done each room immaculately in Farrow & Ball paint and quirky wallpaper, which had made Martina do a funny squinting thing with her eye. All the floorboards were salvaged wood and were covered with giant rugs, and original fireplaces adorned the two reception rooms. Aisha was proud of the work she had done, with the help of a friend from uni who ran his own decorating business. It had been the huge distraction she'd needed after she finished at the Greek restaurant where she had been the manager before she took maternity leave. Whenever Aisha felt bereft and out of control, she cast her mind back to the process of decorating each room over the course of those weeks, then she felt calm again. She tried not to dwell too much on how good she had felt having that project to pour all her energy into. It had been so satisfying because even though she had been heavily pregnant and unable to settle well at night, the days were filled with tasks that could get ticked off so she could see the final results.

She wished she could feel the same sense of satisfaction when she was with her sons, but there was no final goal in sight, and by midday she always felt as though she were ready to just write the day off.

Aisha had the blinds closed over slightly; it had been another lazy morning that may have turned into a lazy afternoon had Martina not shown up.

'What, you mean, "doin' nothin'"? When I was your age, I had three of you running around, plus your cousins, and what's this fourth tri—whacha keep callin' it?' Martina said firmly but in a hushed tone in case the boys were sleeping. Which they weren't. They were ready for a feed.

Aisha blew out a breath, picked up Otis out of his Moses basket. She could tell the difference between the two instantly, even when they were sleeping, because Otis's eyes sloped more at the edges, whereas Jude's were slightly rounder.

'Fourth *trimester*, Mum. It means for the first few months of a baby's life, they still think they are in the womb, so we're trying to replicate that feeling of just being here with them.'

'I see, just a shame you couldn't give them your own milk.'

Aisha looked down solemnly. She had desperately wanted to try breastfeeding, there was no denying that, but the second the babies slid out of her, she panicked. And then the juggling of the two of them just didn't come as naturally as she had hoped. And then the milk just wouldn't come. She was still mourning the loss of what could have been a beautiful journey, and now hid behind the excuse that she and Charley wanted the feeding of the babies to be a shared experience.

'But, that's something I can say I did not do – two at once! You be fine, girl – bottle not gonna do the babies no harm, neither.' Aisha accepted the half compliment; she knew it was the best she would get from her mother, hardened by the sudden disappearance of her father and raising of her own babies and two of her sisters' babies alone. Martina's sister, Lula had suffered 'the darkness' after her babies were born; a common mental state of mind amongst many of the mothers in Brixton. Luckily, in a tight-knit community, there were always women like Martina to step in – someone who was already suffering her own loss and tragedy somehow drew from her reserves to help. When Martina was doing such a selfless act for others, it would have been heartless for Aisha to try to explain to her mum how she had felt back then. How a sort of gaping hole had opened up where the extra time for cuddles and listening had been handed over to her auntie's children, and without a father to step in, it hadn't closed. But she had grown up to love those children like her own brothers, so Aisha could never complain of being lonely in that sense. It was a different sort of loneliness she had experienced then, and one that still seeped through now and then. But she didn't want to talk to either Charley or Martina about how that strange nagging feeling in the pit of her tummy she experienced as a child – when she had worried constantly since the day her father had left – was back.

And the reason she didn't want to mention it was because she didn't understand it. It was clear why she had those feelings back then – Martina's time and patience were suddenly stretched from three kids to five overnight. But this feeling, here, now, didn't make sense. It wasn't in the right context for a start. Where was the real fear factor? She had Charley, who adored her and the boys, a mum, who may have been strict when they were young, but was trying to make up for it now with her time and love for her grandsons. The house she and Charley had bought was all finished, so even when there was a certain amount of mess in the house, it didn't look too grim against the backdrop of the smart walls and minimal furniture. There was nothing – other than the incessant wails of two babies that generally needed tending to at the same time, day and night – that should be stressing her out.

Charley had said if things began to feel as though they were getting on top of her, she would organise a cleaner to come over. *A cleaner?* Aisha had thought. She wasn't sure that someone dusting around her and the boys would help with the tightening of her gut. So why, with pretty much all the boxes ticked, did she sometimes feel as though she was about to topple off the edge of the world?

Aisha pulled Otis onto her lap and picked up one of the bottles she had warmed and brought through earlier.

Jude began his soft mewling, which intensified with every second.

Martina began talking softly to Jude, and Aisha watched in wonder as he seemed to become hypnotised by Martina's voice, which had now morphed into a sweet lullaby. Jude's calming synched with the end of Otis's feed and so the two women made the seamless transaction of the twins so Aisha could begin feeding Jude. She was slowly but surely getting used to managing everything by herself, with only a little bit of help from her mum. She would do this feed, maybe have a little tidy-up and make her and her mum a coffee, then it would be time to do it all again.

Jude began sucking furiously on the bottle as Aisha stared off into the distance and heard her mother's voice.

'You gettin' enough sleep, girl?'

Aisha pulled herself away from the glare of the window and looked at her mum, who now appeared to have a streak of white across her face from the sun that was caught in Aisha's eyes.

She let out a small sigh. 'I have six-week-old twins, Mum. There's no such thing as "enough sleep" right now.'

'Well, if you say so, but what with your modern set-up and all, I figure you girls would have had something sorted. I can't imagine it's like it was when you were young, with your father sleeping all day on his days off. I s'pose you get the help?'

Aisha felt Martina had done well to have accepted Charley as her partner, even if she did insist on referring to it by her little phrase. But there was still something missing. Aisha didn't feel that Martina had fully embraced Charley in the same the way that her sisters' boyfriends had been welcomed into the family. She hoped more than anything that now they were both mothers to Jude and Otis that Martina might find it in herself to be a little more unguarded around Charley.

'Charley has a job, an important one, with deadlines. She helps in the night sometimes, but she has to be up early and at work. She's with me and the boys all weekend.' Aisha heard how pathetic she sounded. She had hoped that Charley would be spending a bit more time with her during the week, but she retreated to her studio pretty quickly after the statutory parental leave was over, even though she was self-employed and could make up the rules as she went. Aisha could barely remember the conversation they'd had about when Aisha would be left with the twins for the majority of the time, since each day had become a blur, and being able to keep her eyes even half open during the day had become such an enormous effort in itself.

Aisha also neglected to mention the part about Charley moving into the spare room these last two evenings. Since the boys had become a little more vocal at night-time, Charley had said it was easier if she wasn't there, so she didn't disturb their night feeds. But Aisha wondered whether it was more that the disturbed nights were throwing Charley's creativity out the window, and concentrating in the studio was a priority. The thought made her shudder, and she wondered if all those months spent discussing Aisha getting pregnant, something, somewhere had got lost in translation. This wasn't how she had anticipated spending her life, and not the image she had conjured up when she and Charley began discussing starting a family over two years ago. Pacing the room alone in the small hours, trying to cradle two tiny babies to her chest, had been an entirely different picture in her mind less than two months ago.

But Martina was here now, and both boys were fed and asleep in the Moses baskets. Both women looked at them for a few seconds. Aisha wished they would just stay this still and quiet for a few hours, but that was not going to be. She knew she had maybe half an hour before one of them woke.

'Let's put that kettle on and I'll show you all them goodies.' Martina brought the enthusiasm for both of them, but as she followed her mother through into the kitchen, Aisha felt the strange sensation dragging behind her like a heavy iron anchor.

3

MEL

Her face burned. Her whole body shook. Mel couldn't believe what had just happened. She wanted to get home, but Skylar had begun screaming for her feed, and so the bench just in front of her would have to do. As she sat down, the rage bubbled up inside her.

'Bess, get here,' she called to the lanky black Labrador. She was only three years old and still acted like a puppy at times. Except for today, when she had reminded Mel that she was a guard dog as well. Skylar had been strapped to her chest and Bess had been walking ahead, sniffing out something on Wandsworth Common, when a small dog – Mel had no clue what kind. It just fell into the silly, small dog category that she detested so much – had approached Bess, barking and yapping the way they do. Bess had snapped at it, and Mel had been ready to begin the usual jovialities about the dogs not taking a liking to one another and maybe theirs was having a bad day (she always liked to pin the blame, however subtly, on the small dog). But on this occasion, Mel was pipped to the post by the dog's owner, who began laying into her, telling her that *her* animal was a beast and that her little

Minky (Minky?!) had been savagely attacked. Mel hadn't hesitated in correcting her that, in actual fact, it was *her* dog's aggressive behaviour that had riled up Bess and made her let out a warning growl. There had been a few profanities (from Mel's end) and some stick waving (also Mel's end), until finally the woman began to retreat, but not before Mel had reached the crescendo of obscenities and hurled the C-word at her. Its crudeness rang out loud and shrill in the woods, and even the trees, swaying in the wind, seemed to whistle their disappointment back at her.

So, there she sat. Angry at first, but the anger was slowly making way for the disappointment that now replaced the heavy weight of Skylar on her chest. She pulled out a bottle from her backpack and popped it into Skylar's mouth, the silence was golden. Or it would have been if Mel couldn't hear the echoes of the blasphemy reverberating in the air around her. She was the world's worst mum. Skylar hadn't even reached three months, and she had already heard *that* word. Mel had been so relaxed for the last eleven weeks since Skylar arrived in between an episode of *The Chase* and *The Martin Lewis Money Show* (which Mel had really wanted to watch because it was the one with the top tips on how to spend well in the new year), but now she could feel the stress and the anger creeping back in. And now that she had dropped the C-bomb, she knew she was slowly coming out of the shell she had been cocooning with Skylar in for the last three months. The babymoon was officially over.

Skylar finished her bottle, and Mel rearranged her into the front carrier, a little skew-whiff, but it didn't matter because Skylar would be asleep in seconds and home was only round the corner.

They ambled back along the common until Mel rounded the corner into Fern Drive – a neat row of four-bedroom terraced houses. Hers was at the very end of the long avenue dappled with trees. She had fallen on her feet, she thought whenever she arrived home, even after ten years of living here. Her husband, Daz, sticking in the same job for twenty years and the few thousand gifted for the deposit from his parents meant they were paying a tiny mortgage, which was great at a time when Mel couldn't go out and work.

She shuffled into the hallway with Bess in tow and dropped her keys on the table by the door. She went straight upstairs and eased Skylar out of her carrier and straight into her cot in one swift movement. Skylar barely flinched. It was a skill she had perfected when she had her first child eleven years ago. Leia was now at secondary school, had TikTok and therefore considered herself practically self-sufficient. But Mel had to keep her head about her, so she could keep checking in on Leia and not be that mum who has a baby and totally forgets she has another child. Leia was at such a sensitive, tricky age. Girls definitely grew up too fast these days, and as Leia practically passed for a teenager, Mel seemed to spend more time worrying about her than Skylar.

She had been sure she was done with one child. Both she and Daz had agreed; they both loved their careers and their lives, and one would suffice. It took them until they were thirty-two to have Leia, and then eleven years later, Mel had a meltdown when she realised that she may never experience giving birth or cuddling her own baby again. They agreed they would casually try – but Mel timed it exactly right and worked out when she would next be ovulating, but still figured she was probably too old now and nothing would happen. The next month, Mel held a positive pregnancy stick under Daz's nose and they both shook their heads in disbelief. 'Basically, I have been this walking fertile creature all this time, think how many kids we could have now?' she said, and they laughed at the prospect. Although the risks of the pregnancy going wrong were higher, because Mel was a 'geriatric' mother, as the doctor had dubbed her, her job as a professional singer and burlesque dancer meant she had always kept herself fit and healthy; she had done HIIT training and yoga right up until Skylar was born. Although she hadn't been on stage for many months. In fact, Mel realised, it was coming up for a year since she had last been in a club performing, even though she had planned to keep singing right up until the baby was born. *It's funny how life has other plans*, Mel recollected as the thought of the last night she had been performing in the club made her shudder.

Many remarked that Mel looked at least ten years younger than her forty-three years. And she felt it. So far things had been going really well in the baby department. Skylar slept well, fed even better and was basically a dream child. Mel had even managed to fit a little exercise in. She had begun to think about the stage again, but with mixed feelings. She missed it, and she knew her clients had missed her too – Robbie from The East End Club had been messaging her since she left, saying how much he was mourning his star act – but she was still nursing the wound of the last night at the club. Soon, she would need to start thinking about getting some gigs booked in, but the slight flutter of terror she felt when she thought about being on the stage again, made her feel as though everything was spinning out of control. And it was something she was trying very hard not to think about. *Just focus on the positives, Mel. It was a one-off. That was all.* But a one-off that had knocked the confidence out of her.

The house was quiet when Mel came downstairs. She pulled her mass of hair – which Daz referred to as her 'mane' – into a messy bun on top of her head. She made herself a cafetière of coffee and flipped her laptop open.

And there they were: unopened emails from her local haunts enquiring when they could start booking her in for gigs again.

There were emails from pub and club landlords looking to get her to perform her Adele tribute and also to perform burlesque dancing – her two most popular acts. Both brought her a tidy salary that almost rivalled Daz's accountant wage.

She scrolled through a couple of the emails, took a deep breath and bashed out a quick reply to them to say she might be ready by April onwards and could they please consider pencilling her in for now. She could always back out at the last minute, because there it was again: the panic. Was she really ready? She needed to just get over her worries and start seeing it as something to look forward to. Although Mel had been thoroughly enjoying her time with Skylar, she needed to get a little bit of herself back, for her own sanity. And Skylar slept so well in the evenings, she knew Daz would have no problems whilst she was out at work.

Mel was just about to close down her inbox when she spotted another email that she'd almost missed amongst all the work emails that had been stacking up. It was from Daz's mother, Irene. Mel's own mother had passed away when she was twenty-one. It had almost destroyed her and made her turn to drink and drugs, but then she found her voice and began to appreciate dance, round about the same time she met Daz. The combination of the three was what saved her.

So Irene had become more than just Daz's mother to her and Mel considered herself *very* lucky to have found a friend in Irene.

She usually emailed at least once a day, even though she lived a fifteen-minute drive away. She never just turned up either. She always called – never texted – first to make sure it was a convenient time for her to drop in. And she was helpful, in a proper way, not in a thinks-she's-trying-to-be-helpful way: washing up and then putting everything back in the wrong cupboards, or saying 'I'll hold the baby for you' whilst you cook tea, only for the baby to scream the entire time, causing you to burn said tea and then end up not eating anything because the baby then needs a forty-five-minute comfort to get over the trauma. Irene was a godsend, if Mel was being honest, and she quite often quipped to many that if she was forced to choose between saving Daz and Irene in a fire, she would choose Irene. She would neglect saying that there would be no hesitation whatsoever.

Irene had sent through her usual daily meme, and then below it a short message and a picture attachment.

Hi Mel,

Hope you and little Sky are doing well today. Here is an ad for a mums' group not far from you, and I wondered if it was something you might fancy? I know you always said you despised the damn things, but this looks like a small group and she does hand massages and tai chi, which is definitely up your street.

Anyway, the truth is, she's the daughter of a friend, and I said I would try to support her. Maybe pop along once, show your face, and if it's too awful, you never have to go back again. Anyway, I was thinking of popping in on Saturday – Mike has a big golf tournament and I'm at a loose end. Let me know.

Love, Irene x

Mel found herself smiling as she always did, reading Irene's notes. She was a kind woman – proper salt of the earth, some people might say. She had done so much for Mel over the years, even back in the day when Mel and Daz were courting and Mel would cause quite a stir with some of her night-time outfits and then come falling through Irene's front door at all hours of the morning, still singing and clomping about in her heels, whilst Daz tried to hush her. Irene didn't tell her off, but would come down, put the kettle on, get Mel settled with a cup of tea and get her talking about her night until she was so tired she almost passed out on the kitchen table. Then Irene would flip out the sofa bed – as no one was strong enough to carry Mel upstairs because Mel was and always had been, as Irene liked to refer to her as, 'a well-structured girl'– and she and Daz would guide her into the lounge where she would sleep in until midday, with everyone else creeping around her. Mel felt she owed so much to Irene, and yet Irene would say that Mel had given her everything she had ever needed by staying faithful to Daz, making him a happy man and bringing her and Mike grandchildren.

Mel messaged back to say she would pop along with Skylar to the baby group, even though the thought of it might bring her out in hives. She could dance around in a skimpy outfit to complete strangers or belt out an Adele number to a room full of corporates, but put her in a room with a bunch of other mums and expect her to talk about weaning, naps and which bottle teat works best for acid reflux and she wanted to run for the hills. But she knew she had to do this for her beloved mother-in-law, although she was positive that a poxy hand massage and some badly choreographed tai chi were not going to convince her to become a regular customer. She was just fine as she was, with her perfect little baby. She didn't need anyone.

4

SOPHY

Sophy wasn't sure how she found herself miles away from home, outside a small community hall on a dull March morning. Her friend Suzi had messaged her earlier in the week and asked her to come and support her at this new baby-group thing she was starting up. Hand massages and tai chi? Sophy wasn't sure it would catch on, but she was giving it a shot. Suzi was charging eight quid, which Sophy thought was a bit steep for women who were essentially knackered and just wanted a bit of peace and quiet. There had been a mention of nettle tea and slices of papaya but Sophy was craving a cup of PG Tips and a bourbon biscuit.

Although loath to admit to many these days, Sophy was from a working-class background, where a proper tea was chips, fish fingers, peas and beans, and dessert was a Battenberg cake or Angel Delight. As much as she had adapted well to her new middle-class life, she occasionally missed the simplicity she experienced when she was growing up. These days there was so much choice for everything, it made her head spin. She craved for the old days, when you could burn your skin in the sun without worrying you'd develop cancer, or not have to separate all your rubbish into six different compartments, complete with the fear of the neighbours banging on your door to give you a rollicking because they saw through their triple-glazed window that you hadn't washed that baked bean can out.

Suzi said she had made an organic banana loaf and the nettle tea was home-made. Sophy really didn't know who she had become. She enjoyed the thought of these things but she couldn't fight off the cravings for a Findus crispy pancake and had to chastise herself; remind herself those days were gone. She was above and beyond cheap convenience food. Jeff provided her with a home, a steady income, a car; they drank champagne on a Tuesday night for god's sake! They ate out three times a week – or at least they did before Max came along. Now it was takeaway. She was slowly building her Instagram account. Soon she would be able to support herself. Sometimes, she thought about her drive for independence, catching herself off guard with it, and wondered why she was so intent on needing to be self-sufficient when she had everything that she had ever dreamed of as a child. Why couldn't she just let Jeff – who was older than her by almost eight years – look after her? After all, that was all she had wanted when she met him. Wasn't it?

Sophy caught a figure approaching along the pavement out of the corner of her eye. She noted the double buggy and straight away felt a sense of competition creeping in. She had the upper hand; this poor woman had two babies, and she only had one. She could not even begin to imagine doing what she did with Max, twice over. Sophy physically shuddered at the prospect as the woman got closer. She put on her best 'mum' face, which was a small smile with a slight raise of the eyebrows. Such a subtle gesture that said so much: *You're a mum. I'm a mum. Here we are, then – being mums.*

The woman, gorgeously light-brown skinned with shoulder-length black ringlets, looked a similar age to Sophy – although it was hard to tell with all the layers on. She began fussing with her prams, pulling blankets that were already perfectly tightened and closing zips that were already fully fastened. Sophy felt obliged to speak. She had never struggled socially – 'a bit of a gobby cow' was how her mum would still refer to her, fifteen years after she moved out of the family home in Milton Keynes. She'd had to find her voice from a young age, what with three little brothers and an older sister to shout over. She had somehow managed to tone down her Midlands accent and adopted a softer, plumper tone, one that she found made people stop and look at her when she spoke.

'How is it with two?' Sophy said before she had time to think about what she was going to say. Already she regretted saying what was probably a cliché to someone with twins.

The woman stopped fussing with the plush grey prams that didn't look as if they had seen the light of day, and looked quizzically at Sophy, as though speaking to a stranger was an uncommon experience.

Sophy waited a beat, felt the old familiar dread in her pit of her stomach when a reply didn't come. Had she misread the situation? When you came from a family of five children, you just spoke when you needed to. Survival of the fittest. She spoke louder this time. 'The twins. I presume, there are two in there?' Sophy laughed to accentuate the lightness of her comment.

'Oh yes, there's definitely two of them.' The woman spoke. 'Are you...?' She looked towards the firmly closed door. 'Are you here for the mother-and-baby group?'

'Tai chi and tea!' Sophy scoffed. The woman looked perplexed. Sophy straightened her expression. 'I know the girl who is running the group. She's a bit eccentric. Doesn't even have kids of her own. Thinks she's just trying to make a quick buck out

of us tired and delirious mothers.' Sophy scoffed and immediately wished she could retract some of that information. She
owed Suzi a bit more than that to this stranger. Why did she insist
on just saying whatever popped into her head?

'Well, I suppose it's nice to be out.' The woman smiled.

Sophy smiled back. Max was beginning to fuss in his pram.
He was flat out on his back. It could be wind. But the day was
grey, and it had started to drizzle, so she didn't fancy getting him
out. She hoped he would go back off to sleep.

Sophy's phone let out a loud ping, notifying her of a text
message. She gave the woman an over-the-top look of shock, as
though getting a notification on her phone at 10.30 a.m. was quite
unusual.

'I'll just see who that is.' Sophy pulled her phone out of her
pocket and scoured the text for the part that was going to defuse
the rage that was building up inside her. 'Fuck's sake,' she
muttered under her breath.

The woman looked at her. 'Everything okay?'

Sophy pushed the phone back into her long black padded
coat, which was so cosy it could double up as a sleeping bag. In
fact, she had actually slept in it once, before she was pregnant
with Max, when she had been too drunk to leave a friend's house
who had been stingy with the central heating.

'That was our host, Suzi. She can't make it.' Sophy frowned at
her phone, still trying to accept she had made the effort to come
all this way for nothing.

'Oh,' the woman said. Sophy thought she saw a glimmer of
relief spread across her face. 'Well, I suppose these things
happen.'

'Oh, no, these sorts of things don't happen. Not to the
majority of the civilised population. They do, however, happen to
Suzi. She's injured her ankle giving her boyfriend a body massage

– apparently it was quite intensive. She could have been walking on him, or just slipped whilst applying pressure, who knows? I never do with Suzi. So the group is off today.'

'The group's off?' came a voice from behind them. They both spun round to see a tall woman with big hair in a messy topknot, arriving with a rainbow-coloured pram with such vigour that she had developed quite a sweat across her forehead.

'Er, yes, apologies sent from Suzi,' Sophy said.

'From your phone?' the sweating woman asked as she came to a standstill next to them.

'Yes. I know her.' Sophy wasn't sure this was something she wanted to admit to anyone any more. 'Do you? Know her?'

'I know *of* her,' the sweating woman said. 'My mother-in-law told me to come – she knows Suzi's mother. Said I'd do them a favour. Anyway, I rushed out of the house to get here and now I'm sweating bloody buckets.' She stooped and looked into the rainbow-clad pram. 'But it got her off like a charm,' she said breezily. She looked at Sophy and stretched out her hand. 'I'm Mel.'

'Oh.' Sophy flung her hand out. 'I'm Sophy.' Mel took it, and Sophy was taken aback by the strength of Mel's grip.

'And this is...?' Sophy paused and looked at the mum of the twins.

'I'm Aisha.' The mum came forward and held her hand out meekly.

Mel and Sophy took turns shaking. It all felt incredibly formal. Sophy wasn't sure why the handshaking had begun in the first place. She was a mum now. Didn't mums hug and kiss?

Maybe not when they don't know each other, Sophy thought. She was new to this game, after all.

'Right, well now we all know each other's names, and this Suzi has well and truly shafted us. I say we head to that café on the high street. I am gagging for a coffee.' Mel looked at them wide-eyed and expectant.

Sophy jumped into action. 'Right, yes, coffee, I'm up for that. Aisha?'

'Will there be room for a double buggy?' Aisha said uncertainly.

Mel pulled a face as if Aisha was clearly mad. 'Don't worry about that, love, we'll *make* room.'

* * *

When they arrived at the coffee shop, Mel helped Aisha through with her twin pram and the three women assessed the space. There were a couple of mums already cosied in a corner with their babies bouncing on their knees, and a young couple sat by the window.

'I say we claim that table.' Mel pointed to a large sofa, coffee table and two chairs. 'We can park the buggies round the corner.'

The three women began arranging themselves, nudging the coffee table to the edge of the window to make room for unbundling of coats and babies. Once they were all sat and settled, Sophy subtly eyed up the other two women. Mel was in good shape – very muscly, perhaps some sort of bodybuilder or gym instructor? Her initial thought was that she wouldn't want to get on the wrong side of her on a night out. Mel had stripped down to a loose grey vest top that exposed a bit of black lacy bra, habitat to an ample breast. Sophy thought the look slutty but stylish all at once. Mel had a tattoo on the top of one her arms and Sophy found herself drawn to the intricate design and Chinese writing that probably told a few tales about Mel.

Then Sophy watched as Aisha consciously removed her black raincoat and placed it carefully over the handles of the buggy.

She was wearing a white plain V-neck long-sleeved T-shirt and jeans. Mel looked across at her and let out a gasp.

'My god! Look at you! You pushed twins out a few weeks ago and you look like that? What's the secret? Good genes?' Mel laughed. 'Get it? Good genes, good jeans!'

Aisha looked immediately uncomfortable and took a moment to adjust her top whilst the joke sunk in. She let out a meek smile.

'I don't think so – I feel flabby still. I am back in my old jeans, but I don't feel like my old self.'

'You won't, love, not for a long time. But that's okay, cos your babies only know this version of you. And they love you, and they will love any other version of you when you start feeling a bit like your old self,' Mel said.

'You sound as though you know what you're talking about,' Aisha said.

'I have an eleven-year-old. Well, going on sixteen. I tell you, there's no in-between bit any more. Girls go from being little girls to teenagers.'

'Wow, you have an eleven-year-old?' Sophy pulled off her oversized sweatshirt to show off a semi-back-to-normal waist underneath, a small part of her wishing to rival Mel's muscly biceps and Aisha's thin waist.

'Yep, I had her when I was thirty-two. Never thought I'd want any more kids. But then never say never.'

Sophy's tired, fuzzy brain did the simple sum, taking longer than she would have liked to have done, but then maths was never her strong subject in school. Come to think of it, she couldn't recall feeling strong in any subjects at school. It was only when she did her Open University degree in business studies when she was twenty-five that she finally felt that she was in the right learning zone. Absorbing information on her own terms. However, the important thing she had managed to work out was that Mel was forty-three, ten years older than she was. Sophy was shocked because she felt she had waited too late to start having babies herself. Thirty-three felt old to her because Sophy herself had been born when her own mother was just nineteen. It meant her and her mum were fairly close and texted most days and chatted on the phone once a week. They hadn't yet visited her since Max was born, but her father was a lot older and retired now due to ill health, and because her mother didn't like driving on the motorways, she would have to get a train. And then recently, somehow, quite out of nowhere, Sophy's mum had developed an acute fear of trains. 'It's all that tight, cramped space moving at such speed, love. No, I'll have to wait to come and see you when your dad is feeling a bit better.'

Sophy knew she would have to be the one to get in the car and drive her and Max up to see her parents at the estate where they had bought their council house and still lived all these years later. She also knew she would be doing it on her own because although she had tried to on a number of occasions, she still hadn't ever fully explained to Jeff exactly where it was her parents lived and she could not imagine Jeff sitting in her mother's cramped sitting room with its late-eighties decor.

Max began making a few mewling sounds from his pram. Mel's baby, who she thought was probably a girl from the pink turban around her head, was still fast asleep, and Sophy could see Aisha had begun fussing with the covers and zips again, even though both her babies were still.

Sophy pulled Max onto her lap, popped the studs on his onesie and pulled off his hat. His hair, which was unusual for a less-than-a-month old baby, stuck up to one side and his cheeks were glowing pink from the fresh air.

'Why, hello, little bubbakin.' Mel leant straight in, smiling and cooing at Max. A huge smile erupted over Sophy's face. She knew

Max was super cute. He had inherited Jeff's ocean-blue eyes – the very thing that had attracted Sophy to Jeff the first time she saw him at an open house he was hosting. He hadn't been shy coming forward and slipping his card into her hand and asking her to call him when she was ready for a second viewing. The next day, she met him and got her very own private viewing, which came with a lot more than pointing out the white goods and the location of the thermostat. Sophy didn't take that house, which would have ended up as a share with two friends from the marketing firm she had been working at. Instead, she moved in with Jeff three weeks later. And hadn't left since.

'This is Max. He's three weeks old. Actually, no, coming up for four weeks. It's funny you don't know whether to say weeks or days, or should I say a month... It all goes so fast...' Sophy felt she was gabbling and trailed off.

She wasn't sure if Mel – who was now squeezing Max's toes gently – was listening any more. Then, whilst still looking at Max, Mel put one hand on Sophy's leg and said, 'You've nothing to worry about – you're doing really well.'

Sophy was shocked to feel the hot sting of tears behind her eyes. The words that Mel had spoken were, of course, exactly what she had been deliberating over these last few weeks. Was she doing a good enough job? She had Jeff, and the house, and Jeff's business and now little Max. She had so much to be thankful for. But it felt as though Mel had just plunged her hand straight inside her and pressed a release button on all her anxieties. But she wasn't going to cry, not here, with these women she had just met.

'Gosh, it's hot in here, isn't it?' Sophy said quickly 'It's hormones though, isn't it? I must be making a ton of them with the amount of milk this one has.' Sophy felt the familiar tingle of her breasts as Max began his usual rooting.

'Oh, you breastfeed,' Aisha said softly and without question.

'Yes. I knew I wanted to even before he was born. It was a no-brainer for me.'

Aisha looked forlorn. 'I would have loved to have breastfed. But I just felt I couldn't, what with two of them.'

'You could have had them stuffed under your arms like rugby balls. I knew a mum who breastfed three. Who told you couldn't?' Mel asked. Sophy reeled at the gall of Mel. She half expected Aisha to stand up and walk out.

'Well, me, actually. I thought it would be better to bottle feed, so my partner could get a go.'

Mel sucked in her lips. 'And you had no one to talk you back into it? I get it. Men can be like that, selfish. They don't want all the crying over cracked nipples and contracting stomachs, leaking boobs and eternal attachment feeding. But they occasionally want the glory photo of them feeding *their* baby. I did it with Leia for ten months. Not this time, though. This one is a bottle-fed baby. Now Daz can crack on and feed Skylar sometimes.'

Aisha's face brightened. 'Skylar and Leia. What lovely names.'

'I have a *Star Wars*-obsessed husband. So they're named after Luke Skywalker and Princess Leia.'

'Oh, I wouldn't have guessed straight away. But now you've said it,' Aisha said looking thoughtful. 'And Max is a lovely name too.' She looked at Sophy and smiled.

'What are yours called?' Sophy motioned to the pram, where she could see movement under one of the covers.

Aisha looked the double buggy. 'Oh, they're probably hot.' She stood up and unzipped both of the prams and pulled back blankets to reveal the babies, one in an orange striped Babygro and one in green with white spots. Sophy and Mel stood and said, 'Ahhhh,' in unison. Then they both looked at each other and laughed, and Sophy felt a tingle of joy surge through her. There was nothing better than having this sort of interaction with another female, when there was a hint that the two of you might actually hit it off.

'Both boys, Jude and Otis.' Aisha pointed to the baby on the left and then the right. 'They will be looking for their food soon'. Aisha began searching in her baby caddy and pulled out two bottles, each filled a quarter way with milk.

'Shall I give you a hand?' Mel leant forward to take one of the bottles. 'May as well whilst madam is still asleep.'

Aisha looked doubtful. 'I really ought to try and learn to do both of them myself when I'm out.'

'Not when there's three of us here, you're not.' Mel snatched one of the bottles from Aisha's hand. Aisha looked shocked, but put the remaining bottle on the table whilst she carefully handed one rousing baby to Mel.

'Who've I got then?' Mel looked down at the baby as she cradled him.

'That's Jude.'

'How do you know the difference?' Mel carefully popped the small teat into Jude's mouth, and he began drinking furiously. 'My, my, he's got a strong suck!'

'I go by the shape of their eyes. I know it sounds silly, but I really can tell. Other than that, Otis has a birthmark on his bum and slightly crinklier ears!'

Mel examined the baby's ears. 'Good lord, so he does. Bless you and them. They'll be messing with you for sure when they're older, won't they?'

'They play me up now!' Aisha said loudly with a slight shake to her voice and both the other women looked at her. 'I mean... What I mean is, two is hard, you know,' Aisha added.

'Yeah, I get it,' Sophy said softly. 'I find the night feeds are the hardest. Especially as it's only me who can do it.'

'God, yeah. It's that 3 a.m. one that's a killer, right? When they were only up three hours before,' Mel said. 'Oh my, he's almost finished this one. Hungry bugger.'

'That's the one I find the hardest to get back to sleep after,' Aisha said. 'The middle-of-the-morning one. I'm so glad it's not just me who feels that way.' Relief flooded Aisha's face and voice. She was feeding Otis, who was almost back asleep at the bottle. Mel leant Jude forward and gently patted his back. His eyes began to droop. Both women were tuned into Aisha. She clearly had stuff on her mind.

'I find it so... lonely. Like I'm the only person awake in the world. I know there are millions of other people up and about, working, but right then, in that moment, in those wee small hours, with such a small person – or persons – reliant on me, I feel so incredibly alone,' Aisha said.

Sophy felt a huge sense of relief that matched Aisha's expression and tone. She wasn't the only woman who felt like this. There were other women too, women like Aisha, who were trying to feed *two* babies at a time when it felt like you were the only person in the world. As Sophy absorbed this new information, she realised she had been quiet for some time and a pang of panic struck for what Aisha must be thinking. Sophy thought it would be Mel who spoke first, but she too still seemed to be mulling over what Aisha had just said. She was surprised to hear it was her own voice that spoke next.

'You know you could message me. At 3 a.m. or whenever the babies are awake and you feel lonely.'

Aisha laughed, a short, sharp hoot through her nose that suggested she appreciated Sophy's sentiment but that it was nothing more than that.

'No,' Sophy continued. 'I mean it. The chances are I might be awake with Max at the same time as you. I can't say I always will be and luckily once I'm asleep after I've fed him, I generally only tend to wake up to his stirrings or cries, so you wouldn't wake me if you text and I was already in bed.' Sophy pulled out her phone, flipped to the contacts section. 'Give me your number.'

Aisha called out the digits and Sophy punched them into her phone.

'I can second that. I'm a really heavy sleeper. Sometimes Daz has to shove me to let me know Skylar is waking up. Sounds terrible, but I've let him off the night feeds. He's an accountant and forgets how to count if he's not had a full night's sleep. But if I'm awake, you only need to holler, and I'll send you some cat memes or something to cheer you up. Then you'll know you're not all alone in the world. In fact, I might do the same to you both, if you don't mind?'

'Fab, what's your number, Mel?' Sophy brought up a new contact on her phone as Mel began reciting the mobile number.

Jude was now fast asleep; his little chin resting in the crook of Mel's hand.

'We could start our own club.' Sophy put her phone down on the table, a small spark of something igniting within her; a notion that this was something more than just an impromptu coffee with two mums she had only just met.

'The 3 a.m. Club!' Mel scoffed.

'The 3 a.m. Shattered Mums' Club,' Aisha said triumphantly and finally with a genuine smile.

Sophy and Mel exchanged glances and grinned.

'Good one!' Sophy said.

'Credentials for exclusive membership include: bags under eyes, stitched perineum, leaking boobs and a twitchy right eye,' Mel reeled off in a heartbeat, making Sophy and Aisha roar with laughter, and Sophy had to squeeze her buttocks together to stop any excess pee slipping out. Sophy watched Aisha wipe a tear from her eye as she felt her heart swell and her stomach flip. This, she realised was the most she had laughed in ages. This was what she craved in life: belly laughs with women who understood her. She couldn't bear the blank stares that came back at her from women she had tried, but failed, to connect with, or worse still, that droll tone followed by 'OMG that's hilarious' as they remained expressionless.

When they had all organised themselves and ordered coffees, and slabs of millionaire shortbread and blueberry muffins had been shared around, Sophy raised her half-drunk cup of decaf oat latte – feeling as though she needed to cement this moment in time, for fear it could evaporate as quickly as it had arrived – and said, 'Here's to the 3 a.m. Shattered Mums' Club.'

And the other two women raised their mugs in unison, and they all chorused, 'The 3 a.m. Shattered Mums' Club.'

5

AISHA

Aisha had watched the man walk past the house three times now. Always on the other side of the road, and he hadn't looked anywhere near her house, but it still unnerved her. *He* unnerved her. She had been trying to distract herself with how extraordinarily pretty Holly Willoughby was looking on *This Morning*, and a great distraction it had been from the monotony of changing nappies and wiping up sick, but she couldn't help but feel uneasy about the odd rhythms of the man on the street. During the ad breaks, she kept returning to the window to monitor his movements until she stopped returning to the sofa. She stood by the window, this time with Jude in her arms – Otis was happy lying on his back for now – and she watched the man. He was tall, with a green parka-style coat and a brown leather ear-flap trapper hat that kept his face partially covered. He reached the end of her road then turned around and walked back again. She presumed he went all the way to the other end, as it was several more minutes until he passed her house again. He was wearing biker boots over jeans, but she hadn't seen him arrive on a bike, nor could she see one close by. She was trying to commit all this information to her memory should the police call by with news of a break-in. She would be pleased that she would be able to give an accurate description. Yet she didn't feel that this was someone who was scoping the street to plot a burglary. It felt more ominous. The longer she watched him and thought about why he was here, the more she began to think he was here for the boys. She knew it was silly, but she couldn't help the dark feeling in the pit of her stomach. She watched him walk past a fourth time, and then waited for several minutes to see if he returned. This time, he didn't.

'You okay?' Charley's voice drifted through, breaking her reverie.

Aisha spun around and saw Charley standing in the doorway to the sitting room.

'Er, yeah. Fine, why?' Aisha couldn't help the slight sarcastic tone that had been creeping through when it came to her girl-friend these last few weeks. There was Charley, fully rested, her neat blonde hair tied back in a perfect French plait, glowing skin, on a coffee break from doing something she truly loved *and* that made her money.

'Because I love you and I'm just checking you're okay.' Charley edged into the room. Aisha clocked how Charley was dressed in a pristine white shirt that she had tucked into a pair of light-blue three-quarter-length cotton trousers. Not a hint of baby puke in sight. Her cheeks looked plump and flushed. She was radiant. She looked like a woman who'd had a full night's sleep. Whereas Aisha could feel the tiredness consuming her body, like she had been possessed by it, as though tiredness had been injected into her blood. She wanted to crawl out of her own skin and step into something that resembled Charley's ensemble.

You could have bloody checked in at 11 p.m., 2 a.m. and 6 a.m., Aisha thought to herself as she continued eyeing Charley. She was sure Charley had just had a meeting with someone, so that explained the smart turnout. But it still stung that Aisha could barely cobble together a limp pair of leggings and T-shirt. Aisha remained tight-lipped and didn't return the term of endearment. She was pretty sure she still loved Charley, but she was seeing her through a fog right now. Most days, she had no idea what day it was let alone had time to consider her and Charley's relationship. Charley was good with the boys, there was no denying that. She was one hundred per cent there at the weekends, but during the week she regimentally stuck to her schedule of getting into the bath – where she read a book for half an hour– and was then in bed by ten. She was an ex-Catholic schoolgirl, and an only child of heavily religious parents, who had not only been shocked when she came out but also extremely offended. They now only sent cards at Christmas and on her birthday, and never once mentioned Aisha or had initiated meeting the babies.

But Charley seemed happy with her life and her choices and loved her job. She was inundated with work, was always working on a jingle, a voiceover or narrating an audiobook. But she made sure she only worked Monday to Friday, leaving herself free and available for Aisha and the twins at the weekend. But that two-day bit of respite only made Aisha feel more anxious as she counted down the hours to when she would once again be all alone.

'Anything interesting out there today?' Charley joined Aisha at the window and looked out onto the street of other terraced houses and the avenue dappled with trees.

'Just some man that has walked past four times.'

'Is it that bad that you've started counting how many times people walk along the road?' Charley laughed and Aisha felt something snap inside.

'And that's funny because?'

Charley stopped laughing and put a hand on Aisha's shoulder, which Aisha immediately shrugged off.

'Okay, it's like that, is it? Well, you just let me know when you need to eat your lunch and I'll—'

'Now! Now is when I want to eat lunch.' Aisha took a tightly bundled Jude from her shoulder and passed him to Charley.

'Oh, right. But you know it's only ten forty-five in the morning?'

Aisha stopped on her way out of the lounge.

'Yes, but when your day and night merge together, there are no longer set times to eat. So unlike your regimented schedules – which by the way seem to have become even more regimented since the babies were born – I get to eat when I like.' Aisha tried to keep a lightness to the tone of her voice, the words coming out in a stage whisper. She had vowed once the babies were born, she would not raise her voice nor get angry. But right now, although her voice was tame, inside was a raging fire, and this was not the sort of person Aisha had ever been. It was also not the tone she'd ever taken with her girlfriend before. Neither she nor Charley were the passive-aggressive type. Or hadn't been. That was what had made their relationship work so well.

Aisha had often been the one to break up the kitchen fights at the restaurant she managed before the babies came along, or calm any riled-up customers. Now, here she was unable to get a grip on her own emotions. She was glad she didn't have anything to hand, because she was almost certain she would have flung it at her girlfriend. After she had taken Jude back, of course.

* * *

In the kitchen, Aisha pressed her hands against the cool surface of the kitchen table. She thought about how she and Charley had sat at this very kitchen table when Aisha was pregnant, imagining what their life would be like when they became parents to twins. They talked about a crazy, chaotic, happy world where they both mucked in. There would be laundry everywhere, they mused, but it wouldn't matter, it would get done eventually. And there had always been the romantic notion that life would be like a romcom with people popping by at all hours, and she and Charley racing against each other to see who could change a nappy in the fastest time.

But all those months they had sat at that table – Aisha sipping little bits of Charley's wine because a few sips weren't going to harm the babies – there weren't two tiny humans to care for 24/7, nor the stark reality of spending almost every day alone. It had only been seven weeks, but it felt like seven years. Time had suddenly slowed down and each minute felt like she was wading through mud to get to the next part of the day. And every time one of the twins cried or mewled, Aisha didn't feel the rush of love she thought she would. Instead, she felt her skin prickle, her body tense up and she had an overwhelming desire to run, to hand the babies over to Charley or her mum and say, 'Erm, I think I made a mistake. I'm not ready for this.' Yet at the same time, she felt this obligation to protect the boys. She knew they needed her, and although it wasn't the romcom-movie life she had anticipated, she knew she wouldn't run. She knew she would stay.

Mel had assumed that Aisha was with a man, when she had referred to – Daz, was it? Aisha laughed to herself. Of course, she hadn't mentioned that she was in a lesbian relationship, but it was funny how people always presumed she had a husband. That didn't really bother her. Once she corrected people, most were very apologetic. Most people also wanted to know how the babies were conceived. Aisha considered what it would be like when she finally did get back out into the world again and the prospect of having to explain to more people that she had been artificially inseminated. Would she explain that she and Charley had sat for weeks looking over the profiles of potential sperm donors and that none of it was an easy journey? Not like the traditional method where most women could be chopping carrots for dinner one minute, mutter something about the 'the girth on that vegetable' to the man in her life, who might say, 'I'll show you some girth,' and minutes later, she falls pregnant. She felt like a bit of a cheat, as though she didn't deserve to have babies because she hadn't done it the way every woman she had met had. It was true, aside from the couples they had struck up a rapport with on the support group forum, she hadn't met any other women who had gone through a similar journey to her and Charley. The forum was helpful to a certain extent, but what was missing was being able to talk with someone face to face about it. Aisha hadn't mentioned it to Charley because she was aware of how long they had discussed children before going ahead, but she struggled with the guilt of how many unwanted children there were in this world, and that if she and Charley couldn't create a baby with one part of each of them, that they should have perhaps adopted instead of found a way to create a child with a total stranger. Which then ended up turning into two. Two babies who could go off into the world and potentially end up falling in love with a sibling who had been created by the same sperm donor. That was something that Aisha had considered more than once and she physically shuddered whenever it crept up on her. But Charley had told her it was such a small chance, and Aisha reminded her it was still a chance, and that there would be a film about it soon.

As Aisha stood in the kitchen, she half expected Charley to walk in and say something like 'Rough day, huh?' But this wasn't the set of *Friends*, and Charley was too absorbed in her projects to conjure up words that could be the catalyst to open the flood-gates. However, if she did, Aisha was confident she would crumble on her feet, fall into Charley's arms and tell her she felt like a fraction of herself, and didn't know what was happening or how to fix it. But to do that would be to fail and she couldn't let Charley see her as a failure. It had taken her two years after she had met Charley to come out to Martina and her siblings, and then it was she, Aisha, who had been the instigator to start a family. Charley had always said she hadn't any desire to be pregnant. Charley was thirty-seven and even as a child had never played with dolls, or made-believe mums and dads; or even mums and mums. She had been entirely focused on playing the cello, reading classic novels, and of course – even from a young age – producing songs. And so Aisha knew it was she who would be the primary caregiver. Of course, Charley loved the bones of the boys. She was attentive to their needs when she was with them, but it was Aisha who was doing the lion's share of the work. She tried to tell herself it wouldn't be forever; soon the boys would be walking and talking and wouldn't need her as much. She tried to imagine that day and conjure up the sadness she might feel, so that she could try to live in the now a little harder. It was difficult to envisage a time when she would be able to blow-dry her hair or pop to the shops alone and not feel a tsunami of guilt.

But Aisha needed to crack on and stop acting like such a baby when she already had two of her own reliant on her. She had watched her own mother battle her demons to raise five children by herself. She took a few deep breaths, then went to the fridge. She would make herself a gourmet-style sandwich to cheer herself up, and god knows she deserved it. She knew there was ham and Edam cheese, gherkins and pickled onions. Charley had bought some bread from the artisan bakery yesterday, which would still be fresh. But when Aisha opened the fridge, and although pleasantly surprised she was still shocked when she saw a plate with a fat sandwich, cling filmed, with a note stuck on the top.

So you don't forget to eat. C x

Aisha felt a rush from her gut into her heart. She placed her hand on the wall to steady herself as the tears fell.

* * *

Aisha swallowed down each mouthful of sandwich as though it were clay. Despite it being her favourite of cheese, ham and pickle on rye, each mouthful was like ingesting her guilt over and over. She had so much guilt inside her these days. She never knew it was possible to feel so much of one emotion. She felt guilty when one twin cried whilst she held the other. She felt guilt when she rested her eyes as she lay on the sofa in the middle of the afternoon when the boys were napping. She felt guilt when Charley came into the lounge and she had *This Morning* on in the background to keep her company. She felt guilt when her mum texted her to see if she needed anything and she realised it had been days since she had even thought about her. She felt guilt when she didn't even get the boys out of the house for half an hour some days and she stayed in her loungewear, which Charley still proclaimed were exactly the same as pyjamas. And now she was literally making herself sick with guilt by trying to swallow down the sandwich that Charley had already made. Aisha pulled the cling film back over the other half of the sandwich, put it back in the fridge and went back into the lounge. The TV was off, and the boys were not there. Panic surged through Aisha, even though she knew she was being ridiculous. Charley was their parent too. The panic turned to annoyance as Aisha began fluffing the cushions and picking up dirty muslins and empty bottles. She carried it all through into the kitchen, stacked a few bits into the dishwasher, then stopped as her ears pricked up to the music coming from the basement. She opened the door that led down to Charley's studio and padded down the stairs. Inside the basement, the music was loud enough so Charley didn't hear Aisha arrive. She was standing in front of her desk, which incorporated the recording suite – a mass of metal and buttons that Aisha had no understanding of. Charley had her back to her, and Aisha could see she was wearing the babies – who were still small enough that they could both fit inside the sling. Charley had always been keener on the sling than Aisha, even though she had bought it, imagining herself wrapping her babies up with ease and then carrying on with her daily tasks with their tiny bodies pressed against her, believing that they were still in the womb. But the first time Aisha had attempted to head out for a walk with the babies strapped to her, she had ended up in a twisted mountain of material, two screaming babies on the sofa and a raging anger bubbling up inside her. It looked so damn easy on the video, and why did all those model mums look so flippin' happy, with a face full of make-up and not a stressed baby in sight? She had swaddled the babies in the pram and hadn't attempted to get them back in the sling since. Aisha felt that familiar pang of anger now as she watched Charley swaying side to side. The music was a song from *The Greatest Showman*, one of Charley's favourite films. The image of her girlfriend with their two children was almost a movie moment itself, but Aisha felt like crying for a different reason. How did Charley make it all look so bloody easy? She lunged forward – surprising Charley, who looked shocked to see her – then tried to engage her in a look that said, *How adorable are they?*

Of course, they were adorable now, but not all through the night, or the day when Aisha tried to settle them. Aisha leant over the mixing desk, looking for the volume amongst the chaos of buttons and levers. Charley leant over her and put her fingers on two buttons and slid them down. Hugh Jackman's voice fell to a low level.

Charley turned and smiled.

'I was just coming to say, I'll take them. When you're done. I had my lunch. I'm just going to take them out for a walk,' Aisha said.

Charley didn't say anything about the sandwich. It wasn't her style.

'Seems a shame to wake them.' Charley looked down at the two tiny heads poking out of tightly bound grey material. 'They love music – I should bring them down more often,' she whispered.

'I'm going to start taking them to that music group at the community hall in the summer, when they're a bit older.' Aisha heard the stinging tone to her voice, and she knew Charley had too. 'They need fresh air,' Aisha said flatly, although thinking that, in fact, she could just go and lie down for an hour while the babies slept soundly on Charley, who obviously had a little time to spare this morning. But instead, she looked firmly at Charley and waited for her response.

'I'll bring them up. If you get the buggy ready, we might be able to transfer them without them waking,' Charley said optimistically.

Aisha managed a nod before she went back up the stairs. They both knew it was wishful thinking. Aisha was only going out for a walk to prove a point to Charley, and now she would be walking the streets, angry with herself and with Charley. And with two very awake, grumpy babies. What a joy.

* * *

3.06 a.m. – Aisha: Hi there, girls. Thanks for creating this WhatsApp group, Sophy. I was just up with the boys, and I thought, 'Oh look it's just 3 a.m.,' so I thought I'd message and see if anyone else was up. It's been quite a day and it would be nice to know if anyone else is awake?

3.10 a.m. – Sophy: Hey, Aisha, I'm up. I can't see straight, but I'm up lol 😂

3.11 a.m. – Aisha: It's weird, isn't it? I used to love being awake at this time.

3.11 a.m. – Sophy: Ha, me too – following the milkman home. That's what we did in my home town in Milton Keynes 😵

3.12 a.m. – Aisha: And now here we are, wishing we could be asleep!

3.13 a.m. – Sophy: I know, but these days won't last forever, will they? That's what everyone keeps telling me. Need to treasure these golden hours. It's so good to know I'm not the only one awake though. Thanks for texting. We must meet up again soon.

3.14 a.m. – Aisha: Yes, we must. Good luck with the rest of the feed and getting a good night's sleep.

3.14 a.m. – Sophy: U2 x

6.35 a.m. – Mel: Hi girls. Sky has only just woken up. I think I'm onto a winner with this one. She seems to prefer the latter side of the night, which is good because I loooove my sleep so much.

6.45 a.m. – Mel: Anyone?

6

MEL

'And why aren't you at bloody school, anyway?' Mel shouted to get the last word in over the fence. She had been in the garden hanging the washing out – a rare moment of domesticity had come over her as the sun peeked through the clouds and a warm breeze had filtered through the house, urging her outdoors. Next door's teenage boy had been playing football, and twice the ball had come over into Mel's garden, disrupting her domestic-goddess psyche and filling her with an overwhelming rage.

She had thrown it back over once, but when it came over again, she had seen red and found herself locked in an altercation with a teenager who had more or less no facial hair but was trying to style it out all the same.

He had thought he had ended the argument by calling her a 'menopausal witch' (where do they learn such insults?), except this had only served to rile Mel up even more and she was ready to march around and bang on the door and really tell him what he needed to hear. Instead, she shouted her last words to a closed door and hoped they would penetrate through. She couldn't remember what the lad's name was. He had always seemed pleasant enough in a mute, tracksuit-bottoms-and-hoodie-wearing, nodding and grunting teenage sort of way. His mum, Lucy, always smiled, and they'd had coffee once there just after Mel had moved in. She had also brought flowers when Skylar was born and popped in for a 'quick coffee and cuddle' that had lasted three hours. In the end, Mel was forced to feign sleep and Lucy had quietly left. There wasn't a husband on the scene, just a string of boyfriends, who all dressed uncannily similar to her teenage son.

What had worked up Mel even more was she had planned to remain calm all day. Mel knew she was fighting a losing battle with herself. It was the classic pram-in-the-hall issue for her; Mel was constantly wrestling between wanting to be a good mother, but also needing to express herself through her art – her singing and her dancing. She didn't want to consider herself getting old either and the prospect of reproduction no longer being possible once the menopause set in and she certainly didn't need a little jumpstart from next door reminding her of her age. But Mel couldn't ignore the nagging feeling that was nudging at her, pestering her from time to time. Was this new recent anger to do with what had happened at The East End Club before Skylar was born? Maybe she hadn't given herself enough time to consider the enormity of it. She had always brushed off these kinds of incidents in the past. But none had ever escalated to the extent they had that night. When she was pregnant with Skylar as well. She dreaded to think what might have happened if things had got out of hand. Would Sky even be here now? She shuddered at the thought, and yet again pushed the images that occasionally crept to the forefront of her mind away. She was a big girl, a mum of two now. It was in the past. She just needed to keep it there.

Mel was also dealing with the usual emotions of being a new mum like that dragging sensation of being in a house that was constantly messy, which didn't seem to feel any easier second time around. She really needed to employ some daily routines that Leia could abide by, just some simple stacking of the dishwasher or putting a wash on. She was eleven now. Sometimes, just looking at the mess all around her made Mel want to run out of the house, but the desire to be out singing and dancing did not yet override the fear she felt on the last day she had performed and the very thing that was keeping her away from doing the thing she loved. She had got back to her Robbie who wanted – no, needed her – back at The East End. He said he was sure to go under if she didn't at least give her fans something. So she had confirmed a date. She would be back on the stage within the month. The stage was where she felt most at home, but she felt an underlying sense of dread whenever she imagined herself back doing what she was born to do. Her very last gig at The East End – where she had been performing since she was twenty-eight years old – had been one of the worst nights of her life. She could still see him; still smell him. She wondered if she would ever be able to move forward and find the strength to put that night behind her.

She thought about the girls she had met last week as she finished hanging the washing up and how nice it was for Aisha to start texting. It was a lovely idea of Sophy's, but Mel secretly hoped she would never need the night-time counselling service. Skylar was sleeping in big stints at night so far. But it hadn't surprised Mel that someone like Sophy had instigated the 3 a.m. Shattered Mums' Club chat on WhatsApp. Sophy was a proper yummy mummy; she looked the type of girl who liked to organise things like spontaneous girls' spa weekends away. She had noted that expensive sleeping-bag coat and the way her nails were manicured and painted alternate shades of green and yellow. Mel imagined she would be a riot on a girls' night out. Aisha was different – she seemed a lot more reserved, and almost shy in comparison. Mel was sure that if it wasn't for her own bolshy behaviour, Aisha wouldn't have come along to the café at all. But still, she was glad she had met them both now. She had friends around London, but none that were new mums. Mel had always found meeting new mums difficult. She shied away from all those mother-and-baby groups – she had only been doing Irene a favour that day by showing up for the tai chi and tea thing, which the bloody girl had the cheek not to show up to. It wasn't that Mel was unable to make friends, but the problem was if she met someone she vaguely liked, or tolerated, they would generally want to exchange numbers and meet again, 'Oh, we must get the girls together again. Didn't they have fun?' The next thing, she'd see a photo of her baby next to the other mum's baby on social media with 'BFFs already' written underneath it. This sort of thing happened a lot when Leia was little. So even though Mel had been dreading the tai chi and tea group, she was annoyed that the woman hadn't shown up. She had a mind to pass on her thoughts to Irene to share, but she had reminded herself that she was a changed woman now: no more sudden emotional break-downs. She decided she would put the football-over-the-fence incident into the 'one-off' category where the C-bomb clash was also lying sheepishly. Everyone was allowed an off day (or two). Mel was sure it was because she wasn't dancing. Surely the dancing would give her back her confidence. She knew once she got back up on that stage, she would be releasing all that pent-up energy. All that rage. Again, her mind began to ponder on just where the rage was stemming from.

She reminded herself that she must text the girls tonight. Even if it wasn't during the 3 a.m. feed, which luckily Skylar hadn't shown any preference for. She could even try to get the message in before she fell asleep after the midnight feed, show that she was on board.

Mel spent the next few minutes standing in the doorway and looking around at the mess in the lounge. She knew the bathroom was crying out to be cleaned, hairs and dust were clinging to every surface, and Daz had wiped the mirror so many times after a steamy shower no one could actually see their reflection in it any more. Mel craved a clean-looking house. She wished she could have it all gleaming and organised like those influencers on Instagram – Christ, one of them has four kids and a job on the telly and still manages to hang her crisps from a curtain hook in the snack cupboard. Mel followed them all and bought all the products they recommended and endorsed. She had a cupboard full of shower cleaners and grout whiteners; she'd even bought a Lazy Susan for the fridge because she had seen an influencer put all her condiment jars on one so she could spin it around and find her cranberry sauce without having to plunge her hand into the unknown territory of the top shelf. But despite all the gear, Mel still had no desire to clean. And so the house stayed just that side of messy and dirty.

Mel ignored the ever-evolving cleaning chores and decided to cook instead. It was something that relaxed her. Cleaning was not for her, but an hour making a one-pot chicken dish and some brownies was right up her street. Mel settled Skylar in her bouncy chair on the kitchen island as she cooked, thinking as she bounced her with her hand every now and again that whoever made these things was a bloody genius because she couldn't live without it. Skylar was in hers a lot. Last week, Irene had come over and said to the wee thing 'My, you get around' as Mel took Skylar from room to room with her as she reluctantly did some hoovering, dusting, and cleaned the bathroom, to show Irene she wasn't completely incapable – all whilst Skylar happily sat in her chair.

She popped the chicken dish in the oven and whipped up the brownies and then put them on the lower shelf in the oven. She took herself and a sleeping Skylar into the lounge, and before long, found herself scrolling on her phone. It was a terrible thing to do; her worst habit. She did like a bit of social media but she found she could pass a whole hour and come away feeling as though she had just been released from an underground vault and was seeing daylight for the first time in weeks. She much preferred to be exercising, but recently –well, call it sleep deprivation, if you will – Mel had become hooked again. She needed some inspiration to get herself eating healthier again, and if there was one place to inspire you to make yourself look better, it was Instagram.

Overall, she thought she did pretty well; ate a rainbow from time to time, and obviously her fitness levels were pretty slick, but really she needed to get herself into a routine. But there were times when she did feel exasperated with herself, when she dropped the healthy habits and found herself reaching for the endless amounts of cake there seemed to be in the house. Daz hated sweet things but worked with a bunch of middle-aged feeders who constantly brought sponges, doughnuts and muffins to the office that had been left over from their child's birthday/ graduation/ baptism. The events seemed to be endless. Mel would catch herself in the kitchen, picking at some neon icing and purple sponge that had been lovingly created for a child she had never met, wondering why she couldn't just leave it the hell alone. And she so wanted to not eat that rubbish. She wasn't fat by any stretch of the imagination. But with her stature, or her 'big bones' as her dear poor mum had referred to her, she had to be careful that she didn't add any excess weight, because apart from all the health related issues, it didn't bode well for family photos.

But Sophy had talked of her fascination with nutrition during their café meet. She had told Mel she worked in marketing, learned a bit about social media then used her love of healthy eating to inspire others. She went into the search bar of Instagram and typed in *Sophy West*. She knew that was what she would need to focus on, getting her nutrition levels up there so she had the energy to train, be a mum, run a house and do her job as a burlesque dancer and singer. There were a few Sophy Wests, but Mel soon recognised Sophy, looking smiley and glowing in a bright white T-shirt, hair slicked back in a tight ponytail. Mel clicked on the account, curious and wanting to get a better look. The account was called ThisGirlThisBody and Mel was astounded to see she had 160,000 followers. Her account was pristine. The top few images were of baby Max, but only the first three. One flat lay, one of him in someone's arms and another of just his fingers wrapped around a hand, presumably Sophy's, the wording underneath was that classic poetic Instagram tripe that Mel detested.

Welcome to the world, our little prince. We are so blessed to become Mummy and Daddy to this little beauty today. Our world is truly rocked.
59,000 likes
2391 comments

Mel shuddered as she clicked out. Is that the sort of person she really wanted to be friends with? Sophy had seemed so... so, well, so not like that, when she had met her last week. It was amazing how hard people tried to create this other persona on social media.

As Mel scrolled down through the account, she saw image after image that looked as though it had been lifted straight out of a women's magazine: a trendy-looking pink water bottle perched on a wall with a sea landscape just out of focus. Sophy in a pair of hot pink leggings and blue trainers, against a blue-and-green-graffitied wall. As Mel scrolled further back, she realised that Sophy had managed to maintain a pink-and-blue theme throughout. This was what baffled her the most. How was this possible? How on earth did people find the time to plan all this stuff? It was beyond her. But she did like Sophy. She had liked her from the moment they'd met. Despite the cliché Instagram posts, she thought she had something going for her and that all this Insta stuff was a cover for the person Sophy really was, or maybe wanted to become.

Mel thought that, deep down, Sophy was already a success, without the need for the filters and hashtags. Mel was generally attracted to people like that, and in her experience, they didn't come along very often, but when they did, she wanted to be around them. It was an evolution thing, survival of the fittest; aligning yourself with other like-minded or successful people was what had got Mel all the amazing gigs over the years. Perhaps, if nothing else, Sophy could teach her a thing or two about how to make her own Instagram account look half as eye-catching as hers, because that whole pink-and-blue vibe was really quite striking.

Mel noticed the time was almost 4 p.m. and she realised that Sky had been asleep for a while. Maybe, at this rate, she would be up half the night, meaning Mel might get to chat to the girls at 3 a.m. after all. Even though Mel knew she was setting herself up for a longer night she still couldn't tear herself away from Sophy's feed.

As Mel continued to browse through the page, she spotted

that Sophy had tagged a handle in the pictures of Max. *Ah, so this must be the father*, Mel thought and felt a desire to see who her other half was. Mel clicked on the handle and the account went straight into the account of a one Jeff Haddon. A slim but tall man in a too shiny suit stood next to a desk with a plain white wall behind him. Mel hated to be that person who judged, but she looked at that photo of Jeff with his blond hair sticking up at a funny angle – he looked almost Swedish or Danish or something – and couldn't help but think he was trying too hard to look twenty years younger than he clearly was.

'Oh, Sophy,' she said. She quickly clicked back into Sophy's account and noted that their surnames didn't match. So they weren't married, or Sophy was awesomely modern and hadn't given her surname up. Mel secretly hoped it was the latter, but she had a sneaky feeling that Sophy was merely cohabiting with this... Could Mel really be thinking the word *weasel*? Although, weirdly enough, there was something about him that gave Mel the creeps. She clicked back into his account again, then began scrolling through every picture of him one by one. And there were a lot. A few posing with Sophy at a restaurant, at a beach bar at sunset, and lots more of just him. The man loved a selfie.

Now, Mel had encountered a fair few men in her time and had her fair share of bum slaps, tit gropes and leg grabs, but the longer she looked at Jeff's Instagram account, the more she studied his face, his eyes – which were such a piercing blue she was sure you would never be able to forget them – the more certain Mel was that she knew this man.

Mel's gut dropped and her body shuddered.

It couldn't be. It couldn't be! Thoughts erupted through her mind like a volcano. Thoughts she had vowed to put away some-where and never retrieve, but they were back. And they were staring right at her through the eyes of Jeff Haddon, a man whose name she had never known, but whose face she would never forget.

Mel stood up. She felt her breath catch in her chest, the way it had for months after that night. How was it possible that by just looking at his photo, it could bring it all back again? To some, it would not seem like a big deal, but it had crushed Mel's confidence, even made her reconsider her career at one point. She barely knew Sophy – who was to say that this friendship was going anywhere, anyway, even though Mel was only just thinking what a great girl Sophy was. Oh, why did life have to be so cruel and twisted? Of all the men Sophy could be with, it had to be him. Of course she couldn't be one hundred per cent certain that Jeff Haddon was the same man she had encountered less than a year ago. But 99.9 per cent? Surely that had to be enough.

Mel went through into the kitchen to make herself a cup of tea for the shock. She looked at the state of the kitchen, turned upside down just to cook one bloody meal. She tutted and let out a long sigh. She noticed the bins needed emptying; it was the one job that Daz absolutely failed 100 per cent at every time. Even when she put Post-it notes on the bin to remind him to 'empty the goddamn bin'. She put one on his car windscreen once and had been shocked to discover it was still there when he returned home from the office. She slapped her Marigolds on and hauled the stinking bag out of the bin, the bin juice dripping all over the floor. But Jeff Haddon's face was in her mind's eye. She was pretty sure he would stay there for the rest of the day. She cursed under her breath and carried the dripping bin bag outside.

7

SOPHY

Sophy had begun to see other mums like a mirage – after a month of surviving on sporadic sleep as and when Max dictated, she had managed to open one twitchy eye wide enough to notice there were a few other mums skulking around the local area with small babies, and she had an overwhelming urge to be near them because she felt she was just a chimp clinging to a rock floating in space and needed other mummy chimps to be around her to help raise her baby chimp. But of course, she never said that out loud to anyone, although she might have said it to Jeff once, and he asked her if she had been sniffing Tippex again. She certainly couldn't imagine herself saying that to other new mums, and shuddered at the thought of humiliating herself.

Sophy always used to let every weird and eccentric thing about her spill out, but now, when she imagined being her most authentic self, she would experience a sense of panic that would grow and evolve until she was panicking about other areas of her life too. Like how people believed she knew what she was talking about on social media. But the truth was, Sophy knew very little.

She had done a business degree, and she read up as much as she could about nutrition. Oh, and she liked keeping fit. But what had started out as a bit of fun had escalated, and now people gave her free stuff, which was great, but Sophy couldn't help but feel like a colossal fraud. Mostly because deep down, she wasn't that passionate about nutrition or advocating it. She just liked it a bit, and somehow, she knew how to take a bloody good photo and had managed to create a sort of brand with the pink and blue. And now there was the pressure to keep it going, because who knew what it could lead to. One hundred and sixty thousand followers in just over a year was a fantastic achievement. But talking about women's bodies on social media was all a bit confusing. There was a whole new approach to embracing larger women under #bodypositivity, and with more people coming forward to admit anorexia and eating disorders due to years of dieting and feeling the pressure to look lighter and slimmer, Sophy really didn't know where she stood any more, and she certainly had no idea what sort of content was acceptable. She was completely winging it, and she knew it was only a matter of time before she posted something that offended too many people. She had seen and heard it happen enough times on social media. She had witnessed the shit show as normal, everyday women with lives and families happened to write a post that had caused offence, then the big, long apology post came and they disappeared for months – only a few would return with their tail between their legs, with much more politically correct content, as if they had been away and learned their lesson. But Sophy wasn't sure she was up for that. She wasn't sure she had the strength to satisfy every single angle to cause the least amount of offence.

But Sophy knew one thing, and that was that she was determined to make some true mum friends. She had made a few social-media friends that she had met at events, had a couple of school friends she kept in contact with and a few of Jeff's friends who were married couples who they met for dinner from time to time. But she was in a new phase of her life now and was craving that human contact more than anything.

Sophy had heard a saying recently that it takes a village to raise a child. Her mission now was to seek out these women and surround herself with them. And so far, she was pretty sure she had bagged herself two friends and she was going to cling on to them with all she had. She was spellbound by Mel with her firm body and carefree attitude – she needed both Mel's 'fuck it' philosophy and her bulging biceps to rub off on her. And then there was that tender moment in the café when she had somehow managed to understand exactly how Sophy was feeling without Sophy having to say a word. And then there was Aisha, who remained so calm and collected even with two babies to tend to. They were both an inspiration. And she had felt pretty comfortable around both of them. That was the sort of friendship she needed; people she could be real with. Now she had Max, she felt she was ready to have her tribe, the sort of thing Beyoncé had; safety in numbers felt like the right thing to do now she was responsible for a small person. Who said she had to do it all alone?

Sophy's mum was still dealing with her sudden fear of trains and Jeff's parents were as useful as a condom machine in the Vatican, always there with those half-hearted offers of help but never following through and relieving any of the pressure.

'We can come and help you paint the bathroom next Wednesday—Oh sorry, did you say it was today? I've booked a hairdresser's appointment.'

She had tried over the years to encourage Jeff's parents to like her. She bought a floral blouse so that Jeff's mum, Wendy, would look at her and compliment her. She spent a week reading crocheting magazines and watching episodes of true crime documentaries just so she would have something to discuss with her over dinner, but no matter how many times she dropped in questions about *Abducted in Plain Sight* or asked her thoughts on *The Staircase*, Wendy seemed to shun her every time. Like actually shut her down by asking her to pass the gravy or enquiring whether anyone wanted cranberry sauce because she had bought three for two in the supermarket last week and she wouldn't use them up by 2024 at this rate. Then conversations would invariably turn to what Sophy's plans were once the baby was born. It baffled Sophy that anyone would ask that. 'That child will be taking up the next eighteen years of your life and then some.' As if Sophy was unaware of what giving birth to a child entailed long term. 'I still worry about my little Jeffy baby,' Wendy had gone on to say during one lengthy lunch just before Christmas. Suddenly, all Sophy could see was an adult version of her boyfriend of four years, who was turning forty-two next year, as a snotty little child, and the sponge pudding that had seemed mildly enticing had become a congealed blob of yellow mass in front of her. Wendy also consistently ignored Sophy's successes on her social-media platform; she'd gained so many followers, and her vlogs on health and fitness had won a small award the previous year. 'Vlogging? What is vlogging? It sounds like a form of corporal punishment, love,' were Wendy's words when she tried to explain that she was indeed using the degree in business and management – not marketing as Wendy had suggested – every day when she interacted with humans either face to face or via the internet. But what could you say to a woman who went to the same holiday resort in Tenerife every year because the cabaret act from the hotel bar had once featured on *This Morning* and still considered a glass of tomato juice a luxury starter? The only thing tomato juice was good for was to throw in with a bloody Mary.

But Sophy was beginning to see the cracks in social media. What had once seemed so enticing and gave her goosebumps when she thought about a post going live, now felt hollow and empty. She craved something else. But she wasn't sure where the frustrations with Instagram ended and the loneliness of new motherhood began. There were empty promises of meet-ups with a couple of the mums from her 'Labour of Love' class she had attended whilst pregnant with Max. But she had suddenly realised that meeting mums was worse than dating. If she found just one weird thing about them, then she was completely turned off. At the Labour of Love class, one of the women had such a hairy upper lip that Sophy couldn't stop staring at it. She knew trying to forge any kind of relationship where she would never be able to say 'Must dash' without causing offence, would be impossible. Not to mention that Sophy was sure she would spend any conversation in some sort of perpetual 'tash' trance. The other woman at the class had talked about her carpal tunnel insistently and referred to breast milk as 'milky milk'. Neither of these women were the ideal candidates for the sort of long-term bosom-buddy, tell-each-other-everything relationship that Sophy was seeking.

Tiredness had truly set in, and Sophy walked around that morning as though she were looking at the world through a sepia lens. Sophy pulled on her huge sleeping-bag coat, togged up Max and set off for a walk to try and clear her hazy head. She knew Mel lived fairly close to her – she and Aisha were opposite ends of Clapham and Mel was in Wandsworth. 'What the dodgy end?' Sophy had said quoting her favourite *Love Actually* character and was ecstatic when Mel actually belly laughed because she got the reference. She decided a long walk with the pram there and back, just to suss out her street was in order. And if she happened to bump into her, all the better! Besides, it was near to one of her favourite coffee shops, so any 'chance' meeting wouldn't come across as so weird.

When Sophy arrived in Mel's road, she cruised past the house, then double backed on herself. There was a side gate, but Sophy could just about see the far end of the back garden. Was that a hot tub? Sophy perched herself on the frame of her travel system. Instantly, she felt bad treating such an expensive piece of kit with such disrespect. She had begged Jeff for this particular model, knowing that it cost over a thousand pounds, and ignored his response of 'Well, as long as there's something in it for me' as he took out his wallet and handed her his credit card. Sophy had rubbed her bulging belly at him. Could the birth of a healthy baby boy not just be the 'something in it' for him? So far, in the thirty or so days since Max's birth, Jeff had been very late home for eight of them; after-work drinks, schmoozing clients, showing houses, paperwork that absolutely had to be done there and then. Sophy was fairly sure he could have got himself out of several of those meetings if he really wanted to. When she was still heavily pregnant, Jeff's secretary had taken Sophy aside at the Christmas party. 'I remember what it was like, darling. A baby turns your entire world upside down. You ensure Jeff is at home with you from now on. I will make sure we send someone else out to do the client meets and whatnot. He really doesn't need to do it himself – we have three other very competent sales-men.' Maggie was a slight woman with permanent pink cheeks and a smile that radiated. But when Sophy mentioned what Maggie had said, Jeff claimed Maggie must have been drunk and that his absence would cause massive repercussions for the business. Sophy recollected that night with a great deal of clarity, as she had stood cradling her third fizzy elderflower and watched through the window as a very sober Maggie took her husband by the hand, escorted him to their car and drove them both home.

Sophy stood on the travel system and winced at a pain down below. She had been warned by the midwife to take it easy. Max had a big head; the tears were still healing. Three evenings after Max's arrival, Jeff had turned over in bed in a sulk muttering, 'I have needs too you know,' after she had declined giving him a hand job whilst Max suckled on her breast, where he had been for almost seventy-two hours. Soaked in fresh and regurgitated breast milk, Sophy looked at her boyfriend and wondered was it possible she now had two babies to tend to?

Sophy hadn't been prepared for the loneliness. The tiredness she could just about handle at the moment – there were probably a few hormones knocking around giving her a high, so the hazy, underwater feeling seemed tolerable enough when you didn't have to really interact with anyone other than a snuffling infant. But the lack of human contact was glaringly apparent. She had begun walking the entire street layout of her area every day, determined to get her body back into shape, but the days were long and the nights longer. Jeff seemed smitten enough with Max, the boy he had desperately wanted, but his work demanded him to be up and off by 7.30 a.m. Most days, Sophy had barely finished the night feed and found herself stood in front of him in the kitchen to wave him off. She hadn't ever experienced such aching despondency at not having anyone to talk to all day. She missed who she and Jeff were before Max came along. Then she felt guilty for even thinking that an innocent baby was to blame for the sparkle having gone out of their relationship. Some evenings, she was so tired she could barely speak to Jeff. They used to laugh so much when they first got together. And there had been a lot of sex. She knew Jeff would be missing the sex. But all couples went through this after a baby, didn't they? But, she wondered, was it normal that they were suddenly so distant with each other now that Max was here? It certainly wasn't the picture-perfect family image she had conjured up before she got pregnant.

As she tried to steal a better look at Mel's place, Sophy could feel the structure of the pram yielding under her weight but took her body to the next phase of stretching to get onto her toes so she could see a little more into the garden. She wondered if she and Jeff could squeeze a hot tub into the tiny garden of the two-bedroomed house they lived in. She had already told Jeff that they would need to add an extension to the back of the house to accommodate an office and another bedroom. This, Jeff had said, he would investigate and had booked a building firm to pop in for a survey next week.

As Sophy stretched up, she felt the buggy give way, the brake she thought she had applied had not locked properly and clicked off, and the next moment Sophy felt herself falling forward. Her feet slipped from the body of the buggy and as her knees hit the ground, she felt an actual crack. Her hands took the blow less than a second after her knees, which had already taken the brunt of the fall. Luckily, she was wearing gloves, as the weather had turned chilly again. She cried out as the sting from the sharp pebbly pavement and the hard impact from the fall ripped through her body. Then there was a voice that sounded far away. Sophy had instinctively tried to curl into the foetus position, but the voice was closer and Sophy couldn't bear to look up and see who had witnessed such a catastrophic blunder.

'Sophy, is that you?' The voice began to come through as the pain subsided and Sophy could finally hear properly again. She looked up to see Mel looming over her. Her heart sank. She felt the rage of disappointment at her misdemeanour. Why had she thought stalking the woman who had offered to talk to her at 3 a.m. was a good idea? Mel had seemed like a good human. What the hell had Sophy been thinking? She hated herself right now.

Sophy looked up and smiled. 'Hi, Mel, how are you?' Sophy did her best surprised voice.

'What are you doing around these parts? You're Clapham, aren't you?' Mel had her hand out and Sophy realised she was still on her knees; the buggy had only edged a few feet away from her and she could see Max was still fast asleep.

'Erm...' Sophy raised her hand, and Mel pulled her up in one swift thrust, the act so seamless, they could have been a couple on *Strictly Come Dancing*. Sophy was shocked and thrilled in equal portions at the vigour and strength Mel used. Then began to brush herself down in a show of disbelief.

'Wow, what a fool I feel,' Sophy said, suddenly feeling able to be slightly more honest in front of Mel.

'Good job I was just putting the bin out then, or your face plant would have gone undocumented. You still look fabulous though, by the way. But then I gauged that about you when I met you. I looked you up on Insta. You didn't tell me your account was so popular? You're a social media guru! I definitely want you on my team now,' Mel said putting an arm around her. 'Are you okay?'

Sophy smiled self-consciously. Here was Mel being an open book, whilst she had been skulking around outside her house. 'Yes. I'll be fine.'

'So did you get lost or is this your usual route?' Mel dropped her arm from around Sophy and pulled Max's pram back towards her.

'I love the coffee shop around here, and I was lost in thought walking – I must have missed the road turning.'

'Oh wow. Well, I live just there.' Mel pointed to the house Sophy had just been spying on.

'Oh yes, of course, you said you lived over this way. Nice gaff. Four-bed?'

'Yes. Thanks. My husband is a proper grafter. Left uni with no debts and got straight on the property ladder.'

Sophy smiled. 'Lucky.' She thought of her own poor set-up at Jeff's place, where she was still essentially just a lodger.

'So, you're off to Frank's? Their vegan brownies are to die for. I would join you, but Skylar is still sleeping, and well, I'm enjoying the peace and quiet. And I'm going to get a quick HIIT workout in.'

Sophy surreptitiously looked Mel up and down in her pink athletic leggings and shimmery grey vest top which showed off her perfectly sculpted shoulders.

'Wow, you're really into your fitness. I loved meeting you and Aisha the other day. I think she needs us, you know. Well, I think we all probably need each other. Christ, this parenting lark is proper hard,' Sophy gabbled.

Sophy realised she was still staring at Mel's arms and Mel had said nothing. 'Sorry, you're not cold, are you? I'm probably keeping you from your workout.'

'I don't mind the cold. I prefer it actually to the heat. My Daz complains cos I need a window open in the bedroom all through the year or I just start sweating, like profusely. It's not pretty. I asked Daz what he would prefer: a sodden wet mess next to him or a few little goosebumps.' Mel smiled. 'Anyway, do you feel okay? No sharp pains or dizzy spells? I have my first aid certificate – got it cos I was teaching dance as well as doing it, so you know, you're in safe hands.'

Sophy thought for a moment. There was a searing pain in her knees, and she knew she had the remnants of a few pebbles stuck to her gloves, but she decided to play it down.

'I think I'm going to be okay. Just my ego that's wounded.'

'Oooh, nice line – I like that. Okay, my friend. Take it easy.' Mel turned to walk away, then she stopped and called back over her shoulder, 'And text or call when you're feeding later. I've a feeling I'll be up with Skylar tonight – she's slept half the afternoon and woke up sniffly as hell.'

Sophy waved and smiled through a grimace.

Then she limped away to Frank's café, where she worked her way through three vegan brownies in a state of mortification.

* * *

Just over an hour later, Sophy wheeled the pram into the tiny hallway of the house, left Max sleeping and raced upstairs. After the catastrophe outside Mel's house, Sophy felt she needed to offset some of the negative energy that had been seeping from her since it happened. That negative energy quadrupled when she left the café, three brownies heavier. What kind of influencer was she? She experienced a moment of mortification, a slight bash to her knee and she did the one thing she explicitly told her followers not to do: she had turned to food for comfort.

She quickly touched up her make-up and tied her hair back into a neat ponytail. She held her iPhone to her right side, her better side, and sat in the chair with the wall in the background and pressed record on the Insta stories.

'Hi guys! It's been so nice these last few days with Max – we've been getting out and about without Daddy, as he's back at work, and already we're like a proper little team. I am starting to feel a bit more like myself again, but I am feeding Max through the night, so I can't say I'm not tired. But it's worth it. I'm excited for what this year will bring.

'As we are coming into spring, I am focusing on getting my core strength back in shape, it shouldn't take very long because I continued exercising whilst I was pregnant with Max. But I want to get strong. I have several challenges I have set for myself, which I want to share with you soon, and maybe, just maybe, you will feel inspired to challenge yourself too.

'Our bodies are capable of amazing things. I mean, I just pushed a human out of my nether region – something I honestly thought was an urban myth until it actually happened – so we can really surprise ourselves when we have a little faith and try to push our bodies that little bit more.

'Anyway, I just wanted to pop on, say hi and let you know I haven't disowned you, and I'm not lost in a world of nappies and baby wipes – although there is a lot of that. I am here for every single one of you, to help you, encourage and inspire you. You are all brilliant, brilliant humans – don't forget that. Exercise and healthy heating is a lifelong journey, not a quick fix. It's a lifestyle choice, so make that choice and stick with it. I'm here for you as always.

'See you soon.'

Sophy blew a kiss to the camera then felt the familiar deflation as she thought about what she had just told her followers versus the stark reality of her body currently digesting three brownies. Then she thought about the influx of messages in her inbox that were sure to come from that one post. A wave of despondency washed over her at the thought of having to reply to people. She just wanted to lie in bed and watch *Married at First Sight*. Sophy looked around at the mess in the bedroom she had meant to sort earlier before she left and felt even worse.

She began to tidy up, but, after a few minutes, tiredness overcame her and she flopped down on the bed. Sophy looked at her emails on her phone and saw there were fifty-one new messages. Oh crikey! What did all these people want? Couldn't they just leave her alone? But Sophy knew she needed this job; even if Jeff reassured her that he was the breadwinner and that she had nothing to worry about financially, she did not want to end up as one of those women who had to go to their partner to ask for money. She had to have her own source of income for her own sanity, and maybe – she could admit to herself, after all – as a safety net. Some relationships didn't last, and if that ever happened to her and Jeff, then what would she have as a backup? Her parents were skint and had only manged to buy their house because the council sold it to them for a pittance. She received a modest income in sponsorship from her Instagram account, but she was determined to build it up into a business, even if it killed her. She just had to find a way to love it a bit more, to feel true enthusiasm for the content she was putting out. That way, if she really believed in it, then everyone else would too, and then she was sure the account would grow exponentially. She knew that until recently, she was just riding off the back of a few well-taken photographs, well-timed posts and clever hashtags.

Sophy glanced once more at the messages and then put them to the back of her mind until later. She would reply to all of them in bed tonight.

The house was a mess, and seeing all those messages from followers all wanting advice on nutrition or just reaching out to say hi, made her brain feel messy too.

But claustrophobic as well. The house really was too small. She was frustrated that Jeff, who drove around in a Jaguar F-PACE, had taken so long to commit to the extension on the house when she knew there was enough money coming in from the estate agency to cover the cost. Why *had* he taken so long? Sophy wondered. She tried not to contemplate the possibility that it was because he hadn't seen them lasting. She had definitely felt some tension after they discovered she was pregnant, even though it had been discussed many times. Jeff had been adamant he was ready to be a father. Yet he'd developed a faraway look in his eye once the pregnancy test was sat on the table between them, and it hadn't ever really gone away.

Max was here now, and so far Jeff was showing some promise as a new father. But the size of the house was a problem. Especially if they decided to have more children. It wasn't something they had discussed, but something Sophy knew she would want in a few years' time. She would just need to wait to broach the subject with Jeff once he had lost that look in his eye. Sophy had specifically asked him to do something before Max was born so that they weren't all tripping over one another and the mountain of Max's stuff that was beginning to take up every corner of the house. If Sophy had been a little savvier with money or understanding finances (it was her least favourite module in her business degree), then she would feel more confident speaking to Jeff about his money. But she didn't and so he kept his finances well and truly to himself. And Sophy found she didn't have the foggiest about the ins and outs of Jeff's business. She knew he owned an estate agency, but she was annoyed that she had never instigated finding out more about the financial operations of the business from the outset. But how does one bring that up in the beginning of a relationship? *Wow, I really love your eyes? Tell me how much did your business make in the last tax year?* She had met Jeff, fallen for him, specifically his charming mannerisms and his insistence on paying for everything, so that when it became serious, she didn't feel she could begin questioning anything. Four years later, she was as clueless as the smitten girl who had fallen for him.

She bent down and began tidying the clutter in the bedroom. She was about to start making the bed when the loud trill of the doorbell made her heart leap. She cursed, because she knew that would have woken Max up without a doubt. But it was her own fault for leaving him so close to the front door.

Sophy trotted down the stairs, peeked in at a miraculously still-sleeping Max and opened the front door. There on the doorstep was a tall, tanned man, around six foot with ruffled dark-blond hair and an unshaven rough-stubbled chin. He was wearing the most miraculous smile that lit up his eyes so that they sparkled like hundred-watt bulbs and made his cheeks dimple in an endearing way. She was quite taken aback and seemed to forget all doorstep etiquette. She just stood there, smiling back, until she felt her cheeks beginning to hurt. Eventually, he spoke, and Sophy was treated to the richest velvety Irish accent she had ever heard.

'Hiya, I'm Niall. Me and me lads are doing the extension.'

And then Sophy felt herself inwardly groan.

Oh no, she thought. *Oh. No.*

* * *

2.38 a.m. – Sophy: Hi, girls. How are you all doing?

2.47 a.m. – Aisha: Hey, Sophy, I'm up with the twins. Just finished feeding them. They are both back in their cot. For now. Reckon I might get a couple of hours' kip in. Thanks for texting. Hey, it's almost 3 a.m.!

2.48 a.m. – Sophy: Yeah, I know. This time of the morning, like you say, can be the loneliest time. So good to meet you all the other day. I don't think we were destined for tai chi and tea. Shall we try to meet up again soon?

2.49 a.m. – Aisha: Yes, definitely! It was great to meet you both too. Hey, I guess Mel is having an easier time of it and is asleep!

2.50 a.m. – Sophy: Yep, I reckon Skylar is a champion sleeper!

2.50 a.m. – Aisha: Lucky Mel. Hey, Mel, hello when you wake up and read this message. We were thinking of you.

2.51 a.m. – Sophy: You get some sleep now, Aisha. I promise I will message some dates tomorrow. Night night. x

2.51 a.m. – Aisha: Great. Night night x

5.45 a.m. – Mel: What can I say, I have the dream second child.

8

AISHA

Aisha was almost home after a mammoth walk around the park and the high street. She didn't think she had ever walked so far, and knew already that her legs would be aching the next day.

But the twins had loved it. Their little faces had lit up looking around at the sights and sounds. And, of course, Aisha would then find herself falling easily into conversations with complete strangers, as one did when they had tiny babies.

According to her phone, she had managed five kilometres, and the twins were now sound asleep. She was exhausted and was experiencing the odd heart palpitation, having barely eaten a thing all day. She had been up three times in the night feeding the twins, but it had been nice to speak with Sophy in those early hours. Just being able to reach out to someone at that time of the morning made a real difference. It suddenly felt as though there was a connection there. And that was the sort of thing she was looking for right now – what she was craving. That and a full English breakfast. She could almost taste it.

As Aisha rounded the corner onto her street, she stopped in her tracks. The man from the other day. The one who had walked up and down the road, over and over. He was there again. But this time, he was staring up at her house from the opposite side of the road. She was sure of it. She started walking again, and the man suddenly began moving away, his head bent down into his chest so she couldn't see any of his features. Had he really just been staring up at her house, at her bedroom window? Or was she being paranoid? Perhaps he was a birdwatcher and had seen one on her roof? She stopped herself before she began to overthink it.

She wheeled the buggy through the front door and pushed it through to the end of the hallway. The postman would be here soon, and the clattering of the letter box would absolutely wake the twins up. She put the cooker extractor on for some white noise – and because she was about to fry eggs and bacon – then put the kettle on. She was absolutely gagging for a cuppa.

She looked at her phone again to check her achievement, thrilled to see almost nine thousand steps. She noticed a message on the 3 a.m. Shattered Mums' Club WhatsApp group that Sophy had created. Aisha went into the message and saw Mel had joined in from her and Sophy's chat last night.

11.36 a.m. – Mel: Hey, girls. Sorry I missed you both last night. Skylar had a really long sleep in the middle of the night. She's got a bit of a temperature, and only woke for her 10 p.m. and 5 a.m. bottle. I know, I know, you hate me. It's just luck, that's all. I promise I have no secret tricks up my sleeve. I won't be writing any baby-whispering books soon. Hope you're both okay. Would love to meet up again soon. Sophy, you're our admin! Will leave you to throw some dates at us. Ciao for now! M x

Aisha felt another wave of something that felt like joy. Was this sisterhood? It had been too long. Her own sisters were so busy with their own lives: one had moved to Brighton, the other to Bristol. Her cousins were still around, but where they had been close as kids, the gap had expanded over the last few years. Aisha suspected that they felt she was too middle class for them now the way they would tease her over her fancy wallpaper and Charley's Audi.

She tried so hard to keep believing in who she was; and stay true to her Brixton roots but ever since she was a kid she had always felt as though a part of her was missing. She had spent the last twenty years trying to fill that gap with material possessions. She would use any pocket money from relatives to buy things for her bedroom, which she shared with her two sisters. Her side of the room had been filled with teddies, ornaments and posters on the wall. Her sisters cursed at the way her corner of their bedroom stood out from the rest of the room, but occasionally she would see one of them glancing over, their eyes would focus on a new trinket or bed cushion and she could tell they were envious of her ability to spend her money on things that could be seen and treasured and not wasted on sweets and chocolate.

Ever since she was old enough to get her first job at fourteen in a tea room, with the twenty-five pounds a week she made, she would go into town after work and buy herself new hair clips, stick-on nails, make-up from Superdrug and jeans and tops from Miss Selfridge. When she moved out of the Brixton house at twenty and rented her own flat around the corner, she filled it with furniture, plants, rugs – anything to stop her feeling as though there was something missing.

When she met Charley, her wage as restaurant manager combined with Charley's salary – which was twice what she earned – meant there was always extra money for stuff. So now, as the bacon sizzled in the pan, Aisha found herself heading to her favourite online furniture store and browsing some coloured intricately designed tumblers. A set of six just shy of one hundred pounds. Because when she began to feel up to it, she would want to start entertaining again. And catering for friends and family was what she did best. Her fusion of British and Jamaican cooking was what she was famed for amongst those closest to her. Her dream was to have her own little restaurant one day, serving her signature dishes: her Jamaican take on the roast dinner: garlic and paprika potatoes, with cinnamon lime chicken and sticky ginger carrots. But at the moment, every time she dared think of it, the dream slipped further and further away. The boys were so young – it would be years before she could commit to something like that. It was such a great idea; she was sure someone would open a similar restaurant before she had the chance. She had often thought of buying the domain name now, so she had it ready. But Charley had encouraged her to wait: 'Let the business grow organically – don't force something to be born before it's time.' Charley had a point, but Aisha was mad at herself for how easily she settled down and got cosy, feeling so secure with Charley as the breadwinner when she should have been hustling and getting the business started. And then she got pregnant. But she tried not to think about to it too much, because the more she did, the more she felt the stress build. The boys were here, and they were so perfect. Why couldn't she just live in the moment and feel it a bit more?

'Your mum stopped by earlier.'

'What?' Aisha turned at Charley's voice. She walked into the kitchen and grimaced at Aisha's food frying in the pan. She was strictly 'a bowl of bran flakes for breakfast and salad for lunch' kind of girl; none of this randomly eating at 11.30 in the morning. Charley did not do brunch or afternoon tea. 'Mum never pops round.'

She still had beef at Charley from yesterday, even though she was no longer sure why – she just knew she was mad, and she had to make her know it for a few more days.

'Right. What did she want?' Aisha said absently as she put a teabag into the mug and poured freshly boiled water over it.

'Just that, she was just passing and thought she'd pop in.'

Charley had one of those doorbell app things on her phone for when she was down in the basement and couldn't hear the front door.

'Were you in the middle of recording?' Aisha wondered if her mum messing up one of Charley's jingles would make her feel better about whatever was still eating her up.

'No, just an edit. I asked her in for a coffee...'

'... But?'

'She made her excuses. Said she had errands to run.'

Aisha pulled her mouth down. 'Weird.'

'I thought so too.' Charley leant over the counter and looked down at Aisha's phone. 'Thinking of buying those? Ninety quid is a bit steep?'

Aisha snatched her phone up away from the kitchen side. She had forgotten she had extended the screen saver timer the other day when she was trying out a recipe and had meant to put it back to thirty seconds.

'All right, touchy!' Charley said, reaching for a mug and taking the rest of the boiled water for a coffee.

'I thought it was "our money",' Aisha said.

'It is. They're just a bit expensive, that's all.'

'I wasn't buying them – I was just looking. I'd like something similar when I start the restaurant.'

Charley's silence was deafening.

'At least say what you're thinking,' Aisha snapped this time.

'That's the joy of thinking – no one has to know.'

Aisha took the milk out of the fridge, squeezed out the teabag and added a splash.

'You don't want me to have dreams? Is that it?'

'God no, Aisha. I love your dreams. Your dreams are my dreams.'

'Yeah, so you say,' Aisha mumbled.

'I just want you to focus on the babies, enjoy them now, because they won't be little forever, and you have all the time after that to focus on your career. You wanted them so badly, and now they're here...?'

'And what? You didn't want them, is that what you're saying? I'm thirty years old, Charley! If I don't start at least thinking about the business now, it will be too late! I'll be nearly thirty-five by the time the boys go to school and I have some time to spare.'

'That's if we don't have any more,' Charley quipped.

'God no!' Aisha said too quickly and too loudly. She saw Charley's expression: a mixture of relief and surprise. 'What I mean is, I think we've been lucky getting two at once. I don't think we need any more children. Do you want any more?'

Charley shook her head. 'Two's good for me. And stop worrying about your age – thirty-five isn't old, and you'll never look older than forty as long as you live.'

'Well, it's okay for you. You have your career, and it's not as if you really wanted them in the first place, did you?' Aisha spat out the words she had been holding on to since they first found out she was pregnant.

'Come on, now. I love our boys.'

'*Now*, but you would have been happier without them?' For some reason, Aisha felt an incessant need to keep pushing and pushing.

'I was always happy with just us; I didn't have the same... needs as you.'

'Well, sorry for wanting a family!' The volume in Aisha's voice had gone up.

Charley backed away.

'I wasn't as keen to start a family as you were, that's no secret, but I'm glad they're here. We have some really exciting times ahead of us. Let's just be grateful for what we have and live one day at a time, okay?'

Aisha had her back to Charley but even without seeing she could feel that she had turned and was walking away. For a split second, she had wanted to turn and grab Charley, pull her into an embrace and tell her she was sorry. But instead, she let Charley go and felt the gap opening up between them.

* * *

Later that day, as Aisha was calming down after her cross words with Charley, she began to assess her emotions, tried to break them down so she could work out what was really eating her up. And as she did, she felt a strange longing, a need to speak about the man from the street. Under normal circumstances, these were the sort of things she would talk to Charley about. But after the falling-out and how stupid Charley had managed to make her feel yet again about simply looking at some coloured tumblers, Aisha stopped herself bringing anything up on the several occasions throughout the rest of the morning and into the afternoon they crossed paths. Each time, she could feel a void deepening between them. She felt like a stranger around Charley these days. Charley manged to keep acting and looking like the same person she always was, whereas ever since Aisha had become a mother, she felt like she'd stepped into someone else's body. She was probably just tired and hormonal, and she needed someone to reaffirm that.

She messaged the girls on the 3 a.m. Mums' group.

2.55 p.m. – Aisha: Hey, ever feel as though you're going totally mad?

Mel's reply came back straight away.

2.56 p.m. – Mel: Yep, every day. I spent the entire day with my top on inside out. No one said anything. I only noticed when I went to change out of it after Skylar threw up on me.

Aisha laughed out loud. She understood that completely. It was exactly the sort of thing she could imagine herself doing.

Mel: Can you top that?
Aisha: No. Nothing that bad. Although that was pure lol. Just checking I'm not the only one who feels like they're losing their mind!
Mel: I'm with you there, girl. I sometimes think I'll pass myself coming back the other way, I'm that busy at the moment.
Aisha: Well, take it easy. Let's wait to hear from the admin with a date. But I'm pretty free most days. And I haven't been to any baby groups, is that bad?
Mel: Maybe we could go to one together? Safety in numbers!
Aisha: Yes, could we? I do want to do it for the boys, but the idea of a baby group terrifies me!
Mel: I'm a veteran of baby groups. I'll find us one and we can all go together.
Aisha: Ha-ha! I look forward to it.

As Aisha put down her phone again, she found that she was smiling. The boys were laid out on their activity mat in front of her, *Orange is the New Black* was on quietly in the background – that was one thing she was going to make the most of – watching programmes that would be deemed highly inappropriate if the babies could sit up and see. She got down onto the floor and lay closest to Otis. He gurgled and made a squeaking noise. Aisha tried to do what she was being told to do by Charley and just live in the moment, but the happiness that she had felt after Mel's reply on the WhatsApp group had passed as quickly as it had arrived, and Aisha felt a sudden sense of foreboding, a hint of a gut wrench that was trying to sneak back in. Why couldn't she hold on to the happiness? Why was it so difficult? She tried to replay Mel's message in her head, and relive how it had made her feel, but it was gone, and the strange tingly tummy feeling was back again.

Aisha had always been an optimistic child. When her father had left, she had comforted her mother daily, telling her that things would be okay. That was where her love of cooking had come from, as she had begun to assist her mum in the kitchen to feel closer to her. So, Aisha tried to use some of that optimism now: she'd felt a sense of joy when she had read messages from the 3 a.m. Mums, so if she could feel little else for now, at least she had hope.

9

MEL

The small, skinny woman who had claimed her spot directly in front of Mel at her yoga class was stretching enthusiastically even before the instructor had arrived. Was that not the point of a yoga class? To stretch? It had been a fair few months since Mel had been to one of Doug's classes at her local gym, and she wondered if she had missed a vital new addition to the timetable. Was stretching prior to stretching now mandatory? The woman in front of her was in a downward dog but was so damn flexible that her head was almost coming all the way back through her legs like some sort of stretchy cartoon character. As a result, Mel got not only an intimate view of the woman's backside but also at her strange elastic neck as her head poked in between her tiny legs. It was comical to look at, and Mel was half inclined to stay put and not move twelve inches to her right so she would be able to see Doug when he arrived and instead remain highly entertained by Mrs Incredible throughout the class. But before she had time to think about it any longer, a woman arrived next to her and began setting up her yoga mat. She flung it out and Mel was hit by a waft of lavender. She turned to the tall, thin woman next to her.

'Wow! That smells amazing! Is that you?' Mel said to the woman.

'Ya, it's my mat. It's fluffy too!' the woman said in a South African accent

Mel looked down at the mat, which had a mound of fluff on the top. 'So, it is! I have never seen one like that.'

'Ya, t'was a present. From me!' The woman guffawed loudly. Mel flinched at the noise and thrust herself into a downward dog. *Ahh*, she thought, *so stretching before stretching is a thing*. She buried her head between her legs and avoided any further eye contact with lavender woman or Mrs incredible. Doug arrived, looking fit with his usual golden tan. The thirty-something dark-haired yoga instructor strode into the room and immediately all eyes were on him. A few women began chatting intimately, clearly discussing Doug's Greek-god-like status as he went straight down almost into the splits and lay his entire body along one leg. Mel heard one woman three mats away outwardly gasp.

'Okay, Okay!' Doug got himself back up and began fiddling with his iPad, attaching a headset over his bouncy barnet. Soft music began playing out of the speakers around the room and Doug got settled back on his mat at the front of the room.

'Right, ladies, who do I have today? Any newcomers, any injuries, show your hands now!' Doug's Essex accent rang out around the room.

Mel stood up straight and caught Doug's roaming eye.

'Mel!' he said brightly. 'Welcome back! Ladies, if you haven't yet met Mel, she is our super-star yoga enthusiast, been here as long as I have. So good to see you again, make sure you grab me at the end. And take it easy!'

Mel smiled and nodded and avoided the gazes of some of the other women, a few of whom she remembered from when she came before but had never really engaged in conversation with.

Doug began the class with a tai chi warm-up and then began the yoga. Mel quickly drifted off into her own world with the dulcet tones of Doug's voice lulling her into a meditative state. It amazed Mel how he lost his high Essex accent somewhere after the first sun warrior as his tone morphed into hippy yoga instructor: deep and melodic.

Mel was feeling completely relaxed and was thrilled her body had sunk back into most of the positions as though no time had passed, as though she hadn't given birth at forty-three and put her body under a massive strain at such an age. Doug's voice oozed itself out around the room and spread itself amongst the ears of the women. Mel wondered why it was indeed *all* women in this class. She remembered a man from a couple of years ago. Doug had made a lot of references to his sex, singling him out for commentary throughout the class, and perhaps, Mel thought, he had become tired of being the only guy amongst fifteen or so women. Doug was sweet but lacked tact and occasionally good social etiquette.

'And into a downward dog.' Doug's voice trailed slowly and smoothly. Mel slid seamlessly into the move, but not before she caught the eye of the woman in front of her and her stupid upside-down face that hung between her legs. She looked between her own legs and tried to pretend the woman wasn't there. Mel was feeling smug with how easily she was able to make the transition between each move so seamlessly and could feel her muscles tense and relax again with each move.

'Now warrior two, right leg turned out, third toe in line with knee and sink as far as you can go.'

If Mel had felt the sudden sucking of air into her vagina during the last downward dog, she chose to ignore it, because in the time she had been away from this class, she had not thought about the loosening of the muscles in her nether regions very much. When she had given birth to Leia, she had been over ten years younger; things had popped back into place a lot quicker then. So, when she had followed Doug's instructions and sunk a little lower into the pose, she was shocked to hear the sound that trumpeted from beneath her, initially unable to believe it had come from her or a hole that had brought two babies into the world without creating such a hullabaloo before. But the shuddering sensation between her legs that accompanied the loud expulsion of air confirmed her worst fear. Doug remained calm and focused, continuing his honeyed words, encouraging breath and spiritual connection. Heads spun this way and that, searching for the culprit, and Mel remained tight in her pose, her cheeks burning with mortification, but her head held high. With the music playing and Doug's voice coming through boldly from the speakers, it would have been impossible for anyone to know, and Mel was certainly not about to hold her hand up and admit to doing something that, until then, she had thought only happened to other women, women with incontinence or who had given birth to fifteen babies. So, it was with the greatest confidence that Mel sunk back down into another downward dog, this time tightening her pelvic muscle to ensure no entry to any unwanted air. Just before she tucked her head down, she caught the eye of the upside-down woman in front of her again. And even at such an awkward angle, it was impossible for Mel to ignore the face that was trying to say something. The woman held Mel's gaze for enough time for the message to come across loud and clear. 'I know it was you' said the upside-down eyes, and Mel sunk into her pose, suddenly feeling half the size she was when she arrived.

* * *

Back at home later that afternoon, Mel allowed a slight tingle of excitement to sweep through her as she began putting down the dates of gigs in the calendar. It was as though she had opened herself up to opportunity.

Now she had the shows to think about, they managed to keep most of the negative thoughts at bay. As soon as she had agreed to one gig, then they just came flying in. She was now booked up from April to September, putting on her Adele tribute act and burlesque dancing twice sometimes three times a week. She was confident that at three months old, Skylar was showing signs of a good night-time routine. She could hardly believe her luck, really. Daz would do the 10 p.m. feed on the weeknights she was out, and she would do the early-morning feed when she came home. Of course, she would be exhausted, but eventually it would get easier. And if it meant she could return to her beloved gigging, then she was happy.

Of course, as she noted down the latest bookings, there was the slight niggling feeling that she had been trying to ignore. The incident that had occurred on her final gig. She still felt the twinges of something in her gut, the reminder of what had happened that last night she had performed, and now she knew she was almost certain that the perpetrator was Sophy's other half, well, she just couldn't bring herself to tell lovely, kind Sophy. How would that make her look? She already knew how some women viewed her: as someone who was gagging for it, as harsh as it sounded admitting it to herself, it was the truth. Mel knew she emitted a certain look that some women took to mean she was a husband stealer. She was certain that Sophy would perceive her that way too and think she had been responsible for what had happened.

She had been six weeks pregnant; she knew she had to stop the dancing, no one wants to see a dancer with a massive belly.

She was feeling as sick as dog, anyway. But then it happened, and by the end of that night, she went home feeling as though she wanted to rip herself inside out. She hated her body, for what it had attracted, for what that man felt he had the right to do. Of course, she didn't tell Daz. He was still none the wiser even to this day. She wasn't sure exactly what he would have done if he did know – he wasn't the kind of guy to get into brawls or confrontations. She was able to block all thoughts of Jeff when she was with Daz. It was in her blood, the ability to switch emotions on and off. The show must go on and all that. It was what she did. If she couldn't perform, she would shrivel up and die. As much as she loved the bones of her daughters – and she did with a fierce lioness's force; she wished to protect those girls from everything that was bad in the world – she knew she couldn't live every moment of her life for them. Doing things for herself was what made her. Mel always felt like a much better mum when she could go away, do something creative. And every time, she would come back, refreshed, ready to perform her duties much better.

* * *

That night, Mel had tried to put Skylar down after her 10 p.m. feed, but instantly, she could sense something was different. The baby seemed fractious and unsettled. It took Mel a good half an hour of extra burping, then cuddles, and before she knew it, Mel was walking the length and breadth of the house just to get her back to sleep.

'Good grief, Skylar, why are you testing Mummy this evening. I thought we had come to an understanding – I feed you and you go back to sleep until morning.' But Skylar whinged on until eventually she tired herself out again and was a dead weight on Mel's shoulder. When Mel put her down in her cot, she could feel a little milky dribble damp patch on her shoulder. She stripped off her top and threw it in the laundry basket and pulled a white vest out of her drawer. Daz was already asleep on his side of the bed, snoring inoffensively. Mel knew she was lucky, that Daz may not have been everyone's idea of a sex god, but she still fancied him, and besides, he was a steady guy, who always put the toilet seat down and didn't move furniture with his breath when he slept.

* * *

Mel was startled awake. She looked at her phone. It was just after midnight. Sky was crying in the cot next to the bed. Mel jumped up and lifted the baby up to her chest. She wasn't wet, but she couldn't be hungry again after two hours. Mel lay Sky down on her bed whilst she pulled her dressing gown on. Sky opened her lungs and an almighty cry exploded from her mouth.

'Okay, okay, sweet one.' Mel lifted her back into her arms and hurried out of the bedroom, just as Daz began to stir. Leia's door was ajar as Mel tiptoed onto the landing; Skylar was feeling a little more settled in her arms. Leia's little face was peeking from the gap in the doorway.

'Is everything okay?' she whispered. Her dark raven hair was pulled up into a messy bun, almost identical to the way Mel wore hers.

'Yes, she's just a bit unsettled.'

'Okay,' Leia said, Mel could tell she was still half asleep. It was times like these Mel wondered what the hell she had done having another kid when she had an almost teenager who slept most of the day, their two worlds were so far apart. But Mel walked downstairs and began the pacing of the house again, listening to the creaking of the radiators that were still kicking in during the night as the temperature dropped. Perhaps that was what had woken Sky – she was chilly. Mel took another blanket from a pile in the lounge and wrapped it around Sky.

She began her shhh-shhh sound, which Daz claimed drove him to distraction and Leia said made her sound a little bit mental. 'Why would any kid want to hear that noise in their ear? It must be pure torture,' Leia had said only last week as Mel did the 'shhh and drop' walk as Leia named it, because she would take long strides but slacken her legs slightly with every step, so Sky would drop ever so slightly, hopefully sending her off to sleep. Daz and Leia had looked on in wonderment.

'You look like Liam Gallagher; you're walking like him,' Leia had said. 'And you're dribbling as you shhh. You're a drunk Liam Gallagher. I'm going to video this and put it on TikTok.' Leia pulled out her phone and started filming, the camera shaking as she laughed.

'Do not make me into a TikTok video, Leia, or I will ground you for life, so help me,' Mel had seethed.

At that, Daz and Leia had lost it and were holding one another up laughing.

Finally, after twenty minutes of walking, Mel felt the weight of Sky on her shoulder and her breathing had become slow and heavy. She took her back upstairs and lowered her into her cot, where she remained asleep.

* * *

Mel sat bolt upright.

'What?' she called out to the room. Daz stirred next to her but didn't wake. Skylar was screaming again. Mel looked at her phone. It was 2.21 a.m. She jumped out of bed and lifted Skylar out of the cot.

'Shhh,' she whispered. Mel had fallen back to sleep with the dressing gown on, so she wrapped it around her and Sky and paced the bedroom. The cries continued, so Mel grabbed her phone and headed back downstairs again.

She had a few bottles made up in the fridge for the morning, so she whipped one out and into the microwave for thirty seconds to take the edge off it. She knew that's not how the formula milk companies recommended you do it, but Mel was past caring, and after breastfeeding Leia, had prepared formula exactly the same way. She shook the bottle, took a sip to test it and popped it in Skylar's mouth. She took the bottle and Mel walked through to the lounge, flopped onto the sofa, and leant her head back against the soft fabric. She must have dropped off again, as her head jerked forward as Sky spat the teat out. She was asleep. Mel reached for her phone: 2.53 a.m. She bashed out a message to the girls.

Mel: Mayday, Mayday, is anyone out there?

The response came quickly from Aisha.

2.55 a.m. – Aisha: I'm here settling the twins downstairs. I know I shouldn't have, but I've put on the TV for a bit of extra comfort.

Mel shook her head at Aisha worrying about what she should and shouldn't do. Who or what book told her she couldn't put her TV on at three o'clock in the morning?

2.57 a.m. – Mel: You do what you gotta do, girl, to get through.

Another message pinged through from Aisha.

2.59 a.m. – Aisha: How come you're awake, anyway? That's unusual for you.

3.01 a.m. – Mel: I know. I've had the night from hell. Sky's had me up three times already. Hoping she'll go through now 'til actual morning.

3.02 a.m. – Aisha: Oh dear, she's over three months now, isn't she? She's out of the fourth trimester and is now a bit more conscious of her existence. I guess we'll be hearing from you a lot more during the night!

Mel looked at the message in bewilderment. What was this fourth trimester that Aisha was talking about? And why didn't she, who had been a mother once already, know about this? She googled it and read quickly about the phase straight after birth, where the mother can help ease the transition between the womb and the world by keeping baby close at all times. Well, Mel had not done any baby wearing; Sky had been happy in her cot and slept for almost six hours most nights for the last six weeks. Occasionally, she would wake for a feed at about four, but would always go straight back to sleep again until at least seven.

Mel threw the phone on the sofa and hoped that this was just a slight blip. Skylar was having a mere moment and, hopefully, normal business would resume the next night. She was forty-fucking-three – she couldn't cope with being woken that many times in one night.

She pushed herself to the end of the sofa, lay her head on the cushion and put her feet out along in front of her. She would just stay there for a moment until she was sure Skylar, who was flat out on her chest, was definitely not going to wake up again.

* * *

'What are you doing down here?'

Mel opened her eyes. Well, one eye. The other seemed to need a little more encouragement. Daz was standing in front of her and there was light streaming through the curtains. Shit, she had slept on the sofa. Daz was dressed in his work clothes. It must be six thirty already. He was always in the office for eight. Mel wanted to hand the baby over but seeing at how pristine and smart he looked – he always looked pristine and smart – in his suit, she knew he wouldn't take her. She sat up, slowly, Sky still clinging to her chest.

'You'll make a rod for own back sleeping with her like that all night,' Daz said in a half-mocking tone as he walked to the kitchen.

'You don't happen to have one, a rod? I could really do with one right now.' Mel felt a sharp pain slice through her lower spine, which had been unsupported on the sofa for the last three hours. She lay with her head against the sofa and heard the kettle boiling. A few minutes later, there was a cup of tea in front of her on the coffee table. Sky remained glued to her chest, her little mouth open in an O-shape as she breathed. Mel watched her for a few minutes and felt as if all the strength had been sucked out of her. She wanted to reach for the mug, but to do so would wake Sky and she wasn't ready for that just yet. So, she sat there, watching her brew cooling, and in her head, began to invent a machine that would bring hot tea to your mouth without risk of burning mother or baby.

10

SOPHY

The house had taken on the aroma of fresh wood and some sort of chemical smell that wasn't all that unpleasant. This was accompanied by the constant tinny sound of Radio 1 being played and the occasional male voice singing along. Niall had been at the house for three days with his 'band of merry men', as Jeff had referred to them. They were always so jolly – 'Morning, Mr Haddon,' they'd call as they arrived just before he slipped out of the door. The first morning, Jeff had waited to leave the house until after 8 a.m. to make sure they were all there and doing what they should be doing. Not that Jeff had any understanding of what building an extension entailed, but he stood over them for a few minutes as they began unpacking tools, nodding, and saying, 'Good, good.'

Since then, he hadn't bothered, and Sophy had been in the house with them for the last few days and had begun to get used to the noise and the clutter. It reminded her of the house she grew up in, with three younger brothers and an elder sister; there were always people coming and going, and once her parents had bought the house, they spent a little bit of money getting new windows and a new door put in. Sophy realised she had forgotten how much she loved the feeling of a busy house. She had spent so much time simply existing with just Jeff. When she mentioned how she would love a large family like the one she had come from, she saw Jeff physically recoil. She hadn't mentioned it again because, of course, why would Jeff – an only child who had been and still was doted on by Wendy and Al – need a house full of kids with needs and wants? Instead, Sophy had moments of panic that Max would not experience the chaos and love that came with more than one child in a house.

The sun was shining, so she decided she would take herself out to the garden to do her weekly vlog. Max was in the pram in the corner of the lawn. She'd done a walk down to the coffee shop, and he had thankfully nodded off on the way home. She set up a chair next to the small shed, which was still new and modern looking, if a little weather worn, but Sophy felt this added to the background effect she was going for. The shed itself barely contained anything except a few basic gardening tools. No mower either as the lawn was fake grass. She put the camera on its tripod a few metres away from the chair, sorted out the focus, pressed record, then sat down with the empty takeaway coffee in her hand as a prop.

'Hey, guys, hope you're all well. Hope you're all super proud of me for sorting out another video! I do these to motivate myself as much as you, so you know we're all in this together.

'Firstly, sorry about any noise in the background, we're having an extension built, and it's all a bit messy and noisy right now. But that won't stop me getting behind this camera and helping you all stay motivated. That's why I brought myself out into the garden on this glorious morning. It's a bit chilly but the sun is so warm. Remember, sun gives us natural vitamin D, which is essential for absorbing calcium for bone strength, the immune system and for our brains and mental health. We don't get enough sun in this country, do we? So I always take a vitamin D supplement. I will try to add a link somewhere somehow to the one I use. I might stick it in my stories, so check those out too.

'I mainly wanted to say don't forget to look after yourselves today. If you had a bad day yesterday, then wipe the slate clean and start again. My DMs are open if you need any nutritional advice. I study nutrition still every day – there is so much more new information to discover – and as soon as I know it, I'll share it with you. I'll be back to exercising again soon, so I'll keep you posted on how that goes! Eeek, pelvic muscles! I have to give my body a couple more weeks to recover yet. But watch this space! In the meantime, have a great day, guys. And be the very best you can be today.'

Sophy stood up and was about to switch the camera off when she felt the sensation of someone watching her. She looked to her left, and Niall was standing at the back door – which was soon to become one long patio door. He was watching her with a look of curiosity. *Shit*, Sophy thought. She had presumed they were all in the van at the front of the house having their tea break. She would edit it later when Max was having another nap. As she went to take a step forward, a pain shot up through her pelvis.

'Arrrgh.' Sophy went to grab hold of the tripod in an attempt to steady herself, but it was too weak and she watched in horror as it toppled to the ground.

'Hey there, you okay?' Niall was next to her, bending down and picking up the tripod and camera.

Sophy looked at him as he rose back up to her level, then overtook her. He was a few inches taller. With what she now realised were actually green eyes. Had she only just noticed that? Or was this because this was the closest he had been to her?

'Thank you. I'm fine. Just a twinge.'

'You know you shouldn't overdo it. Although, me mammy had six babies and was up the next day with all of us, so who am I to talk.'

'Hey, that's funny, I'm from a large family too. An elder sister and three younger brothers.'

'I thought I could see that in you. You look like a girl who has had to fight for attention.'

Sophy looked quizzically at Niall.

'I meant it as a compliment, even though it clearly did not come out as one. You look like a very assertive young lady is what I was trying to say.' Niall seemed to shake his head in embarrassment.

'Oh, right, well in that case, thank you. And I'm not overdoing it. It's...' Sophy stopped herself. She wasn't about to explain about the searing pain she would get every time she peed that had only just begun to subside, but had now been replaced with occasional pelts of pain through her vagina and into her anus and how she had read up about it and it was all perfectly normal and part of the healing process when your perineum had been ripped pushing an infant's head out of your body. No, best not speak about those things to the builder.

'I get it, as I said, I'm one of six. I know what it can do a woman's body. Anyway, try and rest – just the one you got is it?'

Sophy instantly thought of Aisha with her twin babies. One baby was hard enough. She reminded herself she needed to book in a date where Mel, Aisha and she could all go to a baby group together.

'Yes, my first. It's... hard.'

'I get ya,' Niall said, still holding onto the tripod and camera. Sophy looked at it.

'Here, let me.'

'Just tell me where to put it.' Niall looked towards the house.

'Erm, okay, can you stick it on the island in the kitchen? I need to erm... edit.' Sophy realised she sounded ridiculous.

Sophy walked behind Niall, the camera and the tripod in his hands, his dusty khaki combat pockets swishing as he walked.

'Are you one of those YouTubers?' Niall asked as he set the equipment down on the island. Sophy clicked the camera out of the tripod and inspected it for damage, turning it on and breathing a sigh of relief as the screen came to life.

'Not so much YouTube as Instagram?' Sophy asked as though Niall wouldn't have heard of such a thing.

'Oh right, yeah, me brother is on that. I'll have to ask him if he's heard of you.'

Sophy let out a small laugh. 'ThisGirlThisBody,' she said.

Niall looked her up and down quickly. 'Beg ya pardon?'

'Oh, sorry, I thought you were savvy with the Insta thing, that's my handle. @ThisGirlThisBody.'

Niall pulled his mouth down and shook his head. 'Sorry, it's wasted on me. Not your body.' Niall looked flushed, and Sophy felt herself redden as well. 'The thingy, the handle? I'm not au fait with the whole social-media stuff. I make walls and floors and cupboards.'

'Well, I'd say you made a good career choice. It's not all it's cracked up to be.'

'Oh right, how so?'

Had she really just admitted that to a complete stranger? But she had already just admitted to him that having Max was hard. She hadn't even said as much to Jeff yet.

But Niall seemed... nice. Like the sort of person who would be easy to talk to. She felt a strange sort of comfortableness around him.

Sophy took a deep breath.

'Well, it's a lot of pressure to look and act a certain way and people have expectations you know, like I have to post regular content to keep the audience figures up, so I get the sponsorship, but well, the truth is, I'm sort of struggling with what I want to say. I'm so tired, and everything feels fuzzy and hazy most days.'

Niall nodded. 'I getcha. You're a new mammy, your mind's all over the place – the last thing you should be doing is all that media stuff. You should be on maternity leave or something.'

Sophy looked down, suddenly feeling ashamed. It was strange that she felt an overwhelming desire to keep working when Max was still so little. There were a myriad of reasons, but the two that stuck out were her fear of falling off the Instagram merry-go-round if she kept a low profile for a while. Then there was the other reason. Which she didn't like to think about for too long, but as she was here, just chatting to Niall as though she and he had known each other for a lifetime, she felt the uncertainty of her and Jeff creep in again. How things between them felt different now Max was here, as though all they were ever really supposed to be was just a fling and maybe being a family was something that she tried to make happen rather than something that should have happened organically.

She shoved that thought away as quickly as it entered her mind, because dwelling on the negative things was never going to help them through this blip. And it was just a blip. She was sure of that.

Instead, she said, 'I can't just leave it, I have no one else to take it over, and, well, it's my sort of only income. It's tricky with social media, when it's just you, you see. I can't really get someone to pop in and take my place for six months.'

Niall nodded as though he understood, then he looked around the kitchen where they stood. 'I s'pose your old man will see ya right.'

How could she explain when she wasn't even sure herself

what she was trying to say or how she felt? Because yes, to the outsider, she had a roof over her head and a new baby. She shouldn't really need any more. And yes, Jeff provided. But it just didn't feel right. Because it never felt as though it was *her* home. Jeff always made her feel as though he were doing her a favour.

'Yes, yes, he does.' Sophy sighed. 'I just worry too much. Maybe you're right, I will take a bit of time off.'

Niall just smiled at her, and suddenly Sophy felt as if she needed to breathe a little quicker.

'Anyway, I don't know why I'm telling you all this. I don't even know you,' she said to laugh away some of the fluttering in her stomach, which she suddenly acknowledged.

'Ahh, don't be soft, it's all part of the job. Builders, taxi drivers, hairdressers, we are also paid counsellors. You get two services for one, you see.'

Sophy found she was smiling so much her cheeks hurt a little bit, and was suddenly aware of the heat in her face and the tight grip she had on the camera.

'So, where in Ireland are you from?'

'Dublin,' Niall said quickly. He smiled again, and Sophy noticed how his eyes seemed to glisten.

'Oh yes, Dublin, I know it.'

''Course you do. Everyone does. But actually, I'm from a little seaside town called Killiney, just down the way, but I worked a lot in Dublin. Before I moved to London.'

Sophy noted the confident way in which Niall was speaking to her. He seemed like someone who was sure of themselves, not someone who needed to show off through money or materials. It was strange, because Niall was exactly the kind of guy that she would be attracted to, but back before she got with Jeff, she was looking for someone with a bit more financial stability. And that, she supposed, was what had been the deal-sealer to getting with and staying with Jeff. It was her council estate roots. She didn't want to end up in a shoddy house like the one she and her family had squeezed into growing up. There was never any privacy. And one bathroom between seven of them. She'd had to duck outside on many an occasion as a young girl to take a whizz behind the elm tree at the end of the garden when her dad was in the loo having one of his long sit-downs.

'You know why Dublin is so big, don't ya?' Niall went on.

Sophy shook her head; she genuinely had no idea of the geographical mass of Ireland's capital.

'Because it keeps doublin' and doublin'.' Niall spoke slowly and quietly as though he were telling a child a secret.

Sophy thought for a moment, and then spurted out a laugh. She put her hand across her mouth, as she suddenly remembered Max snoozing in his pram a few metres away.

'A little Irish humour for ya on a Wednesday morning.' Niall grinned and Sophy smiled.

They both stood for a few seconds, and Sophy found her mind was racing with forming questions – things she wanted to ask Niall, about his hometown, his family; why he moved to London.

'Right, better get back to it. No rest for the wicked!' Niall winked and turned back around and walked out of the back door, to the side of the house where bricks and bags of cement were piling up.

'Yes, right, yes. Have a...' Sophy turned, but Niall had gone, and she wondered was she really about to say, 'have a nice day'?

* * *

At lunchtime, Sophy realised she had no food in except bread and a few fillings. So she made herself a sandwich with cheese and ham and sat up on the kitchen island and tried not to assess the calorie content. Max was awake and lying in his baby pod on the island countertop.

Niall walked past the back door and did a double take. He sidled up to the back door and leant on it, looking in.

'Ahh, the wee man's awake.'

Sophy, with a mouthful of sandwich, smiled and nodded. She swallowed.

'Come and take a look if you like?' she said, and Niall came straight through the door. 'I mean, if you like. I'm sure babies aren't exactly your thing,' Sophy added, not wanting to bore him.

Niall looked down at Max, his head cocked to one side. 'Now, why would you think a thing like that? Cos I am a builder, is that it?'

'Oh, no, sorry, I just meant, babies are a bit boring, so I'm sure you have more interesting things to be getting on with.'

'Well, I do, but I do like babies. And who said they're boring? Look at his little face – he is taking in everything!' Sophy looked at Max and tried to see the baby that had been in her life for over a month through the eyes of another. Of course, Niall was right. Max was looking up at the ceiling lights, which weren't on but were reflecting the sun's light.

'He's a very handsome chap. What's his name?'

'Max.'

'Strong name. He'll do well in life. Wish me mam had given me a better name. I have four older sisters, so I think she was still feeling rather feminine when she named me.'

'I like the name Niall.'

Niall stopped looking at Max and looked at Sophy. 'Do you now?' he said brightly.

Sophy felt a rush of colour coming from her neck, threatening to flood her face.

'I do, yes,' Sophy said firmly, not allowing her sudden rush of embarrassment to jar her.

'Well, now, isn't that something?' Niall looked thoughtful. 'Maybe me mam didn't do too badly by me after all. I might even forgive her for all the Findus' crispy pancake dinners then.'

Sophy's face brightened. 'You ate crispy pancakes! I loved those as a kid.'

'Did you now? Oh yes, we ate them by the bucketload. All the flavours stocked up in our freezer. She wasn't much of a cook, our mam – still isn't – but she tried her best. With so many of us running around, it wasn't easy.'

'No, I can imagine. I wish they still did them now though, don't you?'

'Sure you can still find them. They've been rebranded and brought out slightly different flavours, but they're still good enough. I still have one for our tea from time to time.'

Sophy enjoyed listening to Niall's accent. She also wanted to ask if 'our tea' was an Irish was of speaking or if there was indeed a significant other, but decided it was none of her business.

'I do love crispy pancakes – beef and onion were my favourite, and the cheese one.'

'Oh, they still do those flavours. Like I said, not bad.'

'Wow, who knew?'

'You've been shopping in all the wrong places, I'm afraid.'

'Well, you'll have to tell me where you got yours.'

'Oh, I couldn't possibly do that – you'd buy the lot, and I'd be without me tea on a Friday night.'

'Well, maybe if I could bribe you with a posh coffee you might reconsider?' Sophy said, feeling more confident and gesturing to the shiny black machine on the kitchen counter behind her and feeling a ripple of joy at her own flirtatious behaviour.

Niall looked at Sophy for a few seconds as Sophy held his

gaze and smiled up at him. He took a deep breath and turned back to the door.

'I'd best not – the lads will think I've disowned them. Got a flask of builders' brew in the van.' There was still a brightness to his voice, but it had lost some of the vigour that had been there just before.

'Oh,' Sophy started, a feeling of raw disappointment in her gut, but Niall had disappeared through the back door.

Sophy looked at her ham and cheese sandwich, which now felt a bit dry and tasteless in her mouth. and all she could think of was a crispy pancake oozing with cheese or mince.

* * *

After lunch, which ended up being a berry smoothie as well to wash the bread down – but also because it doubled up as a very Instagram-able picture – Sophy took Max out for a walk around the park, stopping on a bench to feed him. She didn't fancy going back to the empty house and wandering around the tiny rooms alone with Max, being overlooked by Niall and his team of builders. She wanted to feel as though she was important and doing something worthwhile, not some sad thirty-something mum messing around on Instagram and fawning over her baby. But then why was she worried about what Niall thought about her? she wondered. It was her house for goodness' sake. Well, not hers exactly. It was Jeff's, and she lived there. Sophy felt a sudden burst of panic. Jeff had said he would put her on the deeds to the house when Max was born. It had been almost a month, and he hadn't mentioned it, and she, well, she had just given birth, was breastfeeding, being up all night and trying to run an Instagram business, so it had slipped clear from her mind. After a moment, the panic subsided and Sophy considered it all for a moment. It was fine, she would speak with Jeff tonight and get it all sorted.

After his feed, Max had a marathon snooze, allowing Sophy time to sit on the bench, occasionally giving the pram a rock when she heard Max stir. She scheduled a few posts on Hootsuite, she had some pictures of Max and a few staple images on her phone she could use for general content – an image of a Nike trainer, a glass of water on the kitchen island – so she added some relevant content to them and scheduled them all to come out over the next few days. Then she saw her DMs had stacked up again. Jeez, did people never stop? She typed out a few replies and thank-yous, then she sat back and raised her head to the sun, grateful for what a warm spring it was turning out to be.

* * *

Jeff was home just after six that evening. Sophy heard him slap his briefcase on the island and fling open the fridge. The beers she had been instructed via text to buy earlier rattled on the inside shelf.

Sophy had just finished bathing Max, and came downstairs with him tucked snuggly into the crook of her arm.

'Is that my two favourite people?' Jeff said without turning around. 'Anything good for dinner, babes?'

Sophy reached Jeff's side, and he turned, letting go of the fridge door so it closed.

'Here he is!' He looked down at Max. 'My god, he gets more handsome every day. Just like your daddy!' he said, touching Max's cheek with his finger. Sophy did an inward eye roll and suppressed a sigh.

'Do you mind washing your hands before you hold him?'

Jeff looked at her quizzically but walked over to the sink and rinsed his hands then dried them on a tea towel. Sophy had hoped for some involvement with soap, but she knew when to pick her battles. She was tired, like she always was at this time of day. All she ever wanted to do when she had bathed Max and handed him over to Jeff, was to sleep. But that would mean she would need to leave putting Max down to Jeff, and well, she was breastfeeding him right until he fell asleep and so that wouldn't work. She handed Max over to Jeff, who began chatting to him about his day as he walked out of the kitchen into the lounge. 'Bring us a beer, babes!' Jeff called from the lounge. 'Actually, scrap that, I'll go straight for a gin and tonic. It's been a beast of a day,' he called again. Then he carried on speaking to Max. 'Yes, it has, Daddy has been working very hard to buy you lots of nice things, yes, he has. Cos that's what daddies do. What would you like when you're bigger, shall Daddy get you a Tesla, shall he?'

Sophy stood in the kitchen, half listening with irritation to Jeff babbling on to Max and getting riled up over the fact she'd made a detour on her way back from the park, with a fractious Max after his long nap, to get Jeff the beers he no longer wanted.

She took down the gin bottle from the top cupboard and bent down to the lower cupboard to retrieve a can of tonic. She sucked her breath in at the sharp pain down below. When was it going to stop hurting?

She took out Jeff's favourite heavy tumbler and placed it on the counter.

'Loads of ice, babes!' Jeff hollered. This time Sophy openly rolled her eyes. She opened the freezer and was startled to see the top section, which was a large space for trays of ice cubes, was almost spilling out with three, no, four, red, brown and blue boxes of crispy pancakes. Sophy let out a loud hoot and then put a hand over her mouth. She slid one box out and looked at it. Cheese and ham. She slid it back and found a minced beef one.

She put it on the kitchen counter, finished preparing Jeff's drink with the ice and then ripped open the box and turned on the oven.

Twenty-five minutes later, with Max lying in his pod on the island, Jeff looked curiously at the funny-shaped orange bread-crumbed food on his plate – that Sophy had spruced up with a rocket and tomato salad – and then at his girlfriend, who was eating her dinner happily – smiling as though she were sharing a secret with herself.

* * *

3.46 a.m. – Mel: Does anyone know if this life-awakening thing, fourth trimester goes on for long?

3.51 a.m. – Aisha: You'll have to ride it out, but if you want an enlightened child, hopefully for the rest of her life? 😊

4.00 a.m. – Sophy: Just woken up with Max. He's having a feed and I'm texting. Check me out multitasking!

4.02 a.m. – Mel: Why are you all so happy at this ridiculous hour of the morning?

11

AISHA

Aisha dressed the boys in orange, blue, green and pink romper suits. That would confuse the mums at the music group Sophy had booked them all into today.

Charley came into the lounge as Aisha was finishing packing the nappy bag.

'All set?'

'Just packing for every eventuality.' Aisha zipped up the bag, which was bulging at all sides.

'We should get a bigger bag, maybe? Order one if you like?'

'Are you sure?' Aisha said, the sarcasm was obvious in her voice.

'Yes, Aish. The boys need it, you need it. You can't keep squashing everything into that tiny bag.'

'Okay! I'll order one later,' Aisha sang.

Charley seemed unfazed by Aisha's continued irritation. She bent down to the sofa and kissed each twin on their little O-shaped mouths.

'We'll have to start watching them on this thing soon – they'll be wanting to roll off!' Charley said.

'I know, but not yet they won't. Few more weeks yet. That's what the book says.'

'The book isn't always right, though, is it? These boys are both strong, aren't you, babies?'

Aisha turned to Charley. 'Are you saying I don't know my own sons? I'm with them all day – I would think I would know when one of them is going to roll over.'

Charley sucked in her breath but didn't rise to Aisha's frustration. Instead, she leant in and kissed her softly on the cheek.

'Have a good day.'

'We always do.' Aisha fixated on the rearranging Otis's sock until she heard Charley leave the room.

She tucked the boys into their pram and navigated it carefully down the hallway and out of the front door, which were both only just big enough to fit the travel system.

Once outside in the fresh air, Aisha felt better. Despite her mood with Charley – she still wasn't exactly sure where it had stemmed from, but it was there all the same – she decided it was going to be a good day. After the music group, the girls were going to have coffee, which took them up to lunch, then she planned to have a long walk in the afternoon.

As she stepped onto the street, Aisha saw the man standing on the corner at the far end of the road, facing her. He was wearing that hat again which flapped over his ears and a green coat pulled up to his neck. Again, it was hard to make out his face. She was headed in that direction, and suddenly filled with an intense desire to know who he could be, she began walking at a pace to the corner. The man had already gone by the time she reached it, and when she turned onto the next road, she could see no evidence of him. She stopped in the middle of the path and sighed. What was wrong with her? Why was she obsessing over this person? He obviously lived on the street, which had over sixty houses on it. Perhaps he just enjoyed watching people but had little social skills.

But what she was really thinking and had been for some time, she was far too ashamed to admit it to anyone. When she and Charley had picked the sperm donor for their twins, she always had this uncomfortable feeling about the father. What if they weren't just a donor? What if they wanted more? She had mentioned it half-heartedly to Charley when they were searching through the files of the donors. 'What if he comes looking for us, for his kid?' she had said, trying to keep the tremble of concern out of her voice. Charley let out a loud trumpet laugh, and Aisha realised she thought she was joking. But she never was, and now it seemed as if her nightmare theory had come true.

So, when she arrived outside the community hall at quarter to ten as they had arranged, she was glad to see both Sophy and Mel were already there. The two of them were deep in conversation but stopped talking and stepped aside to make a gap for Aisha and the prams in the middle of them.

'Hey,' she said quietly.

'Hey, are you okay?' Mel said, perceptive as ever.

Sophy stepped closer to Aisha.

'I think so... No, I am... It's nothing,' Aisha said.

'Hey, hey, there's no such thing as nothing. Your nothing is our something, I bet you any money,' Mel said, and Sophy nodded. Aisha swallowed and began to speak.

'Well, it's stupid, really, but well, for a few weeks now – well, ever since I had the twins, so really it is probably just tiredness and paranoia – I've been seeing a man, lurking—Well, not lurking as such, it's a free county, just standing on the street, at various points, sometimes looking at my house, sometimes just walking past and now, just now, before I got here, he was on the corner, and it looked as though he was waiting for me, but when I started walking towards him, he moved on, round the corner, then I lost sight of him.'

'Hmm,' Mel pondered.

'Well, I'm sure you're not imagining it.' Sophy looked at Mel for reassurance and Mel nodded firmly. 'Is it perhaps someone you know on your street who might just want to congratulate you on your babies?' Sophy said, and Mel turned and looked at her, pulling her chin into her neck in disbelief and widening her eyes.

'People don't lurk on the street when they want to congratulate you on the birth of your baby. They knock on the door with flowers and balloons.'

'I don't think we should scare Aisha – she seems a bit shaken up already.' Sophy put a hand on Aisha's arm. Aisha noticed her nails were freshly painted a light pink.

'Like I said, he wasn't lurking, so I think I'm just being paranoid.'

'Well, what do you think? Who do you think it could be?' Mel said.

Aisha took a deep breath.

'You want to know what I really think? I think it's the babies' sperm donor. I think he's somehow found me and wants to know where his sperm went, but I can't say that to Charley because—'

'Hold up, wait a minute. Rewind, sister. Sperm donor?'

Aisha looked at the girls in turn. 'Yes, sorry, I should have clarified that I didn't conceive naturally, because I'm gay. Charley is my girlfriend. Sorry for not saying earlier. I just hate having to explain it when heterosexual people never have to.'

'Oh, wow, Aisha, that's amazing. I feel like I'm seeing you brand new all over again,' Sophy said.

Aisha smiled coyly.

'Shit! I'm so sorry. I presumed you were straight, didn't I? And

I was ranting about men being arseholes. Sorry,' Mel said and put her arm around Aisha.

'Oh, don't worry, we have our moments, and we argue. In fact, that's why I don't want to say anything to her about what I'm thinking. She'll think I'm mad.'

'I don't think the sperm people give out the addresses of the recipients to the donors. I mean, I'm no expert, but I'm just guessing that's not how it's done,' Sophy said, and Mel nodded.

'Oh no, you're totally right. I just... like I said, I'm tired and I'm overthinking.' Aisha began to turn the prams around. 'We should go in.' She immediately regretted saying anything – she must sound like a complete lunatic.

'Yes, yes let's,' Sophy said and threw her coffee cup into a bin.

'How can you drink so much of that stuff? I can manage one before my heart feels like it's about to pop out of my chest,' Mel said.

'Decaf all the way, that's how,' Sophy said.

'Oh wow, I would never have guessed,' Mel said, sounding impressed.

Aisha pushed the pram in front of the girls and listened to Mel and Sophy chatting, wishing she could feel as carefree as they were. She longed to be able to stop worrying enough so that she could just enjoy one full day. Sophy jumped in front of her, opened the door to the community centre, and Aisha navigated the pram through the door whilst trying to push all thoughts of the man to the back of her head.

The group was run by a woman who referred to herself as Minnie Music. She was probably in her fifties, wore a bright orange shirt and had pigtails. Immediately, Aisha knew she was going to hate every second.

They camped down on one side of the semicircle that Minnie

was busy orchestrating, and were asked to lay their babies out in front of them, like some sort of sacrificial offering.

Minnie said they were going to start with some vocal warm-ups because babies were happier when their parents were singing their most confidently. Aisha knew that neither of her boys would feel any happier if Aisha began to get confident with her singing voice. She had hummed and sang at a reasonable level to the boys regularly, and whilst they had never put in any formal complaint, they had sort of looked at her with complete bewilderment and hadn't even cracked a smile.

'We don't want any mumbling in this class – you sing loud and sing proud,' Minnie called to the room.

The women warbled and gargled their way through the warm-up. Mel sang out loudly like the professional she was, and Aisha realised it was the first time she had heard her sing. Sophy turned and caught Aisha's eye, and Aisha knew they were both thinking the same thing: Mel had a lovely voice. Aisha joined in sporadically but focused on the boys who were wriggling and unsettled.

'Right. Now, it's time for our welcome song! When I point to you, you must say the name of your baby – or babies.' Minnie beamed at Aisha, who physically recoiled. She glanced at Sophy, who was glowing. Even Mel, who claimed she detested this kind of thing, looked mildly amused.

'Okay, let's go.' Minnie thrust her arms into the air and began singing an annoyingly catchy tune. At the end of every chorus, there was a two-syllable bar for each parent or carer to squeeze singing the name of their child in. Mel and Sophy each sang theirs, and when it came to saying Otis and Jude, which was clearly two syllables too long, Aisha felt her face flush with heat and her armpits prickle. Mel and Sophy gave her the thumbs up – both of them seemed to be getting into the vibe. Aisha felt a pang in her gut as the jingly jangly tone of the music reminded her of something Charley would write, and she felt an overwhelming desire for her to be here with her, mocking the woman under her breath, saying something about how she could write something better in her sleep and generally making Aisha feel like less of a colossal fool than she did right then.

Things felt a little easier when Minnie brought the percussion out. There were some older babies, who were now sitting up and putting the little egg shakers in their mouth, dribbling all over them. The boys seemed to look more engaged as Aisha shook a jingle-bell stick in time with the song. Their little eyes seemed to brighten as they tried to focus on the instrument.

But the end couldn't come soon enough, and Aisha took one twin at a time to the pram and tucked them in.

'Well, I'm ready for a coffee!' she said to Sophy and Mel.

* * *

They found themselves in a roomy coffee shop that was a lot more child-friendly than the last one. This one had a box of books and toys for older children and more space between the sofas and tables.

'Well, I had a thoroughly good time. Same time next week?' Sophy said as she sipped her peppermint tea.

'Mmm, yes,' Aisha said. Mel and Sophy looked at one another.

'That wasn't very convincing.' Mel laughed.

'Well, it was fine. Just not my sort of thing, really, I guess. The boys loved it, though.'

'Okay, well, we can try another group,' Sophy offered.

'It was a bit cringey,' Mel said.

'It was super cringey,' Sophy replied.

'At least Aisha had the balls to be honest, whilst we just played along like two insane fools,' Mel laughed.

Aisha laughed along, but she could feel her stomach tightening and a fluttering in her chest. She thought she had tried to push the thoughts of the strange man away, but it wasn't that which was bothering her. It was the fact that whilst the other two seemed to be able to have a laugh at themselves and the situation, Aisha had felt as though she were trapped in her own body and had felt an overwhelming desire to step right out of it.

* * *

When she arrived back in her street, Aisha stood and listened to the wind whistling through the trees and the sound of the cars in the now busier street. She was waiting for the man, she knew that, but the road was empty, save for a dog walker and a woman with two boys on scooters.

She felt an overwhelming tiredness come over her and a longing for a bath. Once she had done that, she would get Charley to put the boys to bed – it was Friday after all, and tomorrow was the weekend. She could finally relax and maybe get a little bit of respite. Maybe then she would start to feel a little bit more like herself.

12

MEL

'What even are bags, babe?' Mel asked Daz as she pulled and poked at her skin in the mirror in their en-suite bathroom.

Daz was holding Sky and standing in the doorway. Sky was looking around at the lights of the bathroom and making a sweet cooing sound.

'I thought it was when the skin under your eyes went all... bag-like. Bit baggy, maybe?'

'Oh, I thought it was dark rings. There're definitely dark rings, aren't there?'

Daz pulled his mouth down.

Mel clocked his response in the mirror. 'Yep, there definitely are.'

Last night had been another bad night with Skylar. Mel had tried everything: extra feeds, winding, teething powder. In the end, all she seemed to want to do was fall asleep on Mel's chest. Mel could feel the nagging pain in her lower back, the area that was already fragile from carrying a baby inside her for all those months.

'Mum, can I have a sleepover tonight?' Leia was next to Daz in the doorway. Daz moved away and walked Sky to the window in the bedroom and started chatting about birdies.

'Yes, who with?' Mel said absently.

'Maddy.'

'Yep, no probs.'

'Thanks, Mum – you're the best.' Leia came into the bathroom and kissed Mel's cheek. 'What are you doing today?'

'Not a lot. Mainly chilling out. I have a HIIT workout I want to do later – need to get back in shape to start working again.'

'You look great, Mum,' Leia said, as she left the room.

'Oh, Nanny is coming over for lunch,' Mel said as it just came to her. Shit, she thought. She had nothing in.

Mel looked at herself in the mirror again, trying to see what an eleven-year-old girl saw as she examined her hair. No greys. She was lucky, her mum didn't have a scrap of grey in her hair when she died at fifty-one. If she wanted to remember what her dad looked like and if there were any greys in his hair, she'd have to look at Facebook and his annoying profile picture with him sidled up to his girlfriend. There was too much water under the bridge between them. He had, over the years, tried to maintain some sort of half-hearted relationship with her and Leia, but Mel had never quite bought into it. He hadn't been to see Skylar yet. Apparently, he'd been feeling under the weather and didn't want to pass it on to the little 'uns. Mel found her body had tensed up thinking about Gary, as she referred to him because Dad didn't always feel like the title he deserved. She went into the bedroom and put herself into a downward dog where she had a flashback to Doug's yoga class and so quickly tightened her pelvic floor.

'Woah there,' came Daz's voice from behind her. 'Now there's a sight for sore eyes!'

'I doubt it's your eyes that are sore this morning, babes. It was me who was up with Sky from two until four remember?'

'I know, darlin', but it's you she wants. You smell so much better than I do.' Mel felt both of Daz's hands on her hips, he began embedding his crotch between her buttocks. She swung her head over her left shoulder.

'Where's Sky?'

'With my mum.'

'Shit, she's here already?' Mel pushed herself to standing, sending a perplexed Daz to one side.

'It's nearly twelve o'clock. She said she was sorry for being a bit early.'

'Shit, I've nothing in, Daz. I have to run to the shops – you make your mum a brew. I'll be back in ten minutes.'

Mel flew down the stairs, taking two steps at a time. It was just when she had reached the third step from the bottom that she felt her ankle go over on itself and felt a very definite crack. The pain seared through her like a knife stabbing through her leg. She cried out as she fell to her bottom. But as she sat there, pain shooting through her whole body and feeling as if she could cry like a baby, the first thing that occurred to her after the realisation that she wouldn't be doing any burlesque gigs for some time was that she could get a cleaner now.

* * *

'You just put your feet up there, love, and I'll see to the lunch.' Irene gently laid Mel's foot, which was tucked into a special boot on top of a pillow. Bess pushed her wet nose against Mel's hand, forcing it to her soft head for a pat. It gave Mel some comfort and reminded her why she loved dogs so much. They were the best companions when you really needed them.

'I came as soon as Irene called,' Mike, her father-in-law, said from the other side of her. 'Fancy that! A fractured ankle. Could have been much worse, love.' Mike scratched his head, then went and sat down on the sofa where Sky was in her bouncy chair. 'Hello, little lady.' He took Sky's little hand as she thrust it out towards him, trying to grasp at him. 'Are you saying hello to your grampy?'

'Sexy boot, babes!' Daz came over and kissed her on the forehead. 'And there and back to A&E within three hours. That's not too bad, is it?'

'Yes, but I have no lunch. Irene has looked after Sky and bought and prepared lunch and is now running around after me? What kind of bloody host am I?'

'A tired one, I imagine, with a little baby to look after,' Irene said. 'Now don't you worry, dear, Mike is here now – he left golf early to come over. Nothing usually gets him away from his game.'

'No, only my favourite daughter-in-law in peril,' Mike said, still looking at Sky. Mel smiled despite the pain. Then she looked at Irene.

'But what about your afternoon tea with Gail?' Mel said.

'Oh, don't you worry about Gail – she's big enough to look after herself. Besides, she always eats all the best cakes and leaves me with the egg sandwiches. I hate egg sandwiches, don't I, Mike?'

'That's right, love, gives her terrible wind, Mel,' Mike said.

Mel frowned. 'Why don't you just tell her you don't like the egg, or get the staff to bring you more salmon and cucumber?' Mel said wincing at the pain in her ankle, which had dulled but still came through in short bursts.

'Oh, you know me, love, I don't like to make a fuss. Now what can I get you? Tea? How about one of my nice hot chocolates?'

'I don't want to put you out any more, Irene – you've done so much today already.'

'Not at all, love. Sky and I have had a lovely afternoon.'

Mel couldn't help but smile. Irene was just too bloody good to be true. How had she got so lucky with a Daz and an Irene?

'I tell you what, let's start with that tomato soup and crusty bread, and then we'll all have a nice hot bevvy. How does that sound?' Irene patted Mel on the shoulder.

Mel dropped her head back against the armchair, closed her eyes and held her hand out to Irene, who took it in hers.

'Thank you, Irene.' They stayed that way for a minute until the doorbell let out a loud, invasive ring.

'I'll get it!' shouted Leia as she ran to the door. There were whoops and screams of delight as Mel could hear her daughter greeting her friend at the door.

She opened her eyes. Hold on, wasn't she supposed to be dropping Leia off at Maddy's? But Maddy was already in the hallway with what looked like an overnight bag in her hand.

'Maddy's here, Mum.'

'I can see that, love.' Mel smiled through the pain.

'You did say I could have a sleepover.' Leia looked forlorn. Mel had thought she meant that she was going to Maddy's. Now she would have two tweenagers and a baby to tend to.

'I did, love. How are you, Maddy?'

'Good thanks, Mel. Sorry about your leg. Can we do coloured hairsprays? My mum got me some for my birthday.' Maddy smiled through her braces.

Mel found the strength for one more smile. 'Of course.'

The girls ran upstairs, chatting excitedly.

Mel looked at her foot and thought about the dates building up in the diary, the mess in the house, and Sky gurgling away happily for now with her grandad, but come the middle of the night, it would be a different story. More sleepless nights were imminent, and Mel knew she would not be able to manage keeping up with the washing and all the other general house-work. She reached for her phone, went straight to Gumtree and typed in *cleaner*.

Mel scoured a few adverts and was drawn to one where a woman had taken a selfie of herself. She had brown bobbed hair and a thin pointy face. Mel read what she had written underneath.

Hi, my name is Ksenia. I do domestic cleaning with five-year experience. I love to clean – it make me happy and I take pride in everything I do. If you think you need my service, reply to this advert and we discuss further.

PLEASE DO NOT DISTURB FOR SOMETHING ELSE. I ADVERTISE FOR CLEANING ONLY. NO MASSAGE. NO SEX!

Thank you.

Right then, perfect, Mel thought. *A woman with no desire to bonk my husband and who loves cleaning. The exact antithesis of me!* She clicked on reply and asked Ksenia when she was able to start.

* * *

1.53 a.m. – Mel: Anyone awake? I know it's earlier than the 3ish slot, but Sky has woken up three times this evening already. And oh, yeah, I bust my ankle legging it down the stairs, and so I'm hobbling around in a space boot and high on painkillers.

2.56 a.m. – Sophy: Shit, Mel, that sounds awful. You must be feeling like hell. Are you getting any help from Daz or his mum? How did you do that?

3.10 a.m. – Aisha: Oh, that's awful, Mel. Sounds so painful. Charley is doing the night feeds, but my body is so used to being awake, I am lying here listening to the boys crying and her trying to manage it all by herself, and I am this close to just going downstairs and taking a twin.

3.11 a.m. – Sophy: You stay exactly where you are, you do more than enough all week. Try and close your eyes and get some sleep. The boys will be fine. Mel, will text to get the details on the ankle tomoz x

3.12 a.m. – Aisha: Okay, thank you, Sophy. I will. Mel, take care x

4.39 a.m. – Mel: Holy shit, she's awake again.

13

SOPHY

The lights in the restaurant were too bright, the Thai food was tepid and tasteless, and the man sat opposite her was drunk. And it wasn't even 9 p.m. Jeff had started slurring his words at the waitress about twenty minutes ago when he ordered another bottle of wine that Sophy had no intention of drinking with him. She had managed to down one glass and looked unenthusiastically at the second glass in front of her. Luckily, Jeff was too far gone to notice that Sophy hadn't been keeping up. After a too long and complicated conversation with the waitress, Jeff managed to order a gin and tonic the way he liked it. The waitress smiled and said no problem. Sophy gave her a sympathetic look: a secret coded apology for her inebriated boyfriend. The waitress reciprocated with her own sympathetic smile for Sophy, who sat back in her chair, slightly perturbed.

Sophy surreptitiously gave each of her boobs a quick squeeze. She had pumped a little milk just before she came out, but only enough to soothe Max if he woke. But it seemed the pumping had only encouraged more milk flow and now both breasts were filling up rapidly. The right more so than the left, and she was sure they would be looking wonky by now. Not that Jeff would notice – she was sure his eyes were slightly crossed as he looked down at his phone and tried to bash out a text.

'Is Max OK?' she said to him.

Jeff shrugged and continued texting.

'Is that not your mum you're texting?'

'Nope.'

Tap, tap, tap.

Sophy felt her gut tighten and her heart speed up. She had Wendy's number but hated texting Jeff's mother for anything. She had left Max with her once a couple of weeks ago to pop to the doctor's to have a mole removed. In hindsight, she could have brought Max with her and he would have been perfectly happy in his car seat out of the way whilst she had the procedure done, which only took five minutes. It was the time in the waiting room that had got to her the most. When she finally got into the doctor's room, she was half an hour past her appointment. In all that time, she had texted Wendy twice to check if Max was okay and she hadn't replied to either of them. Finally, her phone had beeped as she had been driving home. She had taken a sneaky peek at it at the traffic lights, and it had been Wendy saying he had been asleep the whole time. It had riled her how Wendy took nearly an hour to reply.

She had gritted her teeth when she got home ten minutes later. Max was in Wendy's arms, rooting for her nipple.

'I told him he won't get much out of that thing,' she said through her throaty laugh.

'Thanks, Wendy.'

Sophy had taken Max from her and Wendy had said, 'All sorted, no cancer or anything?'

'That wasn't why I had it removed. It was just annoying me.'

'Well, right then. If you don't need me for anything else, I'll be on me way. Got the shopping to get. I'm cooking liver and onion for Al's dinner tonight. His favourite.'

Sophy had grimaced. 'Lucky Al.'

As Wendy was putting her coat on, Sophy had looked at the empty coffee cup on the table, a screwed-up empty packet of biscuits and the TV still blaring. In the kitchen was a pile of wet washing that Sophy had pulled from the machine just before she left, and a sink still full of breakfast dishes.

'What a darling little boy. No bother at all.' Wendy had kissed him on the forehead. 'Any time you ever need me again, love.' And she had left, slamming the door so loudly behind her that it had made Max jump.

So, when Jeff said they should go out for a bite to eat on Sunday night, he suggested they get Wendy over again – 'because she had been so fantastic with him last time'.

Sophy had tried to explain that Max had been barely out of the womb, Sophy had breastfed him to sleep before she had left, and he was conked out until she returned. This time, things were different. In those few weeks, Max had become accustomed to her smell and favoured her over anyone else. He was waking more sporadically and not sleeping for hours and hours in the early part of the evening as he had done before. So, Jeff suggested she try the pump again. This time was more successful, but Sophy hated the idea of Wendy using her breast milk. And she had a funny feeling that Wendy would be feeling equally disgusted by it.

Jeff finished his text and put his phone on the table just as his G&T arrived.

'Thanks, darlin',' he said.

The waitress smiled and said, 'No problem.'

She went to walk away, and Jeff called after her, 'Hold on, love.' He sat up from where he had slouched into his chair and pulled his wallet from his pocket. The girl looked at Sophy briefly, as though she might offer some light-hearted conversation as Jeff struggled to pull out a wad of twenty-pound notes from his wallet.

He finally slid two out from the stash and handed them to her.

'There you go, love. That's for you.' The girl looked down, impressed with her tip.

'Thanks, sir.'

'Don't spend it all at once,' Jeff said, and let out a loud laugh. The girl laughed politely back, then scuttled off to the dumb waiter where her colleagues were waiting for her. Sophy watched as she indulged them by repeating everything that had just happened metres away from them, then watched as they turned and looked back at her, then regrouped and all started laughing.

Sophy stood up.

'Right, that's it. We need to go. I have to feed Max – he'll be waiting.' Sophy felt a fierce tingle thrust through her breasts into her throat, where it morphed into an intense thirst.

'Eh?' Jeff looked confused. 'The night is young, babes.' He gestured to the almost empty restaurant.

'It's Sunday night, Jeff. Everyone is at home watching *Line of Duty*. My boobs hurt. I need to feed my baby.'

'I told you Mum hasn't called. Everything is fine.'

'Well, I'm telling you that I need to go.' Sophy looked at the group of staff who were all now looking over at them. 'Can one of you please call us a taxi?' Sophy called to them. The waitress who had been serving nodded and picked up the phone. 'I'm going, Jeff, so feel free to stay and party the night away.'

Sophy walked to the door and waited, looking anxiously up and down the street. Then she looked back at Jeff. He was trying to type in his pin number, but the machine kept bleeping. Eventually, Sophy marched back and put her card in the machine. An awkward silence ensued as the card machine printed out the receipt and Jeff began to stand up, knocking a full wine glass over. Sophy shook her head and didn't even begin to apologise. The staff had had their laugh *and* made forty quid out of them.

In the taxi, Jeff kept sliding towards her every time the driver took a turn. He was barely conscious, and Sophy wondered what the hell was making him drink so heavily. She looked down at her boyfriend and found her thoughts wandering to Niall and something he had said in the kitchen that had made her laugh so hard she had to run to the loo and change her trousers (she really needed to work on her pelvic floor). It was a story about the first job he did, and he reminded her so much of some of her own childhood friends. She tried to think back to what she and Jeff used to laugh about when they first got together, and it dawned on her that it hadn't been anything like the way she had laughed with Niall; it had been more superficial stuff about people they knew, places they had been, TV shows and so on. The conversation with Niall had been so relaxed that just being with him made her feel so familiar. It was hard to put her finger on exactly what it was at the time, but sat in the back of the taxi, bracing herself for another impact from Jeff's lifeless body as the driver took a sharp corner, she realised what it was. Being with Niall, and laughing and talking, felt like home.

* * *

The taxi pulled up outside the house, and Sophy's boobs had now begun to leak. She left Jeff, who she had jabbed awake, trying to tip the driver, and she could hear Max screaming as she struggled to get her key in the door. When she finally opened it, his cries filled the hallway, and her heart began to hurt. She found Wendy in the kitchen with the bottle in one hand and a flailing red-faced Max in the other.

Sophy didn't speak a word. She just took Max and went straight into the lounge, where she lifted her sodden T-shirt and unhooked her nursing bra. Max latched on and began sucking furiously, his little jaw working harder than she had ever seen it work before. He made soft animalistic noises and choked as the milk came shooting out, as it always did for the first few seconds. Sophy pulled him off whilst he coughed, but he barely paused before he began rooting again.

As Max settled into the feed, Jeff stumbled through the door into the lounge followed by an anxious-looking Wendy.

'I tried to settle him, but he wouldn't have any of it. I don't understand, me and your father used to go to parties all the time when you were a baby, and we left you with babysitters. You took that bottle every time, no problems.'

Jeff sank down onto the other sofa.

'Don't worry, Mum. You did great.' Jeff's eyes rolled to the back of his head as he slid down into the fabric.

Sophy cocked her head at Jeff. Why didn't he explain to Wendy that a breastfed baby generally favours the mother's nipple over a silicon teat, and it wouldn't matter if Wendy was Mary bleedin' Poppins, there was no way Max was ever going to be happy taking a bottle from anyone, let alone at only a few weeks old? It was a bad decision on her part. But Sophy was past trying to explain it all to Wendy, who had one child forty-one years ago and seemed to think that never in the history of humankind had anyone ever or would ever concede to do things differently.

'Well, you all seem to be all okay here, so if I'm not needed any more, I'll get on home. Al's paused *Line of Duty* for me and we usually have our Horlicks about now.'

For a second, Sophy felt her emotions lift as she imagined Wendy and Al sitting down with their nightly malted drink until Wendy spoke again as she bent down and kissed Jeff's head. 'Night night, son. I'm glad you've had a good night. You deserve it with how hard you work.'

Sophy felt her insides clench again as she shook her head in disbelief, even though she knew no one was watching her. It seemed that nothing Wendy said would ever cease to amaze her.

Next, Wendy went to walk over to Sophy, presumably to kiss Max on the head, but stopped herself midway as she clocked Sophy's semi-exposed chest and turned to the door instead, pulling her handbag tightly onto her shoulder as she did. 'Night night, Sophy,' she said as she walked out of the room, having the decency not to slam the door this time.

'Night, Wendy. Thanks for babysitting,' Sophy mumbled.

Sophy waited until she heard Wendy's Fiat 500 start up outside, and then she spoke.

'I can't do it again, Jeff. I just can't leave Max with your mum or anyone, not whilst I'm breastfeeding. It's too stressful for him and for me. I don't enjoy myself when I'm away from him, and well, let's be honest, your mum is not the most maternal of women.' Sophy paused. Max had slowed down his feed and was sucking at a slow and steady pace, his eyes firmly shut. His hands squeezed into tiny fists. She looked up at Jeff to gauge his response, but his chin was rested on his chest, a small bit of spit dribbling down his chin, as he emitted a tiny snuffling snore.

* * *

3.52 a.m. – Aisha: Things are a bit ropey at this end. Neither of the boys are settling. I have a craving for Pop-Tarts. Does anyone remember Pop-Tarts?

4.15 a.m. – Sophy: I should advise you against it, being your nutritional expert, but you have the metabolism of an eight-year-old boy, so I say go for it. Just make sure you eat some fruit in the morning. The actual morning.

4.16 a.m. – Aisha: I don't have any Pop-Tarts in the house. And I'm really craving one. I can't wake Charley up: she has work tomorrow.

4.17 a.m. – Sophy: Cravings? You're not pregnant again?

4.19 a.m. – Aisha: Ha! No spare sperm flying about the place here.

4.19 a.m. – Sophy: Join the club.

4.20 a.m. – Aisha: There's nothing nice about sperm is there?

4.20 a.m. – Sophy: You're not wrong there.

6.32 a.m. – Mel: Morning, campers. Why on the night when Sky sleeps for five hours do I miss out on a conversation about sperm?

14

AISHA

Martina laid a large roasted chicken in the middle of the table next to a giant bowl of rice and peas and a platter of festival and fried plantain. Aisha's cousins Ruben and Marcel oohed loudly.

'You didn't need to go to all this trouble for us, Mum.' Aisha looked at Charley, checking she was okay with this amount of food on the table. She wasn't a big eater and preferred a very small plate in the evening.

'It's ma birthday, and I cook if I want to!' Martina bellowed her rendition of the classic song by Lesley Gore. Aisha smiled and looked back again at Charley who was smiling as she watched Ruben and Marcel belly laughing, falling about the table, slapping each other on the back and holding their stomachs.

When the boys had settled down, and Martina gave the sign for everyone to help themselves, Charley picked up a serving spoon and put a small amount of rice and peas on her plate. Martina set about slicing through the roasted chickens, which had been marinating all afternoon in a plastic bag filled with jerk spices.

'It smells amazing, Martina,' Charley said.

'Thank you.' Martina nodded and then looked at Charley. Aisha put her hand on Charley's knee and Charley took it and squeezed it. Martina left the sliced chicken on the platter for everyone to help themselves. The cousins took a leg each, looking at Martina as if she would tell them off for snatching at the meat – a habit from childhood when there were five hungry mouths to feed and it had been a race to see who could finish first and get seconds.

Everyone ate quietly until one of the twins let out a pitiful cry from the pram, where they were parked up next to Martina's giant cooker. Martina stood up, scraping her chair back and wiping her mouth with her napkin.

'It's okay, Mum. I'll see to him.' Aisha went to stand. Martina waved her back down.

'You sit and eat. I don't s'pose neither of you get the chance to eat together at the moment.' Martina was up and with her back to both Charley and Aisha when she spoke, but Aisha felt her heart begin to swell as she felt some meaning in the words coming from her mother. What felt like a sense of understanding for both she and Charley. A sense that maybe her mother was finally taking her relationship with Charley seriously. Aisha had always felt that Martina saw what she had with Charley as more of a 'good friendship' than a traditional couple, as she saw it, but now, the way she had spoken of them as a team, as one entity rather than two separate people just living together, made Aisha feel as if maybe, just maybe, her mum was beginning to finally get it.

Aisha hovered between standing and sitting. 'But, Mum, it's your birthday.'

'And I got the best presents right here, these two. I don't need nothing more.'

'It should have been me cooking for you, Mum, not the other way around,' Aisha said solemnly as she thought about all those hours she was at home in her own kitchen; so much time, yet so unable to use it in the way she wanted to.

Carmel, Aisha's elder sister, reached over and touched Aisha's hand. 'It's fine, sis. You're busy. Your time will come again.'

Aisha relaxed back into her chair and picked at some plantain. Martina lifted Jude out of his pram and laid him on her chest. She sat back down and carried eating with one fork. Aisha noticed Charley look on with interest at the easy way Martina was with the baby. After a few minutes, Jude let out a loud belch, and the table erupted with laughter, mainly from the cousins who at twenty-four and twenty-six were still juvenile in their ways and minds and found goofy things hilarious.

Aisha watched Charley eat slowly, taking a mouthful of rice, then cutting her chicken up. She would then take a tiny portion of the plantain and carefully cut into it. On the other side of her the cousins were wolfing down their food. Charley was so different to her family that she was proud of her mum for accepting Charley in any way at all for all these years. Martina's life had been in Jamaica and now in Brixton amongst a close-knit Jamaican community – there had never been any Charley-shaped holes in her mother's life, but for the first time today, Aisha wondered if Martina had made one.

* * *

After the lunch, Aisha brought out some ginger cake she had managed to make over the weekend whilst Charley had the twins. It was one of those recipes you throw everything in the blender so it hadn't taken too long, and she had iced it that morning and it had set hard; only a small piece had chipped off on the drive over here this afternoon. Aisha put the cake on a platter in the kitchen whilst the cousins entertained Charley and Martina with their antics about town and then she put four candles in a neat straight line. This was the sort of cake Aisha wanted to serve in her Jamaican/British café and was going to bake it often to perfect the recipe even more.

Martina whooped and slapped her thigh when she saw Aisha bringing in the dessert – she was still holding on to Jude, and Charley was now holding on to Otis. The babies' eyes were trying to focus on the flickering candles. Everyone sang loudly, and Martina blew the candles out in one blow.

'Make a wish, Mum,' Aisha said as she stood behind her, one hand on her shoulder.

Martina patted her hand. 'I made my wish.'

After cake, the boys were fed a bottle whilst Charley and Aisha did the dishes. Martina's kitchen was still the same as it was when Aisha lived here over ten years ago. Faded wood cupboards and units, orange and blue walls, turquoise curtains and brightly coloured bowls and platters that had come back with her from Jamaica before the children were born. The familiar scent of incense sticks burned day and night.

'Why don't you go out for a walk whilst I give them boys some fresh air in the garden? Reckon they might fall asleep for an hour. I used to keep all of you outside for your naps when you were little,' Martina said to Aisha. Then she turned her head ever so slightly towards Charley and said, 'Go on.'

Charley smiled and took Aisha's hand, and Martina looked at their tight grip before turning away.

* * *

They walked as far as Kennington Park. Charley's hand slipped into Aisha's again once they were outside.

'This feels strange,' Aisha said.

'Really? Strange? Or familiar, wouldn't you say?' Charley said and turned to grin at Aisha. 'It was nice of your mum to suggest we get some time on our own.'

'Yes.' Aisha laughed. 'I think she might have been a bit tipsy from the rum in the ginger cake.'

'She sometimes finds it hard though, doesn't she, acknowledging us?'

'She does. But I definitely sensed something change today. Did you sense it? I feel she may have turned a corner, finally seen us as parents and not just housemates. It's been hard for her.' Aisha felt her voice break at the last word and Charley squeezed her hand harder.

'Do you ever wish things were different? I mean, it's a complicated old set-up, your mum, cousins, sisters, and me?' she said after a beat.

'I wish so many things were different. I wish my dad had never left and that my mum hadn't lost a tiny part of herself. You know it's been twenty years this year since I saw my dad.'

'I had no idea. I'm sorry.' Charley gave Aisha's hand another squeeze.

'Oh no, it's fine. I'm not marking it with some sort of ceremony. I mean, I remember him, what he was like when I was a kid. It's just strange that he hasn't been around for such a long time.'

'Remind me, what was he like? You mentioned him in the beginning of our relationship, but you barely mention him any more.'

'Because he's not part of my life and hasn't been for so long. But I remember him laughing. He had the loudest, kindest laugh.'

'Ah, that's lovely.'

'But then I do remember the sadness too. The way his eyes

would lose all their glow on some mornings. He would go for big, long walks. I thought the day he left, it was just another of those long walks. Except he never came back.'

Charley sighed. 'And you've still never spoken to Martina much about this?'

'She said it was a closed chapter in our lives. He had made his decision and we couldn't change his mind.'

'And you've never heard from him since?'

'Mum said he moved back to Birmingham. Started a new life with another woman.'

Charley pointed to a bench. 'Shall we sit here for a minute?'

The sat quietly. Charley closed her eyes and basked in the afternoon spring sunshine.

'I love the boys so much, you know,' Charley said after a minute.

'I know.'

'And I know you do most of the childcare, and I'm busy a lot, but my mind is always half on you, and if you ever need me, just come and find me. Don't feel you have to do everything all the time.'

'I know. But I can't just keep bothering you all day, can I? I have to find a way.'

'And you will find your groove eventually. But just know I am here, you know, Aish.'

Aisha closed her eyes and absorbed the warmth and energy of the sun. It felt very different not to be with the boys, and she felt freer than she had in weeks. So, she knew how easy it was for Charley to say the words she had just spoken, because Aisha felt it too; the freedom felt intoxicating. They truly were another version of themselves as they both sat without the responsibility of the two tiny babies. Charley had taken the afternoon off work to be here with her today. It was rare for her to do that, but tomorrow she would be back down in the basement again, away from the healing rays of the sun, away from the natural warmth that went straight into your soul and reminded you that you came from the earth and brought you right back down to it. Tomorrow, Aisha thought, Charley would forget this.

* * *

Charley was tucking Otis into the pram, helping them get ready to walk home, when Martina announced that there was an explosion in Jude's nappy.

'What! Again?' Aisha said. The familiar tension that had momentarily faded on their walk was back. 'I only had one spare suit and Jude has that one on. I can't walk him back in the pram in just a nappy and blanket, it's cooler now than when we left.'

'Don't worry, girl, I have a spare one – there should be one in the little basket next to my wardrobe. I kept a few of Ruben and Marcel's suits – it don't feel two minutes ago they was in nappies.'

Aisha went into Martina's bedroom. The scent of vanilla was strong and through the thin patterned curtains that were closed bar an inch, the hazy afternoon light cast a streak of light across the room and landed on Martina's bed. Aisha turned to the wardrobe at the side of the bed, and sure enough, there was the basket of clothes. She picked one Babygro off the top of the pile quickly and spun around to leave, and as she did, the sleeve of her cardigan caught a small bowl, which contained bits of jewellery, on the edge of Martina's dressing table, sending bits flying everywhere.

'Shit.' Aisha fell to her knees and began grabbing at earrings and bracelets that had fallen around the bed and under it. She lay down flat on her front, and it was then that she noticed under the bed an open box stuffed full of white envelopes. She stuck her arm right under the bed and pulled the box closer. The box was full of opened letters, fifty or sixty all addressed to Martina. She pulled one out and read the first few lines. Suddenly, her head began to spin.

'Aisha, girl, whacha doing? Little man gonna freeze to death here.'

'Coming. I'm just coming,' Aisha called and pushed the box back further under the bed. She stood up; the letter she had been reading still grasped in her hand. Without hesitating, she quickly stuffed it into the pocket of her jeans and left the room.

* * *

Later that evening, when the boys were asleep and Charley was in bed, Aisha sat downstairs on the sofa and, by the light of a lamp, read and reread the letter over and over until her eyes were so blurred with tears she could no longer see.

She was reading words written only a few years ago. Words written by her father. The man who she thought had left her without a care. It turned out the man she had thought about every day for the last twenty years had also been keeping her in his own thoughts for just as long.

* * *

2.15 a.m. – Aisha: Hi, girls. Hope you're both okay. I'm a bit sad tonight.
2.46 a.m. – Sophy: Oh shit, Aisha, what's happened?
2.51 a.m. – Aisha: I read one of what appeared to be many letters from my dad. I thought he had disowned me and my sisters. He has been writing to my mum for years.
2.54 a.m. – Sophy: Oh my goodness. That's… sad and amazing.

2.56am – Aisha: I hope you don't mind me telling you.

2.57 a.m. – Sophy: Of course not. Why would I?

2.58am – Aisha: It feels quite personal. We've not known each other long.

2.58 a.m. – Sophy: That's true. But I feel I can tell you things, so I'm glad you feel the same way. This feels like the deep and meaningful conversations I would have with a stranger at two o'clock in the morning in a nightclub toilet, minus the sticky floor and neon-coloured cocktails. I feel women can open up in any environment if they just trust that other women will listen. Obviously the two-for-one Harvey Wallbangers helped in that other situation.

3.00 a.m. – Aisha: Yes, and it feels like the quiet of the night means I have the space in my head to say what I want to. Does that make sense?

3.01 a.m. – Sophy: It does. x

15

SOPHY

'It's an annual thing, and it's not as if I ask you to do much for me, is it?' Jeff said as he ate the curry Sophy had prepared earlier that day.

'It's fine, Jeff. I said I'll come. I just have a lot on at the moment.'

Jeff had just reminded Sophy that his annual charity fundraiser for the elephant sanctuary in Bali was next week. She and Jeff had been on a holiday to Bali when they had first met, and Sophy had insisted they go to the elephant sanctuary. Thinking that Jeff would absolutely hate it, she was surprised when it turned out he thoroughly enjoyed it and talked about it as the best part of the holiday when reminiscing. He gave a hefty donation to the charity, and when they returned home, he vowed to raise money for them annually. So since then, he would hire a room somewhere each year for a fundraiser. Jeff would stand up and do his little speech, then a couple of conservationists would talk – last year Jeff bagged a celebratory vet to talk. There was a lot of alcohol during the event and guests would inevitably spill out into a bar afterwards and then a nightclub. Sophy was tired and as much as she wanted to support Jeff, the idea of getting dressed up and getting over to the venue with Max was a little bit overwhelming. She couldn't bring in a babysitter because of the milk situation and the venue was too far away. If Sophy was going to go, Max would have to go too.

Jeff stopped eating and looked up at Sophy. 'A lot on? You're at home all day, and also, I was thinking about this the other day, it's not as if you have to make bottles or clean bottles like my mum had to do. He has it all on tap. You're not going to many of those baby groups that you said you'd be at every week. And you're not back to training. It's been nearly two months.' Jeff used his fork to emphasise the next part. 'You said to me, "Six weeks and I'll be ready to get back out there again." And don't get me started on our sex life.'

Sophy was dumbstruck for a moment. But once she had absorbed Jeff's harsh words, she spoke up. 'Jeff! It's just... harder than I thought it would be, the recovery. I didn't expect to tear and be stitched up and for it to still hurt. I think I was probably a bit too optimistic when I said six weeks. The reality is it could be months.' Sophy felt a sharp pain in her abdomen, followed by a dull ache. She had winced, but Jeff hadn't noticed.

'Really?' Jeff said, a vast amount of surprise in his voice. 'Months?' he said.

'Er, yes, Jeff. Giving birth is not like ripping a plaster off and all will be well. I birthed a human! I was speaking to Aisha the other day, and she told me that mothers still have parts of their baby's DNA inside them for up to a year, that means, I still have bits of Max inside me!' Sophy said with a hint of melancholy to her voice, which Jeff did not detect. For a second, she thought she might cry.

'I'd rather you had parts of me inside you,' Jeff quipped.

Sophy folded her arms and looked sternly at Jeff.

'Oh god, not the look. I'm just saying, Soph, it's been months. He was inside you for nine of those months. Surely, it's my turn again. Isn't that how we're supposed to keep our relationship going?'

Sophy felt her gut tighten with fury this time.

'Erm, no. We keep our relationship going with mutual respect and admiration for one another.' Sophy thought quickly if the latter was true for her. Did she admire Jeff? She considered his successful estate agent business. And nice car.

Jeff put his fork down on his plate with too much force for Sophy's liking. She had bought those plates in the John Lewis sale last year with one of her first sponsorship payments. She narrowed her eyes at Jeff.

'You've been spending too much time with those new friends of yours. You said one of them was a lesbian, didn't you?' Jeff leant back in his chair.

'And what does that mean?'

'That she's not, you know, getting it.'

'I'm sure Aisha gets plenty of *it*, Jeff. But I imagine, like me, she is feeling a little sore down there after giving birth to two babies.'

'Twins? You didn't say she had twins.'

'I did, Jeff. I did.'

Jeff shrugged, and they both sat in silence for a few moments. Then just as Sophy was thinking of getting up to clear the plates, Jeff's phone rang at exactly the same time as Max let out a piercing scream from upstairs. Jeff picked up his phone to answer it.

'Don't you dare, Jeff. It's half past seven. You finished work over an hour ago.' Sophy leant forward as Jeff tried to bat her away.

'Work doesn't finish just because I'm not in the office, Soph.'

'But your son is crying.' Sophy threw her hands open in despair.

'Well, you'll have to see to him, babes – I need to take this call.'

Jeff stood up and walked out of the back door, and as he closed it behind him, Sophy couldn't be sure with the increasing volume of Max's cries, but the way he answered the phone, the way in which he said, 'Hello,' was done in an endearing and familiar way. Not the way he would speak to his mother or a male friend or colleague, but someone who required a softer touch. A woman.

* * *

Sophy had been mulling over Jeff's phone call as she had soothed Max back to sleep with a quick comfort feed and continued to stew over it as she sat in the bath. Once she was back in the bedroom, and Max was sound asleep in his SnuzPod, she dressed in some sexy loungewear, checked on Max again, made sure the monitor was on and then crept downstairs. Jeff was sitting in his joggers and T-shirt on the sofa, remote in hand.

He smiled at her as she came into the room.

'I thought you were doing your Instagram thing.'

'Not tonight.' Sophy slipped into the space next to Jeff on the sofa. He lifted his arm up and around her, and she rested against the side of his chest. He began softly stroking her arm and side, occasionally his hand would land near to her breast and after a few times, when Sophy did not object, he finally slipped his hand up inside her T-shirt and began stroking her breast, moving slowly up to her nipple. Sophy felt a hint of desire and thought perhaps she could manage something if Jeff instigated it, which at this rate he most certainly would. It was a bit like going to the gym or doing a workout; the thought of it was worse than the actual act. Once she had done a workout, she was glad she had put in the effort and could tick it off for another few days. Sophy wondered if she succumbed to Jeff's obvious desires, and her ever-so-slight pang, she could earn herself a few weeks of safety space. Jeff was so busy at work and usually so tired when he came home most days anyway that he was nowhere near as demanding as he used to be, so for him to be complaining was probably down to tiredness because when she thought about it, he hadn't exactly instigated much beyond that first week after Max had been born. The more she considered it, the more irate she began to feel and then she wished she had not bothered making any effort as the aggravation began to consume her. Her mind swirled back to his tone on the phone earlier when he answered the call. Was she being paranoid?

The caressing moved closer to, and eventually onto, her nipple and Sophy gasped at his touch. Her nipple had become so sensitive since breastfeeding Max. Even still, when Max latched on, the first minute was pretty painful. But Jeff worked on, oblivious to Sophy's squirms, which he seemed to interpret as enjoyment. He grabbed her right hand and placed it between his own legs – where she could feel the hot, throbbing heat – and began murmuring into her ear. Then he quickly moved her backwards, so she was lying down. He lifted up her top and began sucking on each breast so furiously that all Sophy could do was imagine Max in her mind's eye. Nothing about it felt pleasurable. He then stood up and whipped down his joggers, then began working Sophy's loungewear bottoms down.

'Wow, I love these, babes,' he murmured.

He put his hand between her legs, which Sophy knew would be dry – she was practically clenching her butt cheeks with fear of any pain that could come. Jeff licked his hand and put it back between her legs and then brought himself down and on top of her. He fiddled with himself for a second, trying to get to where he needed to be, and then finally, he slowly began pushing himself inside Sophy. Instantly, Sophy let out a scream and pulled herself backwards; Jeff popped out of her like a champagne cork.

'What?' Jeff looked down at her.

'It hurts. I told you it would hurt.' Sophy whipped on her loungewear bottoms.

'Okay, I'll be gentle.'

'You can't, Jeff. That's the problem. It's a penis, entering a healing vagina. A person came out of it a few weeks ago. It's sore.' Sophy wasn't sure why it was taking so long – it was almost two months. Shouldn't she be feeling much better down there by now?

'Well, what am I supposed to do?' Sophy looked at him, her boyfriend who she had once fancied so much, who now had an expression of a small boy who had been told he couldn't have any more cake.

Then they both flinched as an ear-splitting scream came from through the monitor.

'Shit, sorry – I had it turned up earlier when I was in the garden.' Sophy leant over and turned it down.

Jeff looked at Sophy with doe eyes. 'I can be quick. I won't hurt you.'

'Max is crying, I need to feed him,' she said as she sat back, wondering if she actually cared enough to try to make Jeff feel a little bit better about any of this, when she herself felt rotten, sore and exhausted.

Then Sophy felt a wetness on her chest and stomach as she looked down at the one exposed breast, which was leaking milk down into her belly button, the other breast was saturating her top.

'Oh great.' Sophy stood up, sending Jeff lurching backwards until he was sat back on the sofa again, his penis shrivelled in the middle of his thighs.

Sophy pulled off her wet top and stood there with milk dripping from both breasts. She hadn't worn a maternity bra or any breast pads, thinking she would feel sexier without them. How wrong had she been?

'I'm sorry, Jeff,' she said as she walked from the room but as she turned back to wait for him to say something, anything, he was pulling his joggers on and was then back on the sofa with the remote in hand.

'That was a bit mean, getting me all riled up and then *nothing*,' Jeff snapped.

Sophy shook her head and ran upstairs. Max was flapping his arms around in the cot next to the bed, and so Sophy grabbed a towel, tucked it under one breast to catch the excess milk and keep from soaking Max's Babygro, and latched him on to the other breast.

She sat there feeding Max, waiting for the guilt to come, for the part where she was supposed to start worrying about how she was ever going to make it up to Jeff. But there was nothing. She thought about the position she had just been in minutes before, under Jeff with his throbbing manhood waving about near her sore nether regions, and realised right there, with Max tucked into the crook of her arm, was exactly where she wanted to be more than anything.

* * *

When Max woke that night, Sophy smiled when she saw it was exactly 3 a.m. She bashed out a quick message on the WhatsApp group.

3.00 a.m. – Sophy: Hey girls, it's exactly 3 a.m.! Max's just woken up, this second! I fell asleep with him at ten. We had a full five hours. I'm going to feed him and hope I get a few more hours!

3.13 a.m. – Mel: Wow, that's amazing. I've been up since 2.15. Skylar is wide awake! Been watching some trashy American thing and now made jam on toast and tea.

Sophy paused for a second and thought about what she wanted to say but wondered if it was appropriate. Then she thought about what Aisha had said in one of the recent messages about feeling safe telling her things. She bashed out the message.

3.15 a.m. – Sophy: Hey, Mel, is it normal that I don't feel horny and all I want to do is cuddle my baby and not Jeff? I still feel sore.

Sophy sat and chewed the side of her finger, waiting to see if there was any typing. Minutes passed. Oh shit. She shouldn't have said anything. That last comment was probably crossing the line. And Aisha would see it too. Oh Christ, was it too late to delete? She looked to see who had read the message, and she saw that Mel had. Fuck. The minutes ticked by and Sophy's eyes began to close when she heard a soft ping.

3.23 a.m. – Mel: Absolutely not, babe. It's your body and your choice. You should never compromise that for anyone. EVER.

Wow, Sophy hadn't been expecting such a strong response. But she felt better.

3.35 a.m. – Mel: You should get checked out by the doctor if you're still feeling sore, though. Promise me you will?

Sophy felt her heart swell with joy again. It felt good to be cared for by a female. In all her years of friendships, she had never experienced stomach flutters when talking with another woman. This was completely platonic, pure sisterhood love. And it felt great.

3.36 a.m. – Sophy: I will. I promise. x

* * *

'I'm really sorry about last night,' Sophy said to Jeff the next morning as he ate a bowl of cornflakes at the kitchen island at 6.30. She had been up with Max since five. He had managed another couple of hours. Which was fine. He'd go back down soon and Sophy could get herself showered and ready. Niall and his boys would be here in an hour and a half. Eight on the dot every morning, and Sophy hated the thought of not being dressed and looking semi-presentable when they, or anyone else for that matter, arrived so early and ready for work. She tried not to pay much attention to the nudging thought that it was indeed Niall who she did not want to see her looking any less than her best. It was a woman's prerogative, after all, to look presentable for visitors.

Jeff mumbled something into his cereal bowl, and Sophy wondered for a moment why this was still his breakfast of choice when she had tried so often to interest him in so many other more nutritional options.

'What?' Sophy said.

'I said, it's fine.' Jeff stood up and put his bowl on the counter directly above the very open and empty – because she had emptied it at 5.30 a.m. – dishwasher.

Sophy really wanted to make things right, to bridge this gap and for them all to feel close like a family should.

'I will come to the charity thing. I'll rally as many people as I can. I'll invite my new friends, let's make it the best one yet, hey?' Sophy edged forward until she and Max were touching him.

Jeff welcomed Sophy and Max into his arms and they all stood there for a few moments. Sophy tried to breathe in his scent, to really appreciate the moment and the closeness they were all experiencing. Only instead, she wished there were someone close by so they could snap a photo of them, because this, Sophy thought, was the perfect Instagram image and would do wonders for her following.

* * *

Niall and his boys arrived at eight o'clock, as always. Sophy was showered and dressed and sat at the table eating a bowl of muesli.

She had already thanked him for the crispy pancakes in the freezer and they had laughed about how Jeff had clearly not shared the crispy-pancake love.

Niall popped his head into the kitchen as usual and called good morning. Then he said to his boys, 'Say morning to the lady of the house, lads.' And the two builders mumbled an awkward hello.

'Not as outgoing as you?' Sophy said to Niall as the boys went outside and started up the concrete mixer. It was a sound Sophy had begun to get used to hearing every morning now.

'Ahh, they're good lads. What's on the menu this morning?' Niall motioned to the bowl in front of Sophy.

'Oh, just boring old muesli.'

'A good Irish fry-up is what you want.'

'Is that what you've had already then?' Sophy asked.

'Oh yeah, every morning.'

'And do you make that for yourself?' Sophy asked hoping that Niall wouldn't be perceptive enough to understand her line of questioning.

'Oh yeah. Eggs don't fry themselves.'

Sophy stayed quiet. She could see no ring on his finger. It was possible he could live alone.

'Just me and the cat. See.'

'Oh, you have a cat!' Sophy exclaimed so loudly, Niall stepped back in astonishment. For some reason, Sophy found she was glad Niall lived alone with just a cat for company.

'Woah. Someone loves cats, do they?'

In fact, Sophy had no preference for cats or dogs or any furry friends. She had surprised herself with how much energy she had used to expel her last sentence. The thought of Niall home alone with no other human contact had somehow titillated her.

'Jeff hates animals. Well, all animals. Except elephants.'

'I don't think this extension will be big enough to accommodate one of those.'

'No,' Sophy scoffed.

'Well, I'd better be off to work.' Niall stood and looked at Sophy for a moment, then he stood up straight, gave Sophy a quick salute and went to join his colleagues outside.

Sophy finished her muesli, and with a growing image in her head of Niall sat in his home all alone with just a cat for company, she found she was smiling.

16

MEL

'I do bathroom. Make taps very shiny, make loo no shit on it, I get dust off light shade, use long brush – no ladders. I only work alone or with woman in house. No alone with men.' Ksenia stood in the lounge in a blue boiler suit and white plimsoles. Her hair was tied back, making her features look particularly pointy.

Mel wondered if it was appropriate to ask exactly how much hassle her new cleaner had had from men. She was interested in this woman's past – Mel worked in an industry where she would get the occasional jeer from a man, but only once in over twenty years of performing had she found herself in a situation where she had feared for her own safety and that of her unborn child. There was something fabulous about Ksenia, and Mel liked her more with every minute.

'Great, Ksenia, it all sounds fabulous. And you can come every week?'

'Yes, this time every week. I very prompt. I take cash, no cheques.'

'Fantastic. I'll have the cash ready for you. My husband is always at work at this time, so it will usually be me here or I'll leave you a key.' Ksenia nodded. 'And your accent? Where are you from?'

'Russia. I live here three years. I clean all that time. I clean in Russia before. My name, in Russian it mean "hospitable and welcoming".'

Bess who had been bounding around Ksenia, sniffing her feet and panting wildly, nudged her wet nose into Ksenia's crotch.

'NO!' Ksenia hollered down at her, and Bess retreated backwards and sat down about two feet away from Ksenia.

'Wow!' Mel said. 'I've never been able to get her to listen to me like that in three years.'

'I have many dogs in Russia. Dog like men – sniff, sniff, sniff.' Ksenia did a funny pig-like impression with her nose and lips.

Mel pulled her lips together tightly and tried to suppress a smile. She bounced Skylar in her arms. Skylar let out a tiny happy scream, followed by a gurgle. Ksenia bent forward and peered at Sky in Mel's arms, as though she were inspecting a stain on a carpet. Then, without smiling, she said: 'Your baby very cute. He remind me of ex-boyfriend.'

* * *

'I don't know why you are so stressed about going out for one night. You'll enjoy yourself,' Daz said as Mel pulled off another top and threw it onto the growing pile of discarded outfit choices. Aside from the redundant ensembles, Mel and Daz's bedroom was spotless; Ksenia had done an amazing job of the entire house and a few clothes on the very clean carpet gave her zero anxiety.

'Yes, but nothing I wear is going to go with this stupid space boot, is it?' Mel shook her foot out to remind Daz, in case he had forgotten about her bust ankle and thought the hefty cast was now part of her anatomy.

'It's only for a few more weeks, babe,' Daz said, holding a grizzly Sky to his chest.

'Are you sure you're going to be okay with her? I know it's a school night.' Mel looked on concerned.

'It's okay for one night. She should be settled by ten, shouldn't she?'

Mel raised her head. 'I wouldn't bank on it. Madam's been a right pickle for weeks now. She doesn't know what she wants.'

'You, mostly.' Daz moved Sky onto his shoulder.

'That's true. Well, you can let her fall asleep on your chest, can't you? I'll take over when I get back. I shouldn't be any later than eleven.'

'It's fine. You go out and have a drink with your friends. We'll be fine, won't we?'

Daz spoke across his shoulder to Sky, who stopped grizzling for a moment and seemed to be listening to him. *Why is it such a novelty to men when they have their own children for one night?* Mel thought. She would be absolutely getting the breakdown of the entire evening the next day, as if it wasn't exactly what Mel did every day and night.

'And it's for elephants, you say?' Daz asked.

'Yes, a charity thing.' Mel picked up a white and red spotty blouse and held it against her chest.

'Ahh, well, that's nice. You know I could have come, too. I quite like elephants,' Daz said so softly that Mel felt her heart pang for both him and Sky.

'There won't be any actual elephants there, Daz. Just people talking about elephants. And alcohol.' Mel chucked the shirt in the pile.

'I know, but Mum could have babysat. I could have been your date,' Daz said so earnestly that Mel couldn't help but feel guilty even though her body had gone rigid. The idea that she was going to this thing in the first place was a miracle. She had toyed with the idea when Sophy had sent the message explaining how this was an important night for Jeff and since Max had come along, she had not had much time for him, and she wanted to help him make it a really special night this year. Mel got it, she really did. But as if she wasn't feeling awkward enough about it as it was, now Sophy was confiding in her about her sex life. She was in such a rigid dichotomy between wanting to be a supportive friend and feeling completely repulsed by any mention of that man and his sexual needs.

Of course, Aisha had replied straight away, saying she would absolutely be there for her and was looking forward to it. Mel could not think of any plausible excuses to get out of this evening other than her foot, which wasn't stopping her doing most things now that the pain and swelling had subsided a lot. But as far as Sophy knew, this would be the first time Mel would be meeting Jeff. And as far as Jeff was concerned, it would be the first time he would be meeting Mel – their last encounter could hardly be described as an exchanging of pleasantries. But Mel had planned the fake expression she intended to pull when Sophy made the introductions, and she would be none the wiser. She could then feel comfortably uncomfortable in Jeff Haddon's presence for the rest of the evening without anyone else clocking what was going on. But Daz, her sweet Daz, he would be all over her like a heartbeat, asking her what was wrong and why she was suddenly sweating profusely, and she could not deal with that the first time. She needed to get it over, this 'fake meet', and if this relationship with Sophy kept growing at the rate it was now, then Mel would have to find a way to bury the incident for good; to protect her friendship and the relationship between Jeff and Sophy. They had a new baby – she couldn't be the one to tear that family apart. Mel was a tough woman; she had been through enough in her life. She could handle this.

'Oh, don't make me feel bad. I really am just going to go and hang with the girls. We haven't been out yet together without the babies. Although Sophy will be bringing Max, cos boobs don't stretch across London.' Mel had given up on clothes and was sat at the dressing table, applying foundation with an egg-shaped sponge.

Daz frowned. 'Quite. Right, I'm going to read to this one, see if I can get her a bit snoozy. She seems quite tired.' Daz brought Sky down from his shoulder and cradled her in his arms.

'Read her one of your accountancy books. That should send her right off,' Mel scoffed.

'Ha-ha, very funny.' Daz shrugged off Mel's quip.

'Seriously though, I tried to keep her awake a bit today to tire her out so you shouldn't have too many problems with her.' Mel thought how this was the sort of thing that women thought about naturally, but would never have crossed Daz's mind.

Daz bent down and kissed Mel on the cheek.

'Have fun.'

Fun, thought Mel. Yes, that was something she once knew how to have.

* * *

The Tube was cramped and hot, and Mel had to keep making people aware of her foot so that it wouldn't keep getting trodden on. She had rushed getting out of the house, had a last-minute flap about her final outfit choice and changed once more. She had missed the Tube she had wanted to get and was now running late. According to Sophy, there was to be a sit-down talk and slide show bit before the drinking commenced, and Mel was sure she was going to be walking in halfway through the talking.

Once she was above ground again, she put the address into the maps app on her phone and followed the route.

It said a five-minute walk, so Mel set off at the fastest pace she could with the boot on. When Mel arrived at the ornate historic building and found the doors closed and locked, she felt a mixture of panic and relief. She could just walk back to the Tube and tell the girls she couldn't get in. But they would have expected her to have called. So she banged hard on the door and waited a few minutes before knocking again. No one arrived. She had rushed out of the house without using the loo and had needed the toilet all the way on the Tube. Stress increased her need to pee, and now it was threatening to seep out. She looked around; it was an old historical building with well-pruned borders. She walked around the corner of the building to see if there were any other doors she had missed. Not even a doorbell. It was no good. She had to pee.

She ducked next to a bush. There wasn't enough room for her to get right behind it, and it had been raining earlier so she didn't want to get her boot wet on the damp soil. So, she crouched down, pulled her dress up, half her body hidden by a bush, the other half exposed, her leg cocked out a funny angle, and peed. Just as she was finishing up, she heard a voice calling. Mel pulled herself together and straightened her dress down just as a young woman with a neat black bob appeared at the corner of the building.

'Oh hi!' Mel said. 'Do you work here?' Mel started walking towards her relieved she might finally get inside.

'Yes,' the woman said. Even from a slight distance, it was obvious there was a stern look on her face. Mel was confused.

Had she arrived at the right building? Or perhaps they were very strict on arrivals.

'And did you hear me knocking on the door?' Mel said.

'No,' the woman said. Mel arrived in front of her and could see the woman was indeed stony-faced.

'Oh. Then how did you know I was out here?' Mel said, slightly out of breath from her panic pee.

'We have cameras.' The grave-faced woman pointed to a camera on the wall of the building that was pointing downwards directly at where Mel had just been squatting quite unceremoniously. Mel looked back at the camera and then down at the little trickle of pee that had seeped out on the stone path. She felt her heart sink into her stomach.

'Oh, great, fabulous. Thanks.' Mel pulled her handbag tight over her shoulder and walked past the woman, round the corner and through the open door, her head held high; the mortification ripping through her body.

Inside the venue, chairs were tightly packed into a room on the right. The dark-haired woman appeared by Mel as she hung back in the foyer.

'It's that room through there,' she said, and Mel was sure she looked her up and down in disgust as she spoke.

Mel ignored the woman's austerity and the raging shame that was throbbing through her body – if there was one thing she had learned in the business they call 'show', it was to get up and slap a smile on no matter how shit you felt.

Mel stopped at the doorway, as standing at the front of the room behind a lectern was the man who she now knew to be her friend's boyfriend. Jeff had that same swagger and confident manner about him even as he spoke about something as important and serious as elephants getting murdered for their ivory tusks. Mel took a deep breath and walked into the room. It was dark and cramped. Chairs were close together, but Mel spotted a seat at the end of a row. Everyone had to stand up to let her through and she apologised to the six strangers as she gave them a full view of her rear end as she scooched along to the empty seat. She got herself comfortable as quietly and with as little disruption as possible, then she sat very still and listened to Jeff speaking. She couldn't see a compassionate conservationist, loving boyfriend and new father to a young baby, which she realised was what everyone else in the room saw. What Mel saw was a monster.

* * *

Thirty minutes later, the lights were up, and everyone was making their way to the bar in the next room.

'Mel.' Aisha was waiting in the doorway to the foyer. She was wearing a blue floral dress that came to her knees with a black leather jacket and Doc Martens. They hugged.

'You look lovely,' Mel said. 'Really fresh and trendy. I wish I could pull that off.'

'Thank you. And you look lovely too. You really do. How are you? How's the foot?'

Mel looked down at her boot, which was a complete eyesore in the long pink and red floral dress she was wearing. 'Annoying me now. Where's Sophy?'

Aisha looked towards the other room, which people were now making their way into. 'Oh she's off. Quite the socialite. She makes it look so easy. And with a baby in her arms as well.'

Mel nodded. Her gut tightened as she anticipated the meet-and-greet with Jeff.

'There are nibbles too!' Aisha said, like an excited child.

'Oh great, perfect for a foodie like you then. I tell you what, I could do with a drink. Shall we?' Mel motioned to the doorway.

Aisha hooked her arm into Mel's, and they strode into the next room.

They took a glass of champagne each from the bar, and then made a beeline for Sophy as they spotted her working the room.

'Mel, you're here.' Sophy greeted Mel with a hug and a kiss. Mel realised this was the first time that the three of them had greeted one another with kisses. It felt good.

Sophy was wearing a pink jumpsuit, and her blonde hair looked as if it had been blow-dried professionally. Max was in her arms, gurgling at the world around him.

'Oh, look at him!' Mel said, touching his little cheek, which was red and warm and soft.

'I know, wide awake and taking it all in,' Sophy said. 'Thanks so much for coming. It means a lot. I know it's bums on seats and all—'

'No,' Aisha butted in. 'It's a really important cause. Jeff is such a great man for doing such a wonderful thing. You should be so proud. He's a really good public speaker. Mel, did you hear his speech?'

'I did,' Mel said flatly. 'It was really great,' she added to Sophy, who grinned.

'Well, it's his thing. I am proud of what he does,' Sophy said, but Mel felt her tone lacked enthusiasm. Sophy scanned the room. 'Jeff's about somewhere, I can introduce you. I know he'd love to meet you – I've spoken non-stop about you since we met for goodness' sake.'

'Don't go out of your way, Sophy. This is Jeff's night, he doesn't need to be chatting with two shattered mothers,' Mel said and Aisha laughed.

'Does he know about our 3 a.m. club?' Aisha said.

'Erm, kind of, I have told him. I think...' Sophy trailed off, quickly scanning the room. Mel was suddenly intrigued, interested in how vague Sophy sounded when she was speaking of her boyfriend. And was it her imagination, or did she seem a little on edge?

'Does Charley approve of our 3 a.m. texts?' Mel turned to Aisha.

'Oh yes. She is just glad I have that connection, you know.' Aisha took a long drink of her champagne and giggled. 'This is my second glass already. It's really nice.'

'You knock yourself out, love,' Mel said. 'Not literally obviously.' She touched Aisha's arm.

'Charley said I could go mad tonight too!' Aisha said in a voice that was a few decibels louder than the one she usually spoke in.

'Sounds like it's doing its job already!' Mel nodded and smiled.

'Oh god, I'm sorry. I don't really drink very often, not because I don't like it, I do, I just haven't been out that much since the twins got here.'

Mel patted Aisha's arm reassuringly. 'None of us have, love.'

'Oh look, there's Jeff,' Sophy said, and Mel looked and saw Jeff walking towards them all. Her heart started pumping harder in her chest as images of how the next few minutes would play out swirled around in her mind. She took a long drink of her champagne, almost finishing the glass. 'Jeff!' Sophy shouted, and Jeff, who looked as though he might have taken a sudden swerve for the bar, stopped, and when he saw Sophy, he gave a quick nod and walked over.

'Jeff, I want you to meet my friends,' Sophy said with a wide smile – that Mel was struggling to invest in – plastered across her face.

'The 3 a.m. Shattered Mums' Club!' Aisha said loudly and

laughed at herself. Jeff smiled patiently. His silver suit was super shiny under the lights of the room and his blond hair was swept back off his face. Then he turned his attention to Mel, and she felt the weight of those piercing blue eyes.

'This is Aisha and Mel!' Sophy said enthusiastically as though she were a presenter on a family TV show and she might also add what they did for a living and where they came from.

Jeff leant over, took Aisha's hand, and then to Mel's horror, leant in and kissed the side of Aisha's face gently. 'It is a pleasure to meet you. I have heard so much about you. Thank you so much for coming this evening.' His voice was low and gravelly.

Aisha laughed again and took another drink of her champagne.

Then he turned back to Mel again, and Mel was certain she saw a flicker of recognition in his eyes, but she was more focused on the fear penetrating through her body and making its way down to her stomach. Her legs felt like heavy weights and every part of her body was screaming at her to run. She should just think of an excuse, run to the loo, anything, to escape from what was about to happen. Before Mel had time to think a moment longer, Jeff had his hand on her arm and had leant in and was brushing his lips against her cheek. The smell of his aftershave was nauseating. How was it possible, after all this time for him to still smell exactly the same? Scent is one thing that the brain holds on to the most and evokes the most memories. Daz had bought a similar-smelling aftershave recently, and Mel had insisted he throw it in the bin and blamed it on baby hormones.

Jeff drew back and his eyes scanned Mel's face for another second. If he had recognised her, he had done a good job of disguising it, but Mel was certain she had given the game away. She could not seem to force her mouth into even a semi-smile.

'Your glass is almost empty, Aisha. Why don't we go and get

you another drink?' Mel took Aisha's arm and began turning her back towards the bar to try and disguise any awkwardness.

'Oh gutted, wish I could have one!' Sophy called after them. And as she and Aisha walked to the bar, she could just hear Sophy hissing, 'I know, Jeff, but I can't. I'm bloody breastfeeding – how many times do I have to say it?'

At the bar, Mel ordered two more glasses of champagne. She looked around the venue. It was not the sort of place where she would have imagined someone like Jeff hosting an event. She knew he was the sort of guy who preferred locations with a bit more glamour; places he could flash his cash and people wouldn't bat an eyelid. This venue was steeped in history and a little too conservative for the Jeff she had encountered.

'Jeff is so nice, isn't he?' Aisha said. 'This is such a great thing to do. I love charity stuff.'

Mel nodded and scanned the room, wondering how much longer she could get away with being here. She looked at Aisha, who was looking around the room and smiling at nothing; she was just happy to be here by all accounts, and Mel felt bad. Out of the three of them, Aisha always seemed to be the one who struggled the most with motherhood, with two tiny boys who she had to look after most of the time alone, and as a new mother, Mel had seen the shock and sadness in Aisha's eyes and recognised the signs from when she had Leia. Of course, she hadn't known she was suffering from post-natal depression then. It was three years later that she read something that described exactly how she had felt and acted during the first year of Leia's life.

So she let this woman she had known for just a few short weeks enjoy the time away from her babies who were being cared for by another woman who loved them just as much and stayed by Aisha's side, topping her up with water in between glasses of champagne – because if she could give any new mother a piece of advice, it would be don't get inordinately pissed in the first place, but if you're going to let your hair down after carrying two babies for nine months and then not sleeping for months, stay hydrated. The sickness doesn't feel half as bad if your body has enough water inside it to counteract the alcohol levels. She didn't bore Aisha with these facts; she would just hand her the water to drink like she was handing a sippy cup to a toddler.

Mel looked at her phone; it was just after 10 p.m. They'd been there long enough now. She decided she would get her and Aisha to the toilet and then get them both in an Uber, dropping Aisha off first.

Aisha was in deep conversation with a rather frail-looking elderly lady a few feet away and had been for some time, so Mel stepped over and took Aisha's hand.

'I'm going to get in a cab soon, and I think it's best we share, so shall we nip to the loos first?'

'Oh yes... yes... absholulee... This is Pauline, by the way.'

The woman looked at Mel. 'It's Doreen, actually. Hello.'

'Hi,' Mel said.

'Your friend is very sweet. Her boys sound lovely.' Doreen smiled.

'Oh yes, yes they are,' Mel agreed.

'Twins are such a blessing.'

'They are. It was lovely to meet you.' Mel began to navigate Aisha towards the toilets.

'Bye, Pauline,' Aisha called over her shoulder.

Outside in the foyer, it was a lot cooler, and Mel felt some relief that soon they would be on their way home. She began to steer Aisha towards the sign for the ladies'.

'Ladies, off to the ladies'?' came a voice from behind that Mel had hoped she wouldn't have to hear for the rest of the night, or indeed, her life.

Mel looked over her shoulder. Jeff was standing two feet behind them.

Mel ignored him and, holding on to Aisha's arm – she was now actually holding her up –continued to walk on. Suddenly, Jeff was in front of them.

'Woah, your friend looks a little worse for wear here.' He reached out and went to grab Aisha's arm. Mel shoved his hand away

'Don't you touch her!' she hissed. Jeff stood back and raised his hands, but with a smug smile across his face. Aisha released herself from Mel's grip and began to focus on the man in front of her.

'It's Jeff... Mel, looks ish Jeff.'

'I was going to see if you needed any help, maybe ordering a cab. But I see you have your bodyguard with you,' Jeff said in a snidey tone.

'He loves elephants soooooo much,' Aisha said and stumbled forward through the toilet door. Mel followed behind.

'Hey, don't I know you?' Jeff said just as Mel was about to follow Aisha through the door.

'Yes, I'm Sophy's friend. Sophy, your girlfriend?'

'Yes, I know who my girlfriend is, thanks.' Jeff laughed.

'Do you?' Mel said and went into the toilet, closing the door behind her.

Aisha was already inside the cubicle, singing softly to herself.

'Shit, shit, shit,' Mel hissed. This was bad news. She had meant to stay perfectly cool, and not let on to Jeff. But she had fucked it up. Jeff was sure to mention to Sophy how she had just acted towards him and if Sophy was half the woman Mel thought she was, then she would definitely say something to Mel when they saw one another next.

'Shit, shit, shit,' Mel hissed again.

'Ishhaaat you, Mel?' Aisha slurred from behind the cubicle.

'Yes, I'm here. I'm just getting us that Uber.'

'Good... cosh I feel—'

But Mel didn't hear any words after that, just a loud retching and then the sound of heavy liquid hitting a toilet pan.

17

AISHA

'Do you want me to take over this morning?' Charley said quietly to Aisha who was lying on the sofa.

'No, you did the night feed,' Aisha croaked.

'Well, it was only fair since you were comatose and the boys needed feeding.'

'Don't. I'm a horrible mother. They're barely two months old and I've turned to alcohol.'

'You got drunk with some friends. It's not a crime. And you're not a horrible mum. You're a lovely mum.' Charley fell to her knees and stroked Aisha's arm. 'Just don't do anything today. The boys are asleep. Call me if you need me. I'm just working out a new verse for this track. I can come back up and help. I'll make you some lunch in an hour. Okay?'

'Okay.'

Charley kissed Aisha on the lips. 'You smell like a brewery.'

'Oh god.'

Charley stood up and said, 'I don't know, I quite like it,' as she walked away.

Aisha kept her eyes closed. The boys had been fed and were

asleep. They could sleep for anything up to an hour, maybe even an hour and a half. Aisha sunk into the fabric of the sofa. They had made a good choice when they picked this sofa; they knew with babies on the way, this sofa was going to get a lot of use for day naps, watching TV and having guests over.

Aisha had never envisioned – as she and Charley had stood in the furniture shop that day, Aisha's belly fit to bursting and the shop assistant looking more uncomfortable every time Aisha sat down – that this sofa would cocoon and comfort her with a raging hangover so soon after giving birth. What was she thinking? She would have to text and apologise to Sophy. And Mel, god, poor Mel, who saw her home in an Uber. She would do it just as soon as she could open her eyes and look at a screen without feeling sick.

Eventually, Aisha dropped into a semi-conscious state where psychedelic colours and images swirled around with no meaning. She could hear snippets of conversations from last night. She could see the inside of the taxi as she bobbed about in the back, accompanied by the sweet sound of Mel's soothing voice. Suddenly, a face cut through the chaos, just a head and shoulders. Their eyes were bright and shining, then they opened their mouth wide, as if to speak or shout, or cry—

Aisha sucked in her breath and half sat up. She looked around the room, disoriented. What day was it? Why was she sleeping on the sofa? Then she heard the cry. It was Jude. He had developed a rhythm to his loud just-woken-up cry that was so distinctive to Aisha she could now clearly tell the difference between the two of them. She wasn't sure Charley had sussed it out yet.

It was the letter. She had been sleeping fitfully ever since she had found it, brought it home from Martina's and read it. The words on the paper played over and over in her mind and there was an aching feeling in her gut every time she thought about what they meant and how she had believed one thing about her life only for it to turn out not to be true at all. She knew she had to confront Martina about it, but how did you confront your own mother about family business that had not been spoken about for over twenty years?

She stood up and waited for a dizzy spell to pass. She looked at her phone; only half an hour had passed since she had closed her eyes. She wished she could crawl into bed and sleep for a week, completely undisturbed.

The boys were in their prams in the hallway. Aisha had managed a short walk with them before the real hangover had kicked in.

She picked Jude up, leaving Otis sleeping, and carried him through to the lounge. She stood at the window, where the wooden shutters were opened just enough for her to peer through. The street was empty. She felt her gut tighten in anticipation, but for what? She wasn't sure. Was it the endless hours rolling into each other? The thought of spending most of the day on her own with two tiny mewling creatures? Was it guilt at getting blind drunk the first time she went out socially without the babies with her new friends? Or was it something else? Aisha strained to look as far as she could along both sides of the road. But she could only see a woman across the street pushing her bin out into the road.

Damn it, thought Aisha, it was bin day. She needed to get the wheelie bin out into the street before the men came. She was sure she could hear the truck in the distance. She slipped on her trainers at the door. Jude was still in her arms. She was noticing the weight of the boys more now; where they were light as feather a few weeks ago, the presence of their little bodies was so much firmer in the crook of her arm.

She opened the door and pulled the everyday bin from the front of the house. She never had any clue which one to take out, and only copied what everyone else in the street did. She wheeled it through the small black iron gate and onto the street.

The lady from across the road was back in her front garden now and looked over at Aisha and waved. Aisha waved back. She went to turn to walk back into the house when she saw the male figure at the end of the road to her left. She stopped and let out a small gasp, her nerves shattered and raw from the alcohol and fitful night's sleep. She looked at the front door; she could be through it in one second and have it closed and locked behind her in another. When she looked back, the man was crossing the road. Aisha stood and watched as he walked closer and closer, and she felt glad she had the safety of the road between them. Eventually, he was close enough that his features were a little more in focus, and Aisha could see it wasn't a man but a woman, wearing a blue beanie hat. This person didn't look like the figure she had seen the few times along the street. The beanie-wearing woman stopped outside the house opposite where the woman who had just waved at Aisha was now tending to some weeds. The two women began to exchange pleasantries. Then they both stopped talking and looked over at Aisha. The woman waved again, this time as if she were inviting her over to join them. Aisha turned and hurried back into the house and closed the door.

Aisha felt a wave of panic flood through her body. *Just breathe*, she told herself. *You're just tired and hungover. There's nothing to worry about.* Why was she obsessing over people in the street? They were just people, going about their day.

'Right, that's it,' Aisha said to Jude. 'We're going out. I don't care where, the park, the supermarket, I just need to get out.'

She thought about Mel. She had been a terrible drunk in

front of her last night. She should apologise. In person. She lived about a thirty-minute walk away. She could manage that if she packed water and snacks for herself. She lay Jude down in his pram, ignored his protests and texted Mel.

* * *

An hour later, Mel opened her front door and helped Aisha wheel the double pram through into the kitchen.

'My god, your house is so huge – I love it!' Aisha gazed around. 'And so tidy!'

'I got a cleaner,' Mel said fast, as though she were confessing a terrible secret.

'I don't blame you! You can't run a house with two kids and a bust ankle.'

'She's a great cleaner. I can really recommend her.'

'I might take you up on that at some point when the boys are running circles around me and trashing the house!' Aisha leant against the kitchen table. 'I wanted to come here to apologise. For last night.' Aisha pulled a small bunch of tulips out of the net basket at the bottom of the one of the prams and handed them to Mel.

'Oh wow, they're gorgeous. I love tulips. Thank you.' Mel began busying herself by putting the flowers into water. 'But you didn't have to do that, and you certainly don't need to apologise. We've all been there. And it's been almost a year since you've been able to have a proper drink. I think you deserved it. Did you enjoy yourself?' Mel said over her shoulder as she placed the vase, now full of purple tulips, on the windowsill that overlooked a huge garden. She turned back around just in time to see Aisha's coy smile.

'I did, actually. I didn't think I would, but as soon as I got a drink inside me, I began to feel so much better.'

'Alcohol will do that to you. And how do you feel today?'

'Awful. I'm really struggling, actually.' Aisha felt an over-whelming urge to spill everything out to Mel, to tell her about the man that she had hinted at previously, and how she felt a wrenching dull ache in her gut most days, and it only ever seemed to subside when she was with Mel and Sophy or last night when she was drunk. How could she explain all this to this woman, with her big perfect house who always seemed so happy and confident?

Mel sat down at the kitchen table and gestured for Aisha to join her.

'Well, that's okay, motherhood is really hard, especially the first year or so, and you have two, don't forget.'

'Oh don't you worry, there's not much chance of me forgetting that there are two of them!' Aisha tried to layer some humour into her tone, but it was no good, and it came out as raw as it felt. Mel gave her a sympathetic smile and Aisha hated herself for feeling so weak.

'And of course, I have a hangover.' She laughed through her pain.

Mel nodded. 'I know. But how are you feeling day to day?' Mel asked and Aisha almost buckled. She couldn't tell her, even though she was sure Mel would be understanding.

'Is this because I got drunk last night and made a fool of myself?' Aisha laughed a hollow laugh. 'Did it look like I was losing it?' she said, trying to keep the lightness in her voice.

Mel looked at her.

'Shall I make us a coffee?'

Aisha looked over at the pram where the boys were still sleeping.

'That would be great, actually.'

And so Aisha and Mel chatted, and Aisha spoke of everything except that each day was like wading through sludge. She told Mel she was tired and emotional, but she neglected the part where when the boys woke and cried, she felt panic rise through her. That whenever they were asleep, she felt a horrible hatred for herself when she closed her eyes to rest because she could be using that time for something more worthwhile like writing her business plan or looking for a small freehold that she would able to convince Charley it would be worth getting an extension on their mortgage or a business loan for. She wished she could just say it as it was, because she was sure it would just rush out of her like a waterfall, but she was worried that Mel would see her as a complete failure and a nutjob. She had already told the girls about the man she thought was out to get her and her babies, and then acting like a drunken teenager on their first night out together, she wouldn't be surprised. Mel was thirteen years older than her; they were a whole generation apart. Aisha had never felt more a part of the snowflake generation, and although she was just three years younger than Sophy, she felt foolish and inexperienced around her as well. They both seemed so much more worldly than her.

When Aisha stopped talking, she went to lift her coffee to her mouth and realised it was cold. She put it straight back down again.

'Wow, sorry. I can wax lyrical sometimes,' she said, although she still felt the bubble of tension sitting fat and redundant in her throat.

'Do you feel better for saying it, though?' Mel asked.

Aisha thought for a moment. There was still so much left unsaid, but she didn't feel armed with the right words to explain. It was just the hangover, she told herself.

'Yes.' Aisha gulped and then smiled weakly at Mel.

She saw Mel look at her uncertainly for a second. 'Well, you know, the more you open up, the easier it becomes. And you have us now, Sophy and me, so don't forget it.'

An hour later, Aisha thanked Mel for the coffee and began the walk back home. There was a light breeze in the air and the sky had clouded over a little since she had left her own house. She didn't have a thick enough jacket on, and she was feeling the cold that little bit harder today. Aisha saw a bus stop and huddled inside the Perspex screen and waited for a bus to come along that would take her almost back to her house.

A woman sat next to her on the tiny slanted seats that weren't quite seats and only allowed you to perch the smallest portion of your bottom on them, and smiled over at Aisha.

'Can I take a look?' she asked, and Aisha smiled and nodded. People were truly fascinated with little babies, and multiple babies always seemed to draw a crowd.

The tall, middle-aged woman stood up and peered into the prams.

'Oh my, what adorable little things! Boys or girls?'

'Both boys.'

'I love how you dress them so jazzy. I would never have had the nerve to be so daring when mine were little. Mind you, there was not the choice then – it was all blue for boys and pink for girls.'

'Do you... do you have twins?' Aisha asked.

'I do. Almost sixteen now. Both boys too.' She stopped looking in the pram as the bus pulled up. She turned to Aisha before she got onto the bus. 'Don't worry, dear, you'll get there. It gets easier.'

Aisha felt her eyes prickle with tears and wished more than anything that she was there already – at the place that people described so often as 'easier'.

* * *

3.15 a.m. – Sophy: I've been watching a programme about the habitats of voles for fifteen minutes. Max won't settle tonight. He's watching it with me. When is it okay to let your baby watch TV with you?

3.16 a.m. – Mel: The rule book went out the window for me when Sky was born. Listen, babes, I thought I had it all sorted until a few weeks ago. Now I have a fifteen-week-old baby who only wants to cuddle me and wakes up constantly through the night. I'm going to be absolutely shattered going back to work next week.

3.17 a.m. – Sophy: Is it next week?

3.17 a.m.– Mel: Yep. A singing gig.

3.18 a.m. – Sophy: Wow! And I still can't believe I haven't heard you sing properly. I'd really like to come along, but I have Max. Maybe in a few months when he's off the boob.

3.19 a.m. – Mel: Yes, I won't be so ropey then either. Give me a few months to get back into my stride.

3.20 a.m. – Sophy: – No Aisha tonight?

3.20 a.m. – Mel: – Looks like she lucked out on the 3 a.m. feed.

3.21 a.m. – Sophy: – Right, I'm turning this off. I now know everything there is to know about voles. I'm going to try and get this one back off to sleep and get some shut-eye myself.

4.56 a.m. – Aisha: I'm here! Anyone?

'How long has it been since I did one of these? First of all, let me apologise. I know I promised regular content, but the truth is, I'm so besotted with my little boy that nothing else seems to matter when I'm with him. But I know you'll all forgive me because you're loyal and faithful followers. I wanted to pop on today and assure you that I haven't forgotten about you and that Max sends his apologies for taking up all my attention.

'I have been talking with a local business who has been developing some delicious health drinks. They've asked me to try all the flavours and help them decide which ones to bring to market. I thought I would share the experience with you guys. Obviously, I'll be doing the drinking, but you can help me decide which flavours work and which you think you'd like to see out there on the shelves.

'So please stay tuned and I'll be back with more info on that soon. In the meantime, I can post a few more photos of Max and I out and about, so comment below if you're happy for some more baby posts!

'Mwwwhhaa!'

Sophy let out a massive sigh and got up and turned the camera off.

The weight of guilt lay heavy on her chest. She hadn't posted a video for a while and she hadn't done a story or a post in days. She knew people still admired her and wanted to follow her, but she needed to keep it consistent. But Sophy felt the familiar pang in her gut when she thought about what it was she did, what she represented. She wondered if it was because she had Max now, but she just couldn't feel the passion. But then, if she was being honest, she had felt that way before Max came along. She always felt a stab of anxiety before she had to post something. She knew she shouldn't feel that way, because surely you were supposed to love the job you did, or at least not feel sick about it. The thing was, she was good at what she did, once she put her mind to it, and she was always happy once a post was done and dusted and the likes came in. Maybe she was in the wrong line of content. But what else was there that she was good at that she could talk about on Instagram?

She had thought about branching out before. Should she talk about babies? Giving birth? But that was all so passé. Her followers had increased since having Max and there was scope for her to focus on baby nutrition once the baby-led weaning stage came in. *Move over, Annabel Karmel*, she had thought when the idea had come to her. She no longer wanted to feel the initial buzz when she had a flurry of likes, only for the flat feeling to return too quickly, and she looked around for ways to bring it back again.

Which was why when Niall appeared that morning after she had finished her recording, she felt something inside of her lift. What was it about this man, a relative stranger in her house? Yet they had shared so many laughs, he had been there for her when she had stumbled in the garden, and the sweet thing he did with the crispy pancakes. She was practically married to Jeff, surely she shouldn't be having these feelings for another man? Surely, it was just the hormones? Surely, she was feeling things about another man because she had just had a baby? Surely?

'My brother said he now follows you on Insta thingy,' he said after they had their usual morning pleasantries – which if Sophy was being completely honest with herself, had begun to feel more and more flirtatious – but of course, it was all on his part. That is what builders are like, aren't they? Very chatty and friendly, a bit winky. It was all harmless jovial fun. Except twice this week and once last week Jeff had gone into work later in the morning, so he had been there when Niall and his lads arrived, and they had gone straight to work. Sophy had felt an awkward feeling in her gut, as though she didn't want to share the same space with both Jeff and Niall. And it was Jeff she would have preferred to have vacated.

On Tuesday, Sophy had hovered in the kitchen, unnecessarily moving things around until Jeff – who was on his laptop at the kitchen island – let out a sharp sigh and spoke. 'Haven't you got mother stuff to do?'

But Jeff had been at work for an hour already this morning and somehow on this particularly warm spring morning, when Max had fallen asleep after his feed and Sophy had managed to get him in his cot next to her bed, Sophy had persuaded Niall to have a coffee with her.

'On the premise that we're talking about flooring, okay? I can't have the boys getting all jealous now.'

Sophy cocked her head to the side. 'Jealous, you say?' She felt her insides flutter at what he was insinuating.

'Of the coffee,' Niall said quickly. 'The nice coffee. That's what I mean. I just bring them the Nescafé stuff. Nowhere near as tasty as this one.'

Sophy looked at Niall, and their eyes locked as he took a sip of his coffee. Milky with two sugars.

'Is that so?'

'Yes. Very tasty.'

Sophy sucked in a long breath and looked down at her phone and felt her cheeks flush red hot. 'I just have to... erm, send this text.'

'Fill your boots,' Niall said. 'So how long have you and Jeffery lived here?'

Sophy coughed out a laugh. 'It's Jeff.'

'But it's short for Jeffery, surely?'

'Yes, but no one calls him that. Ever. Three years, if you must know.'

'Right. I bet his mother calls him Jeffery.'

'Well, she named him. After Jeffery Archer. Her favourite author, apparently, although I've only ever seen one of his books in her house.'

Niall laughed. Sophy suddenly felt uncomfortable talking about Jeff with Niall. Talking about herself and Max felt more natural. It's not that she was trying to deny to herself that Jeff existed as Max's father or her boyfriend, it was just felt a bit unnecessary to bring him up in conversation when he wasn't here and Sophy was. Sophy realised that she had referred to her boyfriend as unnecessary in her mind and let out a small laugh.

'What?' Niall asked.

'Nothing. Sometimes things just pop into my head. You know, like random things.'

'All the time. I have this thing where I suddenly remember something that happened to me years ago, like proper embarrassing stuff, and it will just pop into me head and I'll be like, "Jeez, where did that come from?" It's usually just as I'm about to fall asleep, and then I just lie there, living through the whole mortifying moment again.'

Sophy laughed long and loud. She felt a twinge in her lower abdomen as she did and ignored it.

'No, seriously, it's horrible, and I can't even get away from it. I'm like trapped like a prisoner in me bed, forced to watch me own misdemeanours in me mind's eye over and over.'

Sophy leant on the island for support and crossed her legs as her chest heaved, and she felt the need to pee. The muscles had not fully reformed themselves down there, and Sophy would often find she just couldn't hold it in, especially when she was really laughing. Which, she realised had only happened recently on a few occasions: with Mel and Aisha, and now, with Niall.

Niall carried on his monologue, obviously revelling in the attention and the joy that it was bringing to Sophy. But then Sophy stopped laughing very suddenly as pain so acute hit her abdomen that she had to double over.

Niall clocked the change in Sophy's expression.

'Everything okay? Is it that pain again?' He was up and at the other side of the counter, trying to help Sophy to standing.

'It... really... hurts.' Sophy gasped, the pain akin to labour all over again. Was there another one in there? She had read horror stories of mothers giving birth and then a second baby was discovered, or maybe she'd had an ectopic pregnancy. It was too soon, she hadn't let Jeff near her since Max was born.

'Oh god,' Sophy groaned and before she had a chance to realise what was happening, she had thrown up on the kitchen floor.

'Right. That's it, I'm taking you to A&E – this doesn't look good,' Niall said. 'Where's Max?'

'Upstairs next... to... my bed.' Sophy clung on to the kitchen counter. She heard Niall run upstairs. Before she had a moment to think about what Jeff might say if he could see his builder running up and down the stairs in cement-stained boots, Niall was back at her side with a rosy-cheeked Max in his arms. He was still half asleep, but Sophy knew he would start to cry any minute and she didn't think she had the strength to even hold him, let alone feed him.

'Can you manage the car seat?' Sophy asked.

'I think so. I've done me niece and nephew's a few times. Let's have a look.'

Niall gave a loud whistle using only one finger, and one of his minions popped their head around the corner in the kitchen.

'Gotta take our Sophy here to the hospital – lads, hold the fort.'

The minion nodded, with a slightly startled look in his eye.

Sophy pointed to the car seat on the floor in the kitchen. and Niall lifted it up onto the island counter. After a few moments of placing Max down in it and fiddling and yanking, he was secured in the seat. Sophy let out a breath that she had been holding the entire time. Then Niall took hold of Sophy's arm with one hand, carrying Max in the car seat with the other hand, and they headed out to the car.

* * *

Sophy opened her eyes. She took in the stark lights around her, the muffled voices, the squeaking of rubber on floors and the smell of disinfectant.

Then she heard a familiar Irish accent, and she felt her heart lift. *He stayed*, she thought.

Just a few hours ago, she arrived at A&E, doubled over with pain and vomiting. She had been terrified, but Niall had been there the whole time. She had been taken for an ultrasound and they had discovered something lurking in her cervix. After a painful examination, they removed a decaying piece of cotton that had been left inside her when she had been stitched up after Max was born. Sophy was too tired to think about what had just happened and just felt exhausted. She was on antibiotics and some good strong painkillers.

Niall's head appeared around the cubicle curtain.

'Hey, how are you feeling?'

'Where's Max?' Sophy croaked.

'He's with a nurse. Don't worry, they said they will bring him down soon so you can feed him.'

Sophy nodded.

'That was pretty rough, hey?' Niall said, moving closer to the bed. 'I came to ask if you need me to call anyone before I go?' For a second, all Sophy heard was 'go'. And she realised Niall was leaving. But then Jeff's name crept through.

Jeff. Sophy thought. It had all happened so quickly she hadn't had time to call Jeff. She thought she would have been in and out of A&E.

'Can you call Jeff? I'm not sure I should have my mobile in here.'

'Sure, I'll take it into the hallway.'

Sophy unlocked her phone and handed it to Niall.

'And thank you for bringing me here. I don't know what I would have done otherwise,' she whispered. Niall gave her a small smile and then wandered off into the corridor.

* * *

Back at home the next day, Sophy ignored the persistent texts from friends who lived in the area telling her that if she needed anything to let them know. Because what was she supposed to do with that? Sophy had found since becoming a mother that people spoke a lot of wanting to help, but rarely did they just show up, for fear of stepping over some sort of invisible boundary. When did these invisible boundaries appear? Even just a couple of decades ago when Sophy was growing up, there were no boundaries between friends. People showed up at Sophy's parents' house all the time to help out. 'Geraldine's here to babysit tonight, kids... Sarah is taking you to school today... Sue's son Malcom is here to fix the cooker.' There had been an abundance of people coming and going all through her childhood, and whilst they had been fairly poor financially, there had been the support system they needed so that their parents could raise them. Her siblings all lived too far away now to just pop by and that was understandable. Sophy was the only one who had managed to make it in London and stay living there for as long as she had so far. Obviously a lot of that she owed to Jeff.

So the texts stayed there unanswered. Sophy couldn't even manage to find the strength to send back a quick 'Thanks'. Because what she wanted to say was 'Well, get your arse around here then!' But then she noticed there was a message on her phone from Niall. She hadn't even given him her number? He must have put it in her phone when she had given it to him.

How are you? Delete my number after if you like, I just need to know you are okay.

Sophy thought her heart might explode out of her chest she felt it swell so hard, and with that swelling came an overwhelming feeling of nostalgia, as though she were listening to an old record that her parents used to play when she was a kid. It was that feeling again, the one that felt like home. Sophy could feel the urgency in the tone of Niall's text and could almost hear him speaking the words to her. She realised that in all the time she had been with Jeff, he had never had that effect on her.

After bringing her home from hospital this morning, Jeff had then gone back to work. Although he insisted she call if she needed anything, Sophy knew he wouldn't come running if she did call him. Sophy had half wanted him to stay. But the other half was already finding a way to build a wall between them, or maybe add to the wall that was already there, and as Jeff had left her alone after what she had just been through, she mentally added another brick to that wall. Eventually, she expected it to be so high that either one of them would need a pole vault to get to the other. And Jeff, Sophy concluded, had never been very good at jumping. She could hear Max beginning to get fractious, and she knew she would need to take him out for a walk soon. She could walk fine, she was just a little tender and tired. She would take it easy, a slow stroll to the park and back would be fine.

Sophy felt a wave of sadness engulf her as she rose to stand. She wasn't sure what brought the wave of tears on, but she brushed them away as quickly as they had arrived and carried Max out into the hallway to get him into his pram. There was a loud rapping on the door, and when Sophy had got Max settled, she squeezed past the travel system and pulled open the door. She had never been so happy to see the faces of Mel and Aisha. They both stood there with sympathetic smiles. Aisha was clutching a brown bag to her chest, a small and simple bouquet of flowers poking from the top hinted at some sort of care package, whilst Mel held a Tupperware full of what looked like chilli con carne.

'We know you batted off our concerns last night on the WhatsApp, but we're bloody here anyway!' Mel said, and Sophy burst into happy, relieved tears.

19

MEL

The black shimmery evening gown felt a little tight around the chest where her breasts had not yet settled down after the pregnancy. But apart from that, Mel looked at herself in the mirror and thought it felt good to be back. There was a stirring in her gut that she tried to put down to the anticipation of being back on stage after such a long break, but she knew it wasn't that. It had been eleven months since she had last performed. Sky was only four months old. Her last gig had been when she had just found out she was pregnant with Skylar and she had every intention of continuing to sing and really rocking her pregnancy – in a Melanie Blatt circa early All Saints kinda way – but that all changed. She walked away from that final gig and vowed she would never return. But showbiz has a clever way of calling you back, or rather never really letting you leave. It would always be in her blood; it didn't matter what anyone did to her.

She wasn't on until 9 p.m., but she wanted to get there early for a sound check before the venue filled up. She could then sit out the back and have a drink to calm her nerves before she went on.

'You look lovely,' Daz said as she came downstairs into the lounge. Bess sensed the excitement in Daz's voice and jumped out of her bed and came bounding over to Mel.

'*No, Bess!*' Mel and Daz shouted at the same time as Mel took two steps back, trying to protect the delicate details of her long dress, and the Labrador retreated back to her bed.

'Are you sure you're going to be all right?' Sky was tucked into the crook of Daz's arm. *Midsomer Murders* was playing on the screen.

'Is she all right watching that?' Mel asked.

Daz looked at the screen, then down at Sky. 'She's fine, she loves it!'

'Okay, well, don't keep her up too late – I am trying to get her into some sort of routine.'

Daz laughed. 'Routine? She was up five times last night!'

'Four and a half. One time was just a squeak in her sleep, and I misinterpreted it. I admit I was too hasty in getting her out of her cot that time, but I was on autopilot and I didn't know what was going on.'

'Ah, well, I have a good feeling about tonight. You just have a great gig, darling! Break a leg— Oh wait! You already did that!' Daz laughed long and hard at his own joke.

'Yeah, well, lucky this gown goes down to the floor, and I have a stool to sit on.'

Mel kissed Daz and then leant in to kiss Skylar. As she did, she inhaled her beautiful biscuity skin and freshly washed scalp. She looked so cute sat up and tucked inside the crook of Daz's arm that Mel was quite taken back by the pang of sadness in her gut as she walked out of the front door into the waiting taxi.

* * *

'Darling, you look simply fab-u–lous!' Robbie crooned as she made her way into the bar, trying her hardest to walk as gracefully as she could with the damn boot on.

They air-kissed on both sides – neither of them wanting to bodge their own or each other's make-up.

'Thanks, Rob, but I feel about a hundred and five,' Mel said as she began following him.

'Darling, you can pull off your showbiz age for a few more years yet – thirty-seven, isn't it?'

'Yes, it is.' Mel smiled and wondered exactly how much longer she would be able to get away with that and followed Robbie towards the door of the green room. It was a tatty room at the back of the stage that had never seen a refurb in the fifteen years Mel had been performing here. Rob had had more work done on himself than the entire venue had in all that time, which was why The East End still had a fairly shabby – minus the chic – look about it. Yet, it didn't deter the punters, for once the lights were down and the stage was lit, the room came alive with an energy that, for Mel, any other venue had yet to rival. And that was why she kept coming back to perform and the hundreds of customers came back to watch her and the many other cabaret acts. The East End was her favourite club to perform in. Everyone here felt like family.

'You look amazing, Mel. That dress! Have I seen that one before?' Robbie stopped at the door to the green room.

'Come on, Rob, you know this dress is as old as I am. I'm just glad I was able to squeeze into it.'

'I must say, darling, your rack looks fantastic. Post-pregnancy boobs suit you.'

'Well, it will give the punters something to look at if I cock everything else up tonight.' Mel let Robbie open the door for her, and audibly gasped when she saw what was behind it.

'A little welcome home for you, sweetie.' Robbie stood aside and let Mel walk through into what was now the new green room. The walls that had once been a sickly yellow colour with peeling paint were now gleaming white. The one brown sofa with springs sticking out of it had been replaced with a smart grey two-seater with a dapper black-and-white coffee table in front of it. The mirror that ran the length of the wall behind had been ripped down and replaced with a neat rectangular mirror and on either side two wall-mounted silver stars with bulbs.

'Oh, wow, Robbie, this is amazing.' Mel stood in the doorway.

'Well, we couldn't have our mama bear coming back to a shit tip, could we?'

'It must have cost you a few quid.' Mel looked down at the fresh-looking grey carpet, which had replaced the red sticky pub one.

'Let's just say Uncle Robbie will be getting a little less Botox this year.' Robbie tittered and took Mel by the elbow and escorted her into the room.

Mel slapped his arm. 'Oh honey, you don't need Botox. I haven't been able to tell if you're smiling or frowning for years! I'd say you're literally set for life.'

Robbie let out a guffaw, but as Mel had just pointed out, his cheeks barely moved.

'Now, you go and test that nice new chair – that set me back a few quid – and I'll make you a nice drinky-poos. The usual?'

'Lovely,' Mel said, looking around. Then she turned to Robbie. 'Thanks, Robbie.'

'Anything for you, my shining angel. I'm just glad my Dorothy is finally home. See you in a sec.'

Mel settled herself in front of the mirror and checked over her make-up and then looked around the room. She felt the familiar tingle in her tummy returning. Those pre-show nerves, which weren't really nerves, more of an anticipation for what the night would bring. She looked at herself in the mirror, and for a few precious seconds managed to push all thoughts of Jeff Haddon out of her mind. *Yes, I'm back.*

* * *

Mel sat it in the green room listening to the act that was before her finish their final song. Her tummy tingles had settled with the vodka cranberry and orange that Robbie had brought through earlier. She would wait to have a second one once she had done her set.

Tonight, it was all Adele classic hits. She had done the sound check, warmed up her vocal cords and was just waiting for the sign from Robbie.

'And now, ladies and gentlemen, she's been away for a while, bringing another beautiful life into this world – is there no end to this woman's talents? – please give the warmest of East End welcomes to the gorgeous, the brilliantly talented Melony Fortuna!'

The crowd let rip with finger whistles and foot stamps until Mel picked her way carefully out of the green room, across the hall and up the steps onto the stage.

The spotlight was on her immediately, and Mel went to flinch and duck away from it; it had been such a long time, she had forgotten the strength of it.

The noise of the crowd died down and Mel waited a few more seconds before she settled herself into her stool and arranged the microphone to her level.

'Thank you so much, you wonderful bunch – you are so gorgeous, and I am absolutely thrilled to be back. Let's start with this one shall we…?'

By the time the interval came around, Mel was officially back in her groove.

'Darling, it's as if you've never been away,' Robbie said, and Mel basked in the praise as she had in the applause.

'I have to admit, Rob, it does feel good.' Mel rose from her seat at the bar and turned to go back to the stage but stopped dead in her tracks. She had presumed it had been some freak meeting when she had seen him that first time, that he had never really meant to be there that night, that he had accidentally stumbled into the bar with his drunk work colleagues. Because why would someone so vile frequent a place that was full of such positive energy and joyous rapture? The two just didn't fit together. Yet there he was again, standing at the bar with the same bunch of goofy guys. Of course, he hadn't stopped coming in all that time that Mel had been away, hiding at home from the very thing that gave her life. Mel had allowed him to dictate her life and control it, and now here he was as though nothing had happened. As though the filthy hands he had placed all over her, when she was carrying her beautiful baby inside, had not caused her to run away home and only now finally return.

Mel was certain she would not be able to get through the next set of songs, but she had told herself before she came tonight that if she saw him, she would not run again this time. She had nothing to be ashamed of. So, Mel settled herself back on her stool and during those last few seconds just before the house lights went down, he looked up and right at her, and she knew then he recognised her, that the night at the charity fundraiser had nudged something in his memory, but he had never quite located it. But now, as she sat in her get-up, he knew who she was. But Mel didn't turn or look away. She locked eyes with Jeff Haddon right up until the lights faded to black.

* * *

3.25 a.m. – Aisha: Both boys are up and alert as anything! I'm supposed to be sleeping, but I can hear Charley down there talking to them. Should I go down and tell her to stop it? Aren't babies supposed to start learning the difference between night and day? They can't do that if Charley's rabbiting on to them all night, can they?

3.35 a.m. – Sophy: I say leave her to it. Both parents do things differently. It's just the way it is. Mind you, if that was my Jeff down there waxing lyrical into Max's ear at this time, I'd want his head to make contact with a frying pan. I'd go for an aluminium though, not iron.

3.26 a.m. – Aisha: Well, that's just it, it's really winding me up. I can't sleep thinking she should be at least trying to get them to sleep. They will never get into a routine at this rate. Surely, they will turn into night owls, hardly sleeping at night and falling asleep in the middle of the day at four years old! Oh god, I'm going to have to go downstairs, aren't I?

3.28 a.m. – Mel: Aisha, can I give you some honest advice? Please stay where you are, close your eyes and try to sleep. Your boys won't be ruined, and they will, one day, sleep all the way through the night and you will be dragging them from their beds.

3.30 a.m. – Aisha: Okay.

20

AISHA

Martina was unpacking Tupperware dishes of jerk chicken, goat curry and rice and peas onto the kitchen counter.

'I'll take those other Tupperwares back, if you got them?' Martina scanned Aisha's kitchen.

'Yes.' Aisha bent down and pulled four containers from the cupboard next to the sink, but before she could shut the door, Martina bent down and took a peek.

'Girl, ya cupboards are messy! You ever think about clearing them out?'

'I like to hold on to stuff, Mum – I never know when I might need them.'

'Okay, whatever takes ya fancy.' Martina tutted and pushed the full Tupperware boxes of food into the fridge.

'You never keep stuff, stash it away and forget about it?' Aisha said, daring herself to push it further, to say to her mother, *I know, I know all about it, just from one letter, everything has changed.*

'Oh no, I know where everything is in my house. Thirty-six years I lived in that house, there ain't no nook or cranny that gets left unnoticed by me.'

Perhaps, thought Aisha, *you have forgotten to look under your bed for a while.*

But she decided today was not the day.

Today was to be a happy day. It was early April, the weather was warming up. It was Charley's thirty-eighth birthday, and they were taking a picnic to the park. It was the first time that Mel and Sophy would get to meet her, and Aisha was finding it hard to muster up the excitement she should be feeling that her new friends would soon be meeting her girlfriend for the first time. It had been just over one month since she had met Mel and Sophy outside the community hall, but it felt like a year. Aisha had met Jeff obviously, albeit in a rather messy state, so it would be nice to see him again to apologise for her inebriated state and then she would get to finally meet Daz, Mel's husband. So, in light of what the day was representing, which was a lot of introductions and celebrations, Aisha knew deep down it wasn't a day for confrontations. Martina had made a great effort just by being here and bringing meals for them for the week. She was also going to join them for the picnic. Martina had never spent time with Charley on her birthday in the seven years that Aisha and Charley had been together, so it was even more of a special occasion from Aisha's perspective.

But now Aisha wished that she had prepared something more lavish for her beloved Charley. It had been a long time since they had really let their hair down, and she had put an array of ideas to Charley for ways they could celebrate from a kitchen disco to a big dinner out with friends. But Charley had requested a simple British picnic of sausage rolls, jam tarts and egg-and-cress sandwiches. Aisha said she could just about to stretch to that and somehow whilst the twins had a few hours' sleep in the early part of the evening last night, she had managed to make the sausage rolls and sandwiches, but picked up some sticky buns and jam tarts from the local bakery.

'How we getting this stuff down to the park then?' Martina asked, looking around the kitchen for a suitable receptacle.

'Well, that's where years of camping comes in handy. We have one of those trolley things we took when we went to festivals – it's like one you use at the garden centres to put your plants on, except it has sides,' Aisha said.

Martina looked around the kitchen as though Aisha might have it locked in some special cupboard. 'Sound ideal. Where is it?'

Five minutes later, Martina had managed to drag the camping trolley out of the shed at the bottom of the garden and up the garden path and through the house.

'Careful, Mum, the paint!' Aisha called after her as Martina pulled with vigour and force, not paying any attention to her surroundings.

'There we go. Now you girls can do the stacking. I'll go see to them babies.'

Charley and Aisha piled the trolley high with a picnic rug, plates and napkins, paper cups, cans of ginger beer and sparkling water and all the food.

By the time they had finished Martina was behind them with the babies tucked up in the prams.

* * *

Aisha had just finished laying everything out on the picnic blanket at the park when she saw Mel arriving. Mel parked up the pram and introductions were made all round. Daz shook Aisha's hand, a nice subtle gesture, Aisha thought as she cast her mind back to the kiss she had received from Jeff when she had met him, an act that had occurred at the beginning of the night and one of the few things her memory had held on to. Mel seemed jittery when Aisha hugged her hello. She hurriedly squeezed Aisha and then began looking around. When Aisha asked after Leia, she was still distracted, so it was Daz who answered for her in the end, saying she was well and living her best tweenager life at a park as far away from her parents as was acceptable.

Martina had parked herself in one of the two deckchairs they had managed to squeeze into the trolley, with a large umbrella erected next to her.

'She looks like the queen of Sheba sat there,' Charley quipped to Aisha, who had to nod in agreement.

Everyone sat down and then Aisha saw Sophy trotting towards them, looking hot and harassed. She was on her own, pushing the pram.

When she arrived next to the picnic spot, Aisha was up on her feet and greeting her, followed by Mel. Mel introduced her to Daz and Sophy was her usual overtly charming self.

'No Jeff?' Aisha said, feeling a mixture of dejection and relief. She had been keen to meet Jeff again and to see Sophy and him together as a couple, yet she was still feeling a little awkward about the charity night and was worried Jeff might blurt out how pissed Aisha actually was that night in front of Martina and Charley.

'No, I'm afraid he's had to work at the last minute,' Sophy said in a tone that sounded bright enough and had Aisha not been fully aware of how she herself plastered on a smile when she had been crying, she may not have noticed a redness to Sophy's eyes or how jittery she also seemed.

But Aisha knew Sophy had been crying. Her eyes were normally so sparkly white, and her usually flawless make-up had definitely streaked. But Sophy managed to brush off her less-than-perfect appearance by talking about how hot the weather had turned and how her hay fever had kicked in good and proper.

Sophy had it spot on about the weather, which had brought a sun warm enough for all the babies to lie on the picnic rug in just their romper suits, with the prams used for makeshift extra shade, as Martina sat on unperturbed taking the lion's share with her colossal umbrella.

'This is so nice,' Mel said, she seemed suddenly more relaxed than she had been minutes before Sophy arrived. Aisha knew she had been back to work this week but hadn't really said very much about it to her or Sophy. Which was fair enough, Aisha thought, because it was always so busy with four babies when they were all together. With the partners and Martina here to help, and with Sophy and Charley already in deep conversation as though they had known each other for years, Daz had adopted the role of daddy day care, with four babies wriggling around on the rug.

Aisha sidled up to Mel. 'Hey, how is work? I haven't really had a chance to speak to you much about it.'

'Oh.' Mel's face seemed to drop. 'Yes, it's been fine.'

'Oh no, just fine? I thought you'd be thrilled to be back on the stage!'

Mel smiled. 'Oh I am. Robbie had kitted out the green room – just for my return, it seems – and the crowd are still just as gorgeous as they always were.'

'Oh good,' Aisha said 'I was worried about you, what with your leg and the time you have spent away from "the biz".' Aisha did quotation marks.

Mel laughed. 'It's just like riding a bike – you don't forget.'

'Aisha, baby!' Martina pointed towards the rug behind Aisha where Otis had managed to squirm his way downwards and was almost on the grass. Aisha grabbed the escapee and looked up at her mum who was as vigilant as a lifeguard watching over a bunch of incompetent swimmers.

'Got him!' Aisha called to Martina. 'I'll keep hold of this one, I think.' She laughed and watched as Mel laughed too, but with a sort of sadness in her eyes.

* * *

Aisha brought the chocolate cake out and succeeded on the third attempt to light the candles in the warm spring breeze. She summoned Charley over and they all sang happy birthday, with Mel adding the harmonies. Aisha looked on with delight as Charley revelled in the attention a little and she was glad she had made the effort for her. Charley had been invited out later with some of her uni friends, and so Aisha was making sure her stomach was well and truly lined. Not that Charley was a big drinker, on the contrary, but Aisha wouldn't wish the hangover she had experienced a few weeks ago on anyone, let alone on the woman she loved. And Aisha realised again for the first time in a long time, seeing Charley fresh through the eyes of Mel, Daz and Sophy and even the beady eye of her mother – even though she desperately tried to pretend that the occasion hadn't moved her – that she did truly love Charley so very much. Motherhood had challenged her in so many ways, but it was these occasions when she was able to bring herself away from the four walls and the reverberating incessant cries of the twins that she could see herself as the mother that she really could be. Confident and capable, and not worried about things she couldn't control. But she knew there was one thing she could control: the letter she had taken from under her mum's bed. Aisha knew she should speak to Martina and ask her outright, but why hadn't her mum said something to her about this before? Why had she tried to hide so much from her own daughters? Maybe her sisters already knew. Should Aisha call them and ask them?

* * *

That night, Aisha lay with her body spooned into Charley's, feeling all the tension that had slipped away for a few hours in the park crawl its way back into her body again. Whilst she was thankful that Charley had decided against going out drinking with her buddies all night, Aisha wished she could just enjoy the moment. Even when Charley whispered into her ear that staying in and having an early night had been the best birthday present she could have ever hoped for, Aisha hated herself for not being able to absorb her girlfriend's words the way she used to.

21

SOPHY

Mel and Aisha sat forward in their chairs in the coffee shop. It was Monday morning and the coffee shop was packed with women with infants and small children, catching up with friends after the weekend. Mel and Aisha each had a twin nuzzled in their arm as Skylar sat happily in the car seat attachment clicked into the buggy. Sophy cradled her oat milk latte, looking intermittently into Max's pram and began telling the girls about what had gone on over the last seventy-two hours.

On the Friday night, two days before Charley's birthday picnic, Sophy had laid the table with the better crockery and cooked Jeff's favourite, toad-in-the-hole with Bisto gravy, just the way his mum had always made it for him. It had taken Sophy three attempts to get the batter just right, and the kitchen looked like a scene from an apocalyptic movie. She had also let a few profanities loose and then looked at Max in his little pod on the kitchen island and apologised.

Jeff had said he would be late home, which under normal circumstances would have annoyed Sophy, but it gave her the chance to bathe Max and get him down him to sleep before Jeff came home. She began reheating the toad-in-the-hole about seven, ready to eat at seven thirty, but by eight thirty, the toad-in-the-hole was shrivelled and dry, and there'd been no sign of Jeff. She had called his phone three times and each time it had gone straight to voicemail.

She'd opened the wine and poured herself a glass and sent a text through to Jeff.

Dinner is ruined. Where are you?

Sophy had been about to turn the oven off and go up for a bath when Jeff had walked through the front door.

'Honey, I'm home!' he called. She heard his keys drop on the unit in the hallway and his shoes being kicked off. His laptop landed with a thump on the wooden floor and then he was standing in the doorway to the kitchen, his tie loose and his hair a little messy. He came into the kitchen and bent down and kissed Sophy on the cheek.

'Oh my god, you stink of booze?' Sophy recoiled.

'Just a quick drink with the team to celebrate a successful month. Not bad considering it's only April, hey? The housing market is booming.'

Sophy looked on as Jeff made his way to the fridge and thought how interesting it was that Jeff always seemed to have something to celebrate. She watched as he started making himself a gin and tonic.

'Did you mention something about dinner? I'm starving. I'll wait in the lounge until it's ready. Gimme a shout.'

Sophy stood up and followed Jeff into the lounge. She peered through the blinds and saw his car parked outside.

'You drove home?'

Jeff had already turned the television on and was channel

surfing. 'Eh?' He half turned to Sophy, although keeping his eyes on the TV screen.

'Your car, Jeff? You're drunk and your car is parked outside, that means you drove home.'

'Ah, babes, it's only round the corner.'

'But you could have knocked someone over, killed someone.'

'Have you been watching daytime TV soaps again? Stop catastrophising.'

Sophy took a deep breath. 'Dinner. Is. Ready.'

Jeff had looked up at her. 'Is it? That was quick.'

'It's been ready since seven o'clock.' Sophy had lost all ability to add any expression to her voice.

'Right, okay, better eat it then.' Jeff hauled himself out of the chair, still keeping one eye on the TV as he walked slowly backwards out of the lounge and through into the kitchen.

Sophy followed him, pulled the shrivelled toad-in-the-hole out of the oven and put it in the middle of the table, then she boiled the kettle, pressed three minutes on the microwave to heat the greens in butter. When it was all ready, she brought the gravy and greens to the table. She served Jeff a large portion and watched him tuck in without any complaints. Sophy was thankful the alcohol had numbed his taste buds.

When he had finished and Sophy had eaten one sausage and some greens, she began to speak. 'Jeff, we need to discuss the house.' Sophy continued without waiting for Jeff to respond. 'When I moved in here three years ago, you said you would put my name on the house deeds. It didn't happen, and I didn't expect it to then, but I am earning a decent wage from sponsorships now and, well, we have Max, together. He is our son. If something should happen to you, well then where does that leave me? I'm not very up to scratch with family law, so I really think it would best if you just put me on the deeds now as we discussed.'

Jeff frowned and Sophy felt a sinking feeling in her gut. She knew that look. It was a look that came before Jeff saying something that not only did she not want to hear, but would not make any sense either.

'But I'm the main earner here, I mean my wage pays for everything. It's not as if you have anything to worry about, is it?' Jeff had carried on tucking into his food. 'Great dinner, babes. My favourite. Well done.' He'd pointed to her plate. 'Eat up – you need your strength for the night feeds.'

Sophy took a deep breath. 'I know I don't have anything to worry about now, but things could change. Anything could change.' The image of Jeff a few weeks ago, taking *that* call was always fresh in her mind. The consequences of such a conversation could be bad for her and Max, if indeed it had meant anything at all. But she knew it did. She had that deep, primal feeling that was telling her things weren't as they once were, that Jeff was slipping away. She had to do something for Max's sake.

'Besides, it's time to move forward.' Sophy saw Jeff's face morph into a frown. 'We have Max now and—'

'Yeah, where is he by the way?' Jeff looked around the kitchen.

Sophy let out a hard sigh. 'He's in the lounge, you passed him on your way in?'

'Did I?' Jeff scoffed.

'So, I was saying, that as we are moving on, as a family, we should maybe start acting like one?'

Jeff had let out a loud laugh.

'Act like one? What does that mean?'

Sophy became exasperated. 'I mean, I just mean, we have a kid, I live here, why can't we make it official? Put my name on the house'

'All right, calm down, Soph,' Jeff said. 'You don't need to whine about it like that.'

'But, Jeff, you're infuriating!'

'You're infuriating yourself.'

Sophy took a deep breath and tried to replay in her head where exactly she had gone wrong and allowed Jeff to steer the conversation in this direction. Again. She waited a few minutes until she could see that Jeff had almost finished his food before continuing.

'I am simply asking that we make the commitment to being a family.'

'My name's on his birth certificate, isn't it?'

Sophy had paused. Her mind played a trick on her and for a nanosecond she wondered, was it?

'Yes. Yes, it is.'

'So, what are you talking about then? Marriage and stuff?' Jeff had asked her.

'Marriage and stuff?'

'Yeah, like you never talk about marriage.' Jeff finished his food and put his knife and fork in a straight line in the middle of the plate.

Sophy had thought for a second. He was right. She had obviously thought about marriage, but it was never something she had pushed Jeff on. Perhaps, she thought it was because she didn't want to be married to Jeff. But she needed some security, and it was only fair as she was earning as well that they were both legally on the deeds to the house. Jeff might earn more but Sophy did pay her way too.

'Well, you don't talk about marriage either,' she'd said after a few seconds.

'Well, blokes don't, do they?'

'Er, they do. Would you not like me to become Mrs Haddon some day?'

'I hadn't really thought about it that much, to be honest. I thought we were happy as we were.'

Sophy thought again about her lack of desire to be married to Jeff. 'Well, we are, except for the tiny matter that I live in a house that belongs to you and I'm your son's mother.' Sophy heard the words *son's mother* and how detached they sounded. Shouldn't she be saying *fiancée* or *lover* or *long-term girlfriend*? Something that meant more to her and Jeff rather than basic DNA.

'You want the name on a bit of paper? I get it, if it makes you feel better. But it had better not be so you can try and screw me for every penny I have. I built that business up over years and years of hard slog. It didn't come easy to me – I flunked at school, I was rubbish at maths and English. Only thing I have ever known is how to flog a house.'

Sophy's face softened for a moment and she tried to cast her mind back to the days when she and Jeff had first met and how she had been so impressed with his business, how proud she had felt of him.

'I get that, Jeff, I really do. But I work too, and I contribute to bills and food. See that sausage?' Sophy pointed to the last portion of toad-in-the-hole in the pan that was crispy and burnt at the edges. 'I paid for that sausage and you ate that sausage.'

'Are you comparing a six-hundred-thousand-pound house to a sausage?' Jeff asked her with real sincerity.

Sophy could have cracked a smile, but she was tired, and this conversation had gone on much longer than she had wanted it to.

She took one final deep breath and began very slowly and clearly so that Jeff could understand. 'I. Just. Want. To—'

Jeff cut her off and shook his head. 'Fine, stop getting your knickers in a twist. I'll sort it, all right?'

Sophy sat back. 'You'll sort it?'

'I said so, didn't I?'

'Okay,' she said softly.

'Okay. Can I go and watch the snooker now?'

'Yes,' she said quietly again and watched as Jeff stood up and walked away. Then she waited for the excitement to rise through her, the feeling of pure euphoria that should come when a couple make a big step forward in their relationship. She would want to be calling her mum and letting some of her friends know, surely? Because this was, after all, a big deal – her name on the house deeds. But when nothing came, she simply stood up and started scraping the remnants of the charred dinner into the bin.

When Sophy had woken the next morning at 5.45 a.m., there had been a text on her phone from Jeff. She hadn't even noticed that he hadn't come to bed, as she'd gone to bed at midnight and Max had slept through. At the time, Sophy could hardly believe it and wished Jeff had been there to celebrate with her. But when she picked up her phone to message the 3 a.m. Shattered Mums' Club, she saw the words from Jeff.

Gone to a hotel for a few days, got a few things to think over.

'He said he'll be staying at a hotel for the next few days to "clear his head".' Sophy made her fingers into quotation marks.

'But what brought it on?' Aisha asked as Mel sat tightly in her chair.

'I asked him on Friday to put my name on the house. It's only fair, right? I have lived there for years, I'm the mother of his child, I buy food and pay bills, why can't I legally own half that house?'

'Absolutely! Right, Mel?' Aisha asked, and Mel nodded firmly.

'And surely it's just a phone call or two to get your name added?' Aisha looked at Mel for reassurance.

'Well, yeah, I'm no expert, but I wouldn't have thought it was rocket science,' Mel said.

'Exactly!' Sophy threw one hand up in the air. Then she peered in at Max sleeping in his pram. 'Anyway,' she said more quietly, 'after our chat where he said he would sort it and then his cryptic message about needing things to think about, I finally get out of him that it isn't that simple, apparently! And that I should hold off badgering him – he has a lot on his plate and nothing I would ever be able to understand, apparently. Are you okay, Mel?'

Mel had let out a funny noise and leant back in her chair.

'Yes, fine,' she said as though she were in pain. 'Just a back twinge.'

'Oh, try holding two of them, my back is in bits,' Aisha said.

'Anyway,' Sophy said, bringing the attention back to her. It was cathartic to get it all out. She had found she couldn't open up like this to her other girlfriends who had known her and Jeff for years. In a way, it was better this way, discussing this matter with someone who didn't know them as well. She knew her other friends would give her advice that perhaps she wasn't sure she wanted to receive. 'He left that night and hasn't been back... since.' Sophy lost control of her voice on the final word. 'I just need to keep busy, I think.' She put her cup down and felt a wave of positivity came over her. 'Maybe he just needs time to calm down. I mean, he's obviously overthought the whole thing. And I understand it from his perspective, I really do – he built that business up from scratch and if we split up, then he might lose out—'

A noise came from Mel again, and both women looked at her. Mel was reclining back in her chair with Otis in her arms.

'Is there something you want to say, Mel?' Sophy said, a sharp tone in her voice that she had never used with either of her new friends before.

'Oh, well, all I would say is that, well, is that you only need to ask yourself one question, really.'

'Oh, okay, what is that then?' Sophy said a little more softly, hoping that this one question would also reveal the answer to this big mess.

'Do you love him?' Mel said frankly.

Aisha sucked her breath in and Sophy's face contorted.

Sophy felt her face turn red and her heart began to race. She was astounded that Mel would ask such a thing. She hadn't just spent the last four years with the same man, had his baby, want to share a house legally with him if she didn't... Sophy was floored. No one had ever asked her that question before. In fact, it had been some time since she had even considered it, or even heard Jeff say it to her or vice versa.

She thought back over the past few days. She had done a lot of crying, but with Mel's questions lingering in the air between her and her two new friends, she began to analyse it all. She felt emotional, of course, but maybe it wasn't *him* she missed. In fact, she had found solace in many small things since his absence like the tidiness of the house, and not waiting for him to come home at night only to practically ignore her and Max and then put the TV on and then fall asleep in front of it. She had quickly settled into a routine of seeing to her and Max, and she noticed she did indeed feel different. By Sunday, she had felt a sense of calm spread through the house.

Maybe, she thought with the joy of hindsight, she was actually sad about the idea of her and Jeff splitting up. Of becoming a single parent, raising Max practically alone – although she did that anyway – and just being at home without *anyone* coming home to her, as opposed to Jeff in particular. There would be no sound of someone coming through the door at the end of the day, dropping keys on the side with a takeaway in hand. She was also sad – no terrified – of the status of a single mum and that her son would visit his father every other weekend without her, and, of course, that Wendy would soon be getting her claws into Max without Sophy's supervision.

But maybe, on the other hand, with his presence no longer in the house, she was holding on to the hope that the Jeff who would come back for the inevitable conversation, would be a new man, one with a different outlook on life. He would apologise for his behaviour, for not doing the right thing when it came to the house they lived in together, he would tell her that he couldn't live without her and Max, and how he had missed them both and that life without them was unbearable. That was what she secretly prayed would happen, but the small niggling feeling in her gut was telling her otherwise. And also, the look on Mel's face. But still, she had to remain optimistic. She realised she couldn't answer Mel's question right now.

'He's not good enough for me, is that what you think? I know you only met him once –whilst he was doing charitable work, giving you free champagne!' Sophy could hear what she was saying, and she knew it sounded ridiculous. And she knew she hadn't answered Mel's question.

Mel looked at Sophy. 'Well, I guess when you put it like that, it does sound as though I don't know what I'm talking about. I'm just going off the few things you've said about him, and well, I watched you both at the elephant event, and you seemed a bit... cold with one another.'

'Cold!' Sophy said and felt tears prickle in her eyes. The last thing she had ever wanted to be with a partner, the father of her child, was cold. Was that really what Mel saw?

'Well, you know. You must have seen it, Aisha?' Mel looked to Aisha with pleading eyes.

'Oh, I wasn't in a fit state to see much that night, let alone analyse people's relationships.' Aisha seemed to physically shrink into her chair.

'I wasn't analysing. It was obvious,' Mel said.

Sophy sat tight-lipped for a moment.

Aisha took a deep breath. 'Well, I thought he was very nice, from what I can remember, and to do that every year for elephants, he must have a very big heart,' Aisha said, her eyes pleading with Sophy.

Sophy gave a weak smile and a small, tiny nod and then glanced quickly at Mel who held her gaze. How could she think all that about Jeff from meeting him once and for Aisha to have to have the exact opposite opinion? What was Sophy supposed to think? Oh, it was all so confusing. All she wanted was to be a happy family, of course, with Jeff. He was Max's father, but she just wished... well, maybe things would be different, maybe this was what Jeff needed to see the error of his ways. And wasn't it easy for Mel to think badly of others when she had perfect Daz, who had been an absolute hero on the picnic and held all the babies in turn whilst the women talked.

God no, what was she thinking? Why was she having these thoughts about Mel, who she had liked very much from the day she had met her and still liked very much? The thing that was getting Sophy down was that she didn't want to fail. Being a failure was not on the agenda. And splitting up with Jeff meant that she would have well and truly failed.

She had thought that she had met a man who loved her, who she would stay with for life. Sure, things had been a bit tricky recently between them, with Max needing all of her attention and Jeff off sulking in the corner, but she could understand to a point how he might feel being left out. And yes, she was soooo tired all the time, like unbelievably tired; as though she were swimming underwater sometimes, everything felt muddy and unfocused. And the fact that she had these feelings towards Niall that would come in swells and stay with her for most of the day after he had left was just her hormones. Once she had stopped breastfeeding Max, she could give so much more of herself to Jeff.

Maybe she would try Max with a bottle tonight, and she would ask Jeff to come home. They would talk and make a plan. She would tell him there was no hurry to get her name on the house. Maybe Jeff could sell the house once the extension was done, and they could move somewhere closer to the countryside where Max could run around. Sophy had always wanted to live somewhere more rural. If Jeff could show an interest in elephants, then he might succumb to the idea of easier country living. They could get hens!

Sophy exhaled a long breath.

'And to answer your question, Mel. Yes, I do love Jeff. Very much. I'm just a bit tired. I think Jeff is too. Having a new baby really turns your world upside down, doesn't it?'

Aisha smiled. 'Yes, it does. But you're doing a wonderful job, don't beat yourself up about it. Jeff just needs a little bit more time to adjust to everything that's all.' Aisha lay a comforting hand on Sophy's leg.

'I know, I know our lives have been turned upside down since Max's arrival, and the extension is happening and he's so busy with work, and then I throw in "put my name on the house" into the mix.' Sophy did a strange high-pitched impression of a woman who she clearly did not think was her, and she managed to catch Mel's eye again who gave her a weak smile that did nothing to back up Sophy's own hopeless theory.

Mel then shifted in her seat, lifting Otis with her as she did, then let out a loud 'Ewwwww!' The other two women both spotted the disaster immediately. Otis had leaked bright orange poo straight through his romper and onto Mel's white jeans.

'I wore white jeans! For the love of god, what was I thinking wearing white jeans around four infants.' Mel was holding Otis aloft like a prize. Aisha stood up, still holding Jude. She moved in front of Mel, and there were a few seconds of a failed attempt at a twin swap before Sophy stood up and took the clean twin, allowing Aisha access to the train wreck.

Sophy and Mel locked eyes for a second and whilst Sophy was sure there had been tension between the two of them before, whatever it was that was bugging Mel about Jeff was suddenly forgotten as she began to howl with laughter, which set Sophy off straight away. Aisha was trying to navigate the heavy nappy bag, swinging it onto her shoulder whilst keeping Otis off her clean clothes by holding him under her arm, bum facing up. She turned around and looked at the other two women. Sophy was practically convulsing, crossing her legs because the pelvic muscles still needed some work, and Mel was sitting with her hands held out, her eyes liquid with laughter, whilst the orange mass spread itself around the white cotton of her jeans. Aisha cracked a smile and then clearly found the scene too infectious and began to laugh as well.

* * *

Later on that afternoon, back at home, Sophy had written out the message she was going to send to Jeff. She'd edited it to perfection so there were no negative words; she was focusing on the positives and wanted to make sure she wasn't backing him into a corner. Then she hit send.

She sat back and waited for the response, checking her phone every thirty seconds to see if the two ticks had turned blue.

Max was laid out on his play mat in the lounge. Sophy had some classical music on softly on in the background.

'Just off then!' came Niall's voice from the doorway.

Sophy looked over and smiled, but she just couldn't get it to reach very far. Which was unusual, as Niall would always leave her with a beaming face.

'Long day?' he asked, not daring to tread into the lounge with his dusty boots and overalls.

'Every day is a long day with a little one.'

'I bet it is, I bet it is. You look like you could do with cheering up?'

'Do I?' Sophy tried to smile.

'You should come to The Tipperary tonight. Monday night's a proper Irish night. Folk singing, dancing. Loads of children – you could bring little Max. Maybe see if your husband wants to take you out. I always find a good ol' Irish knees-up brings me right back to me ol' self.'

'That's because you're Irish.' Sophy laughed. 'And he's not my husband,' she said more solemnly.

'Oh, right you are. Sorry, didn't mean to pry.'

'Oh, you weren't. I guess you just presumed like everyone else.'

'I did. And for that, I apologise. You're obviously a very modern girl, you seem to have everything under control.'

Sophy let out a small squeak as the tears threatened to come. She had nothing under control. She was tired, she was the weakest she had ever been physically and mentally. Her boyfriend had left her. She craved a family life where she and Jeff did things together at the weekend, and where there wasn't this constant thing between them, pushing them further apart.

'The pub sounds good. Maybe another time?'

'Right you are. Have a good evening then, we'll see you in the morning then.'

'Yes, thanks, Niall. Bye.'

'Bye now.'

Sophy heaved out a sigh. She lay her back on the sofa and for a moment imagined herself in the pub with Niall. The music was playing, she'd had a few drinks and was feeling free and easy. Then Niall took her hand and asked her to dance, she leapt up and he took her to the dance floor. The music was wild and Sophy felt Niall's arm around her waist, spinning her and pulling her back to him. As the track stopped, he didn't escort her back to her seat, but to a quiet corner of the pub where he took her face in his hands and brought his lips closer to hers. Sophy felt her heart racing and then a loud ping on her phone made her sit up with a start and open her eyes. It took her a moment to readjust to her surroundings. She leant down and picked up her phone from the floor.

There was Jeff's reply. Her heart, which was already beating rapidly from her semi-conscious daydream, began beating wildly as though it might burst right out of her chest. How could four simple words do that to her?

We need to talk.

* * *

3.26 a.m. – Aisha: Morning! Anyone out there? I have been up for half an hour with just Otis. Managed to get Jude back to sleep. I keep thinking if I had just one, I could be back to sleep by now as well. Is that really awful of me to think that? How funny was the poo explosion today? I've never seen one that colour before, I think he saved it just for you, Mel. Can you rescue the trousers? I feel I ought to buy you new pair.
Anyway, text if you're awake.
3.45 a.m. – Aisha: I didn't mean what I said about only wanting one baby. I'm just really tired. Otis is back asleep now, so I'm off to bed for few hours. Wish me luck!

5.35 a.m. – Sophy: We would never judge you. Sometimes, I imagine my life how it was when I didn't have Max and I miss it so much. Things were a lot simpler, that's for sure. But I love him so dearly, I just know I have to find a way through this time. And I wish it was easier than it is. I mean, no one warns you, do they, that it will be this bloody hard? I honestly thought that babies just slept, and when they weren't asleep, they'd be happy lying in their crib, or in my arms and that they would only cry when they were hungry. I mean, crying when they are tired? What's that all about? I'm so glad I have you two to talk to though.

5.36 a.m. – Aisha: So glad you're awake, I feel like I haven't even been back to sleep! Think I've had half an hour, maybe. It's all the other in-between cries as well. Crying cos they might be in pain, or frustrated, or hot, or cold. I mean, I feel as though I have to be psychic.

5.38 a.m. – Sophy: I know. It's such a frustrating time, for them and us. When can we start teaching them sign language so they can communicate better?

5.40 a.m. – Mel: Morning, campers! It is a hard time and all I can say is that everything is a phase and will pass eventually. And we just have to trust our instincts. We are all doing a great job, even though we may not feel as though we are sometimes.

5.41 a.m. – Aisha: Most of the time!

22

MEL

She had been over and over it in her head all day and night. Then after she had left Sophy and Aisha at the café, she had run it through in her mind a hundred times or so. What should she do? How should she approach this? She needed to speak the truth, surely. Let Sophy know that her boyfriend, the father of her child was a sexual predator? That he almost brought Mel, who had always been such a strong and together woman, to her knees.

She had tried so hard to forget that evening and had hoped that by going back to The East End she could carry on as though nothing had happened. But then he came back, and it was as though the whole night was happening all over again. And although it was not something she wished to remember, she had never forgotten it. It was hard enough reliving the memories, but now Jeff was a part of her life – albeit through Sophy – she was really beginning to stress herself out. She needed to do something, she needed to tell Sophy what had happened that night.

* * *

The night it happened, Mel had been part of a dancing and singing act. They were the 'Lady Marmalade' foursome. Mel had taken what the singer P!nk had worn for the video of the song and tried to replicate it exactly. She had done a good job with the fishnet stockings, knee-high boots, pink wig and top hat. She and Daz had just done the test, and she was a few weeks pregnant. They were excited but nervous for a new baby. Mel had decided she would keep working, and stick to the singing sides of things – the burlesque dancing would not work with a belly! But she felt confident that even with the morning sickness that she knew was imminent, she would be able to perform a few nights a week up until the baby was born. The adrenaline would override any other feelings, like sickness, she was sure of it. So, there she was, with her three showbiz friends, all scantily clad. Mel was dressed in what could only be described as underwear. Black pants, black bra, fishnets and suspenders. They show had gone well; the girls had been rehearsing for weeks. Mel was gutted when she had told the girls she could not continue with the show until after her pregnancy, but they vowed to keep her place open and continue as a three piece until she was ready to come back.

When the show finished and the crowd had gone batty, the girls came down from the stage and instead of going straight back to the green room, they mingled with the crowd. Robbie was ecstatic – the bar had never taken so much money that night. There were gays and straights, transgender people, businessmen, hen nights. Every type of person was in the club that evening. Mel had felt his eyes on her before she had seen him. And when she did turn around, she could see why she had felt it so hard. With eyes like that, a blue that had practically pierced her body, they were impossible to ignore. Their eyes connected, and usually Mel would turn away immediately, as she didn't want to encourage unnecessary attention. But before she knew what had happened, she felt herself smile at him. Mel had had plenty of opportunities to cheat on Daz in her time. She worked late nights, was surrounded by men of all ages and backgrounds – she could have had her pick if she wanted to. But she never did. Not once. The urge was never there. Ever. Yet there was something about this guy that made her wonder how easy it would be, should she want to. Not that she had any intention of cheating on Daz. But Mel was a realist, there are billions of people on the planet, and Mel had never thought for one second that Daz was the only man out there for her. But she had made her choice, and she was going to stick with him for life. She loved him so very much. But for just a few seconds that night, she felt she had betrayed her body and mind and heart with that one smile. As she turned away, after he had reciprocated her smile with a sultry look, suddenly there was a seed of an idea that she would never have let ripen to fruition, but still, she had allowed it to cross her mind. What if?

But as quickly as the thought entered her mind, it was gone. She had witnessed far too many of her friends and friends of friends ruin their relationships with one-night stands, or a secret relationship on the side to spice up their life. Mel may have looked like the type of woman who was up for anything – oh yes, she knew what people thought when they saw her, especially dressed the way she was that night – but there was a difference between thinking about the possibility and actually acting on anything. Mel felt surprise and intrigue that someone after all these years had actually managed to catch her eye.

And that evening, Mel was dressed like nothing more than a tart. And she knew it. But it was theatre – the gays loved it, the straights loved it, the hens loved it. It was fun; it was entertainment.

She had asked her friend Jazz to get her a drink and she'd meet her back at the bar. 'Just a cranberry juice.' Jazz nodded and

Mel headed past the green room and through a small fire escape door that was kept open when the club was as packed as it was that night. She had no idea that she had been followed, and when she heard his voice, she turned quickly and with astonishment.

'That set was unbelievable. Not in all my life have I ever seen anyone perform like you did. You are seriously hot.' He leant into the doorway as Mel stood on the other side. Mel had to admit, it felt nice to be adored. It was, after all, part of the reason she was in the entertainment industry; there was nothing quite like the adoration of a riled-up crowd craving more. Mel turned and leant casually against the other side of the door frame, their heads almost touching. It was rare for Mel to meet men who were the same size as her; at almost six foot, she often left men feeling threatened. Luckily, Daz was two inches taller than Mel, at exactly six foot one.

And there were those Mediterranean sea-blue eyes again. *There are worse jobs to do*, Mel thought to herself.

'I say, you're a very naughty boy sneaking back here. Have you seen the size of our bouncer?'

'I'd say it was worth it, wouldn't you?' He shifted forward one inch. She could smell something clean on his skin, like a soap, then a tinge of a something, citrus, perhaps, with a musky undertone. As he spoke, she could smell the alcohol on his breath.

'Well, you will probably be getting into a lot of trouble.'

'Sounds interesting. Tell me more.' His face moved an inch closer to hers.

Mel laughed and moved her head away from the door frame.

'I would love to, but my friend is waiting for me at the bar.'

'Ahh, that old chestnut. Would your friend not mind if you were missing for say, I don't know, a few minutes?'

Mel laughed again. 'A few minutes? Well, you know how to treat a girl well.'

Mel went to walk through the doorway, but he put his foot in the way and his hand against the other side of the frame.

Mel stopped and sighed. 'I see, it's like that, is it?'

'I could give you hours, sweetheart, but there's something, I dunno, pretty sexy about something happening right now, out here. Wouldn't you say? And let's be honest, with someone as hot as you, I'm not sure I could manage much longer the first time.'

Mel was done. She had enjoyed the sensation she got when she smiled at him at the bar, she found it entertaining that he had followed her backstage, but she was starting to feel chilly, and a real thirst had set in.

'I'm sorry, I didn't get your name?' Mel said as she tried to look past him into the hallway. Why was it empty? Where was Danny? He was usually manning the entrance to the backstage to prevent situations just like the one Mel was finding herself in.

'I didn't give it to you.' He smiled.

'Okay, I'm going to need you to move now.'

Then his expression changed, a sort of darkness spread across his face. His eyes narrowed, and he stood up straight, slightly towering over her. Mel's stomach dropped.

'I'm sorry. You don't get to parade around like that, getting our cocks twitching for nothing. Oh no, I don't think so, darlin'.'

Mel half laughed and went to step forward again. 'No, sorry, mate, move—'

He cut her off as he grabbed her arm and shoved her back so hard that she took several hurried steps backwards and the back of her head hit the wall of the alleyway outside. For a moment, Mel was stunned, but then as she came to, she could see he was outside too, closing the fire exit behind him and stepping towards her.

23

AISHA

The boys were crying. They had been crying all night and all day. As soon as she settled one, the other would become unsettled. Charley had popped her head around the door frame – not fully daring to enter the room should she then be pulled into the war zone that Aisha found herself helpless in and therefore would be obliged to assist – but said mostly unhelpful things like: 'Maybe they can sense you're stressed?' or 'Have you tried walking them around in the pram?'

Aisha had thrown a screwed-up wet nappy at her, which missed Charley, hit the door frame and exploded, sending tiny little bits of the absorption pad everywhere.

'When I need your expert advice, I'll email you!' Aisha shouted as she listened to Charley racing back down to the basement, where she could listen to her own noise at her own leisure.

'Oh, bloody hell,' Aisha said, looking at the exploded nappy on the floor.

There was nothing else for it. As much as Aisha wanted to walk upstairs and fall into bed, she would have to get the boys dressed – they were still in just their vests – and take them to the park. The fresh air might do her some good as well. She had been hoping for a nice quiet morning of them rolling around on their play mat whilst she watched *This Morning*. But that was not to be.

She packed and dressed the boys, checked the nappy bag and tucked them into their prams.

Once she was outside, she did feel the benefit of the fresh air and the boys' cries stopped the minute the cool breeze hit their cheeks. It was the one and only thing that worked to get them to relax when they were feeling fractious. It was just that sometimes, just sometimes, she wanted to put a wash on and then sit on the sofa and watch TV without the babies becoming stressed. Charley was right, of course; her own anxiety was fuelling the babies'. She knew she would feel much better after the walk.

Aisha hadn't been thinking much about the figure in the street because her mind was now consumed with the conversation she needed to have with her mum about the letter she'd found under the bed. It all felt like such a cliché, and to have the secret lurking under the bed like that, she realised the truth had been so close to her for so many years.

Since Charley's birthday, things had smoothed out between them. Charley had become a little more attentive and had been offering to do a few extra things to help out during the day, but Aisha still felt the anger bubble inside her when she heard the sound of Charley walking down into the basement. It was her place of escape, and Aisha was jealous that Charley had that and she didn't, especially as she felt she needed it more than her.

It was a warm but cloudy day, so Aisha had thrown on a thin spring jacket she hadn't worn since last year. As she walked and pushed, she slipped one hand into her pocket, which brushed against a pair of earphones. Aisha had subscribed to Audible before the babies were born, thinking she would sit up in bed listening to books as she fed the boys. She stopped the buggy and selected a book – a Women's Prize for Fiction winner. It had been recommended to her over and over by friends she used to work with, waiting staff who were only at the restaurant for the good tips to get them through university. They weren't there because they loved the hospitality industry the way Aisha did. To them it had just been a job but she had maintained a few friendships as well as some good book recommendations. She plugged the earphones into her phone and pressed play. She kept the volume down low, and her eyes were constantly flicking between the boys and the road ahead. They finally began to look as though they were slipping off into a sleep. Aisha prayed it would be a long one after the amount of time they had been awake last night.

As the book began, Aisha found she relaxed into her stride, each step becoming seamless until she was no longer thinking about walking, but simply gliding instead. Her shoulders dropped, and her mind began to wander off to the places she was hearing described in the book. So, when, after a few minutes, she needed to cross over the road, she stopped the pram and looked to her right. Her heart jumped right up into her mouth as she saw the man standing a few feet away from her. She had thought she had imagined him, made him up, but there he was, standing and looking right at her. It was the closest she had ever been to him. He had a green lightweight parka-style jacket, zipped right up so the bottom of his face was obscured. A slight grey stubble escaped above the top of the coat collar. He then pulled the zip down so that his whole mouth was exposed, and then his mouth was moving. He was speaking now, actually trying to say something to her, but all Aisha could hear was the narrator's voice through her headphones. She put her hand to the wire where there was a volume control and pressed the button, but the narrator's voice became louder; she was pressing the volume up. She grasped at the wire again, but could no longer find the control pads. There was a gap in the traffic, and so Aisha dropped the prams off the kerb and made to cross the road, but she had misjudged it and with a blaring voice in her ear, she only just turned in time to see a car careening around the corner, and she stepped back and tried to get the buggy back onto the path but she couldn't pull it backwards – it had begun to tilt at an angle. Now the narration had become heated, and there was shouting in her ears. Suddenly, she felt the weight of the prams becoming lighter and she turned to see the man with his hands on the handle, lifting it, trying to pull it away from her. She should yell for help, she should push him away, but her hands were gripped firmly on the bar, fearing if she let go, he would gain full control. Her mind rushed with all the thoughts she had been having recently, thoughts that she had begun to align with new motherhood tiredness and that were totally irrational. Now, it turns out, they were not. She should have listened to her intuition. And she should have mentioned something to Charley. There could have been an injunction out by now. Why hadn't she gone with her gut instinct and reported it as stalking, which she now knew very clearly it was?

In the few seconds it had taken Aisha to process these thoughts, she realised the prams were back up on the path and the man had released his grip. The narrator talked loudly in her ear as the man in front of her continued moving his mouth. All she could hear was the muffled sound of his voice. She yanked at one side of the wire and then other and both earpieces popped out. The man was smiling inanely at her.

'That was a close one,' the man said with a strong Midlands accent.

'I don't know, I wasn't sure what happened.' Aisha looked around her to see if anyone was close by so that she might be able to shout out to help her. If she just stayed calm and kept talking to him, nothing bad would happen.

'I saved yours and your babies' life.'

'Well, I suppose I should say thanks then,' Aisha said, her voice trembling.

'You don't need to thank me, Aisha.'

Aisha's gut dropped and her mouth went dry.

He knew her name.

He knew where she lived, he knew her name.

He was here to do something very bad and there was no way she could wrestle two babies out of his hands. She would have to choose between one of the twins. This was her version of *Sophie's Choice*. How could this be happening to her?

'Don't you recognise me, kid?' the man said, and Aisha shifted uncomfortably. *He thinks I know him.* Aisha shook her head and looked briefly around again for anyone who might be able to step in and help.

The man reached out and placed one hand on the side of her arm.

'It's me, kid. Ya dad.'

* * *

The sun had come out and Aisha had removed her jacket, so she was just sat in her hoody. The man, who had just proclaimed to be her father, was sat next to her, a metre between them. The initial terror had subsided, and she was now dealing with a whole host of new emotions. Confusion, frustration, sadness with a tiny side order of joy.

'So, you've been following me all this time?' Aisha asked.

'Hey, ain't been following ya, kid, just trying to find the confidence to come a-knocking.'

Aisha shook her head in disbelief. 'I find it really weird that you would just show up like this. What am I supposed to call you then? Dad? Jon?'

'Jon's fine. I've hardly been a dad to you these last twenty years, have I?'

Aisha turned to look at Jon. 'I didn't recognise you. Why didn't I recognise you?'

'That's cos I ain't had your mother feeding me up for the last two decades. Had to fend for meself like. I was always slim compared to ya mum like, but now I can't keep any weight on me. It was all that fried food. But no matter where I went to try to find food like that, I just couldn't. So I've trimmed down. A lot.'

Aisha nodded. Looking at Jon, trying to see the man she knew as a father when she was just ten years old, there was a glimmer. The years hadn't been kind to his face, which was a sea of lines and wrinkles. 'And so you haven't met anyone else in all that time?'

Jon shook his head. 'Na. Met a few women on me travels but no one would have me.' He let out a low, gravelly laugh.

'I read one of your letters,' Aisha said.

'Oh ay.' Jon looked at her intrigued.

'I saw there were more under Mum's bed. Letters you'd written to her. I grabbed one when I was over at the house the other day. It said stuff about your depression. I had no idea. I wish I had known.'

'Oh, so your mum kept them from you, did she? Can't blame her really. How could you have known? You were a kid! Kids aren't supposed to deal with all that stuff. Not at your age. I know not even Carmel and Laila knew much about it. Then, of course, Ruben and Marcel came along. Your mother had her hands full.'

'I remember the day though as though it were yesterday. Mum was cooking dinner. You went out to the shops. You never came back.' Aisha tried to steady her voice, but she heard the tremble and she knew Jon had heard it too.

Jon shook his head. 'I wasn't going to the shops. Me and your ma had talked the night before. She suggested I just slip away. Thought that maybe you lot wouldn't notice if a waster like me wasn't around any more.'

Aisha looked at Jon. 'But you were ill. She shouldn't have sent you away. She should have looked after you. We all could have looked after you.'

Jon shook his head again. 'It wasn't that simple, kid. I couldn't stay, my head wasn't right. I was making things too difficult for ya mum. She had enough kids to care for. She was better off without me. We agreed.' Jon looked at Aisha's forlorn expression. 'But I s'pose in hindsight, it probably wasn't the right thing to do. I was depressed, so I was hardly in any fit state to work out the best way to explain it all to you kids, was I?'

Aisha shook her head. She knew mental health was still a topic that people struggled to get to grips with, so it was almost understandable that her parents would not have been able to have that conversation with her and her two sisters back then.

'So, it took you what? Twenty years to get your head straight, and now you're what? Better?' Aisha felt the sting in her tone. It was a lot to process in one go.

Jon frowned. 'No, no, the depression don't work like that. I finally got some help like, from the NHS, went to some seminars. And I've got tools now, like mental tools to help me deal with it. But it won't ever go away, but I am different, stronger. I can finally go to work and earn a decent buck. You gotta remember, your mum and I was young when we got together. She had just arrived from Jamaica, but she had a strong support unit already there in Brixton, but all my family and friends were miles away back in Birmingham. It was hard trying to fit in with the way of life your mum had set up for herself. We had you girls pretty close together, and then the blues kicked in. It was nasty.' Jon pulled his mouth down in disgust. 'I wouldn't wish it on anyone. Gonna do a course, help other people so they can recover from it too.'

'That's nice.' Aisha felt a pang of sadness for what her dad had gone through alone all these years and that he wasn't bitter, that he now wanted to help others. 'So, you went back to Birmingham? When you left us.'

'I stayed with a few old workmates in London for a bit. I even went to Mexico for a bit, for work, bit of labouring. Tried to put you all behind me, but I couldn't. I wrote to your mum a lot, gave her updates on how I was feeling. She never replied. Eventually, the years just rolled into one. I moved back to Birmingham about ten years ago now. Things didn't get much better for a while, and I was just rolling from one job to the next. Eventually, I got the treatment. I've been feeling a lot better for a year or so now.'

'That's really great, Jon. I'm pleased for you.'

'Yeah, it's not been an easy ride, but I'm glad I stuck around, you know. That I didn't check out early or anything. Anyway, then I got on the old internet, got myself a Facebook account. Our Carmel accepted me as a friend.'

Aisha felt a cold stab of jealousy that he would find her sister before her. 'Figures. She loves a friend request.'

Jon laughed. 'Yeah. I told her I was thinking about getting back in touch with everyone and she told me where everyone was, said if I was going to try and build bridges, I was to start with you and make my way up. Laila next. I never really knew Ruben and Marcel; they were tiny when I left. They don't remember me.'

'Marcel does,' Aisha said looking at Jon. 'He was six when you left. He used to speak about you.'

'Oh,' Jon said flatly. 'Well, maybe, I dunno, we'll see. Think I have enough on my plate with you three girls.'

'Why didn't you just knock on the door? I rarely check my Facebook.'

'What, that fancy London gaff of yours? Na, too scared. I wanted to catch you on the street. I did eventually.'

'Believe me, there are fancier gaffs than ours. And it's gonna get less fancy as these two grow up.'

'I know, it's mad that I'm a grandad now.'

'Carmel and little Hetty are coming to visit again next month. She's really busy at the hospital – she doesn't get a lot of time off.'

'I bet. I bet. Listen, I'm sorry I startled you, kid. And when you see your mum, you mustn't blame her for me not being around all this time. She had her reasons. Her sister was suffering as well, and you kiddies had to come first. I was neither use nor ornament in my condition, and by all accounts, you all grew up very well looked after with all those surrogate aunties and uncles.'

'We were never short of visitors, I'll say that. It's funny, cos I thought I wouldn't miss it, moving out of Brixton, and when Carmel and Laila moved away, I felt relief. But since having the twins and it being just us, I really miss the busyness of a family home. I miss people barging in and the endless meals that were cooked. There was always someone to talk to. So yes, you're right, I was looked after. I was looked out for.'

'That's great, kid. That's really great. Listen, I'd like to stay in touch like, proper, you know phone calls and that, does anyone do that any more?'

Aisha smiled. 'I do. I'd like that. A phone call.'

'Then maybe eventually another visit, so I can meet me grandsons proper like? And that lady friend of yours.'

'She's my girlfriend, Jon.'

'I know, I know.'

'Well let's say ta-ra for now and be seeing you soon?' Jon held out his hand from the other side of the bench. Aisha looked at it and then reached over and took it.

* * *

3.13 a.m. – Aisha: Is anyone awake? My world has just exploded.

3.15 a.m. – Mel: It wasn't another orange poo was it!?

3.16 a.m. – Aisha: No. My dad showed up. I haven't seen him for twenty years.

3.17 a.m. – Mel: What? OMG, are you okay? That must have been a big shock for you.

3.19 a.m. – Aisha: It was. I thought I was being stalked by the babies' sperm donor. But it was my dad all the time, trying to build up the confidence to knock on my door.

3.21 a.m. – Mel: Well, I don't blame you for thinking that. But what a relief it was him. Are you glad? How are you feeling?

3.23 a.m. – Aisha: Glad, but shocked and also a bit angry with my mum for not being honest about everything. She knew my dad had been trying to get in contact with me for some time, but he left because of depression.

3.29 a.m. – Mel: Listen, it sounds complex and I am sure there is lot for you all to talk about, but you mentioned depression and that makes everything so much more complicated. I think you need to cut them both some slack. Sounds like they all went through a pretty tough time. But he's here now, and that's all that matters.

3.40 a.m. – Aisha: I know. Thank you, Mel x

24

SOPHY

She paced the house from room to room, waiting for it to get to seven thirty. She had put Max down half an hour ago for his evening nap so that she and Jeff could have time to talk. She had changed into light grey skinny jeans and a white T-shirt and touched up her make-up. As she read his penultimate text message over again, the anxiety began to build again.

We need to talk.

She had sent a message straight back, not even trying to play it cool, asking when. His reply had just said:

Tomorrow at the house. 7.30 p.m.

Sophy had no idea if she should be making wedding plans or looking for rental properties in the area. Jeff could be vague in his emotions, but on this occasion, she had felt more from looking at one of Max's soiled nappies than she had got from reading that one text. At least by assessing Max's turds she could tell how he was feeling and if his stomach was upset. But this text gave nothing away.

Sophy wondered what kind of son Wendy had raised and had a good mind to ring her and ask. But Sophy had heard nothing from her all weekend. Usually, she dropped in on a Saturday or Sunday, and there was always the odd invitation over to Wendy and Al's for a Sunday lunch. But there had been nothing for days, which made Sophy realise that must have been where Jeff had been staying since Friday. Maybe, thought Sophy, if she'd been a little more 1950s housewife and a little less Instagram yummy mummy, she could have appeased Jeff. It did make Sophy wish that her own mother would make more of an effort. Sophy had wondered about messaging her mum and spilling it all to her, but then that was admitting that she had failed. And whilst Sophy had many doubts about her relationship with Jeff, she wasn't ready to say it was over.

Which was why his ridiculous riddle of a message was making her stomach hurt, meaning she had barely eaten all day. Why she had barely spoken to Niall when he came to work that morning wearing one of his golden smiles.

Sophy stopped pacing. She had heard a car door slam outside. She decided the kitchen was the best place to be. It said casual. Sophy always felt her most comfortable in the kitchen where there was always something she could fiddle with. She poured herself a glass of the Malbec wine she had opened for Jeff earlier. She'd already had a sip when she remembered she wasn't drinking at the moment. It tasted acidic, and she felt her insides burn as the liquid made its way through to her empty stomach.

A key turned in the front door and it swung open. There was no sound of Jeff's briefcase hitting the floor or his keys dropping into the pot on the hallway table. There was just silence, and Sophy tried to imagine him standing in the hallway and what he was doing. She sat there for a few more minutes and then became unnerved. Why was he taking so long? Why was he just standing in the bloody hallway?

Maybe it wasn't Jeff. Maybe it was an intruder, someone who had got hold of a key from Jeff's office; there were always hundreds of people coming and going from the agency all week. Someone must have got wind that she was here alone.

She stood up carefully, sliding a knife from the block on her way past and held it close to her side. She crept across the kitchen and into the hallway.

But it *was* Jeff. He was standing there, wearing a pair of jeans an uncannily similar colour to hers and a white T-shirt, texting or doing something on his phone. Sophy had thought long and hard about what was the appropriate outfit to wear when your boyfriend of four years, who has been living elsewhere for the last few days, comes around to either tell you he's leaving you or he wants to marry you. It really was a hard call, one that fashion magazines ought to pay more attention to and maybe write more features on. What she hadn't expected was Jeff to turn up dressed exactly the bloody same as her.

'For god's sake, Jeff, what are you doing standing there all this time? I thought you were a bloody burglar.'

Jeff looked up at Sophy and then down in Sophy's hand and said nothing.

'And what the hell are you wearing?' Sophy gestured to her own choice of outfit. 'We look like Posh and bloody Becks, circa '97.'

Jeff looked at Sophy and frowned. 'Babes, Posh is at least two stone lighter than you.'

Sophy's jaw dropped open and her knife-free hand fell to her stomach, where indeed there was a very slight mound underneath her jeggings. It was all the middle-of-the-night snacking she had been doing. How was she to curb that hunger any other way at that time of the night when Max was starving and sucking her dry of every nutrient? Perhaps she would start to have some salads prepped in the fridge so she would stop reaching for the cookies.

Jeff put his phone is his pocket and walked past Sophy his arm brushing against hers. 'Are we sitting in the kitchen? Ah, wine.' Sophy trotted into the kitchen behind Jeff and put the knife down on the kitchen counter. He picked up the glass, took a long sip and sat down. He winced as he swallowed. 'Jesus, Sophy, you been nicking the builders' paint stripper?'

Sophy put her hands on her hips and let out a sigh.

'Are you actually going to say anything that isn't an insult? Like where you've been, what you're doing, erm, oh, or how's Max, you know, your son?'

'I know how Max is, he's a baby. He eats, sleeps and shits. When he's a bit bigger and off the knockers, I can start taking more of an interest, can't I? I mean what do you want from me, Soph?'

Sophy shook her head in astonishment. 'I mean, I just don't know what to say, Jeff. You tell me, you're the one with the cryptic "we need to talk" messages. Well, you're here, so talk.'

Jeff gave her a smarmy look as if to say, *Get off your high horse, love.*

'I said let's talk cos we need to talk. This is my house, and I haven't even lived in it for the last few days.'

'That was your choice, Jeff.'

'Well, you sort of had something to do with it.'

Sophy looked puzzled. 'Mmm, I'm not sure how, Jeff, I mean I was asking a perfectly normal thing, for you to make it legal, me living here, for us to share the house we live in with *our* son, and you just upped and left.'

Jeff looked sheepish. 'Yeah, well, things have got a bit compli-cated, haven't they? And yeah, I left, but it's all been a bit weird at the moment ever since Max came along, and well, if I'm honest, since you began spending time with those girls.'

Sophy looked perplexed. 'Mel and Aisha?'

'Yes, those two.'

'What the hell have they got to do with us, with any of this?'

''Cos since you met them, you've changed. Everything is about you and them and you barely stop to think about me and my feel-ings and what I need.'

Was it Sophy's imagination or did Jeff sound a tiny bit whingy?

'What you need?' Sophy asked. She would dance to his tune for a few minutes – maybe she might get something back.

'Yeah, you know, like sex and stuff.'

Sophy closed her eyes and shook her head.

'So, you're telling me, we don't have sex any more because I made two new friends?'

Jeff took a long swig of his wine.

'We don't have sex because *I just had a baby*!' Sophy shouted the last part, and she saw Jeff physically recoil.

'All right, chill out.' He put his wine glass down on the counter. 'I told you, my head's a mess. I just know I would feel better if you weren't seeing those girls so much. I don't think they're having a good influence on you.'

Sophy did a really quick shake of her head. 'So, when you say "not see them so much", what does that mean exactly? I should only see them once a week, or only when you say I can?'

Jeff took a deep breath. 'I just think, Sophy, that if you and I are going to work – like I presume you want us to, otherwise why would you have washed your hair and put make-up on? – then you need to concentrate on us as a family, just you, me and Max.

So, when I say I don't think you should see them as much, what I am actually saying is, I don't think you should see them. Ever again.'

* * *

'He said what?' Aisha poured herself a glass of Prosecco. She had brought the booze, and Mel had brought the nibbles.

After Jeff had left, under the guise of Sophy thinking about his words, she had messaged the girls, and they agreed coffee was not going to cut it; this was a conversation that required wine. The next evening, Mel had jumped in an Uber and picked Aisha up on the way. Max was nestled at Sophy's breast. She was thankful she had decided not to give bottle feeding a go, because right now, she needed the comfort feeds as much as Max did. The girls had arrived and were given a quick tour of the house, which took less than a minute, and then Sophy talked about the extension for a few minutes, mentioning Niall's name a few times. Sophy was sure she saw Aisha steal a look at Mel when she thought she hadn't noticed. She had only mentioned Niall so she wasn't just monologuing about a bloody extension, which sounded so boring and middle class. Niall's presence in describing the work being done seemed to add a sense of joviality to what was, to her, an incredibly boring subject.

'He can't say that sort of stuff to you, Sophy. Has he lost his marbles? Does he not understand the sisterhood? I mean, I know we haven't known each other that long, but we've made a connection, and I really do class you both as two of my closest friends. And right now, we need each other more than anything. Can he not see that this is all this is? We're not a cavern of witches conspiring to cut off his dick in his sleep and boil it in a vat of oil. We need one another the way he needs his friends.' Aisha sat back in her chair in Sophy's lounge, where they were all sat around the table, which was overflowing with nibbles – Mel had certainly taken her role as the evening's feeder very seriously.

'I think he will come around. I think he just needs time out and then he'll come back,' Aisha added.

'Do you think?' Sophy said to Aisha.

Aisha nodded and crammed a handful of honey-roasted cashew nuts into her mouth. 'I really do,' she said, nuts falling down her chin.

Sophy turned expectantly to Mel. She had been a bit off the last time they spoke about this. And so far this evening, she had said very little.

'Mel? Thoughts please. Leave him to sweat it out?'

Mel was silent for a few seconds and then leant forward in her chair, her hands clamped into a half prayer fashion.

'I too have come to respect and admire you both very much, and I have come to rely on our friendship. Especially at the latter side of the night, when things feel a little bit hairy, I've known I can pick up the phone and be connected to you two women. Which is why Sophy and Aisha, I think it's only fair that I am honest with you.'

Aisha and Sophy looked at each other with worried expressions.

'Mel, you're scaring me a little,' Aisha said.

Mel reached her hand out to Aisha who gratefully took it. 'It's okay. It's my own fault. I have been holding on to it for some time, but I've had a word with myself and now I'm ready. Sophy, I have something to tell you and it's about Jeff.'

* * *

Mel had stopped speaking a few seconds ago, and neither Sophy nor Aisha had said a word. Aisha sat open-mouthed and occasionally omitted a squeak, and Sophy had put her free hand – the one that wasn't nursing Max – over her mouth and had yet to remove it.

Eventually, Aisha said, 'So, he...' then dropped her voice to a whisper '... raped you?'

Mel sat up straight. 'Good god, no. I punched him in the face, good and hard. Well, the best way I knew how. I've never punched someone before, so I literally gave it my best shot. He stumbled back far enough away from me so that I could run down the alley and back into the club. He didn't follow me back in, and I never told a soul.'

'Oh my god, why not, why didn't you report it?' Aisha said carefully, glancing over at Sophy.

'Because that club is my life, my livelihood, my family. It has never seen one hint of trouble in all the years I've worked there, and I didn't want to risk it getting a bad name. Besides.' Mel paused and cleared her throat. 'I felt, that maybe – at the time, this was, mind you – that maybe I had encouraged it.'

'What!' exclaimed Aisha. 'No, you can't say that. You were just doing your job, performing. That doesn't give anyone the right to...' Aisha dropped her voice again '... force themselves upon you.'

'I know but all I'm saying is, at the time, I wondered if I had encouraged it in some way with what I was wearing.'

'No, no, no, Mel, you mustn't say that. Did you invite him to the back door? Did you ask him to put his hands on you?'

Mel shook her head. Aisha moved over to the sofa and sat down next to Sophy.

'Sophy, is there anything I can get you? Some tea? Something stronger maybe?' Aisha carefully prised a now full and slumbering Max out of Sophy's arms. Mel came and sat at her feet and gently pulled Sophy's top back up.

'I'm so sorry you had to hear it this way,' Mel said, looking at Sophy. Waiting for a reaction.

'He came home with a black eye a year ago,' Sophy started speaking. 'It must have been that night, because it wasn't long before we went on our holiday when Max was conceived, and I said I didn't want to turn up at the resort with him looking like Reggie bloody Kray.'

'I knew it though. I knew it. Not *that* obviously, but you know, I had my suspicions about him recently, that maybe he was seeing someone else?'

The other two women nodded slowly.

'But I still thought he might want to make a go of it, even when I received that stupid message that said we needed to talk.' Sophy shook her head.

Sophy heaved loud, heavy sobs. Mel glanced at Aisha, unsure what to do. Aisha stepped forward with Max in her arms.

'Sophy, it's okay. It's a lot to take in.'

Sophy's cries came to a sudden halt, and she stood up and brushed crisp crumbs from her trousers.

'Girls, I am going to have to ask you to leave. I need a moment with this. I need to...' Sophy's lip trembled and Mel reached out to touch her. Sophy flinched and stepped back away from Mel, who shrunk backwards.

'I just need to be by myself.' Sophy took Max from Aisha's arms and headed upstairs. She settled him in his SnuzPod, and a few minutes later, she heard the click of the front door as the girls left.

* * *

2.56 a.m. – Sophy: Is anyone there?

3.02 a.m. – Mel: I'm here, Sophy.

3.03 a.m. – Sophy: You know when you asked me the other day if I loved Jeff?

3.04 a.m. – Mel: Yes.

3.05 a.m. – Sophy: Will you ask me again?

3.07 a.m. – Mel: Okay. Sophy, do you love Jeff?

3.09 a.m. – Sophy: No.

3.10 a.m. – Mel: Okay. You don't need to say this because of what happened, I think maybe he could get counselling or something. I don't want to be the reason you and Jeff split.

3.11 a.m. – Sophy: You aren't. I have never loved Jeff. I know that now. I have always known it, really. I have been holding on to the idea of us, of what I want Jeff to be, but he never will. Plus, I am 90 per cent sure he is messing around with someone behind my back.

3.13 a.m. – Mel: Oh. How do you know?

3.14 a.m. – Sophy: He works late when he doesn't have to, and I heard him answer a call the other day in a voice that wasn't one he would use for a work call. He was talking to a woman. Plus, I just know. You know?

3.17 a.m. – Mel: I know.

3.20 a.m. – Sophy: You've done me a massive favour, Mel. I could have colossally fucked my life up if I hadn't had met you. Jeff is rotten to the core, and I just kept trying to see beyond it, ignoring all the times he tried to belittle me. The things that were bothering me more than not being with Jeff were things like: Where would I live? How would I survive? What would I tell my friends about why we weren't together?

3.25 a.m. – Mel: I get it. I did see it too. But I didn't want to be the one to ruin things. I am glad you have realised for yourself. I am here for you for whatever you decide next.

3.40 a.m. – Aisha: OMG, Sophy! Me too! xxx

25

MEL

'You have very sticky table. I wipe with special product, make it better. How you make it this way, I not know,' Ksenia said.

Mel smiled. She had just got back from a check-up on her ankle at the hospital. It had healed well, and the space boot was no more. Mel was getting used to walking around without the footwear on and had walked around the kitchen table six times.

'Thank you, Ksenia. I really appreciate everything you have done.'

Ksenia nodded. 'You make me dizzy with your walking. I see your foot better. You not need me any more?'

Mel's eyes widened, and she shook her head. 'Oh no, quite the opposite. I would love it if you would stay with us. If you're happy?'

'I am very happy working here for your family,' Ksenia said, her face remained taut with no emotion.

'Good, good,' Mel said. 'I just wondered, if you weren't too busy, whether you might be free for a one-off extra job next week?'

Ksenia looked intrigued.

'And I can hundred per cent guarantee not a man within a hundred yards.'

'Okay. I do it.' Ksenia said, and Mel was sure she detected the slightest of smiles twitching at the corner of Ksenia's lips.

* * *

'I'm here, I have snacks, and I have something else,' Mel said as she walked through the open front door of Sophy's newly rented two-bedroom ground-floor flat with Skylar in her arms. Sophy appeared in the hallway, a sleeping Max strapped to her chest, her hair piled high on her head in a messy bun, with a pink floral turban headband across the front of her hair. Her cheeks were a light rose pink. It was lunchtime, May had brought warmth and sunshine and Sophy had moved into her new home just two hours ago.

Ksenia appeared from behind Mel. 'I have brought the cavalry!' Mel said. 'Meet Ksenia! My cleaner.'

'Hello, it's lovely to meet you.' Sophy put her hand out to shake Ksenia's hand.

Ksenia looked at it like it was one of the filthy toilets she cleaned, ignored it and nudged her head up, indicating the way past Sophy. 'Kitchen and bathroom that way?'

'Er, it is yes.' Sophy looked at Mel for reassurance. Mel narrowed her eyes and shook her head.

'Right, I go there and make clean.' Ksenia walked past Sophy, her cleaning caddy in hand. Sophy and Mel watched her go. Mel's look was one of pride.

'What a woman,' Mel said as she watched Ksenia walk to the kitchen at the end of the hallway.

Sophy screwed her nose up. 'A bit rude.'

Mel shook her head. 'Nah, I don't think so. I think politeness is overrated in some circumstances. Ksenia is no-nonsense all the way. I find it highly refreshing.' Mel shook herself away from her gaze. 'Besides, she is a bloody good cleaner.'

'Oh, good, Mel, because this place needs it. They promised a thorough deep clean before we moved in. I told them I had a small baby and they assured me. I would have been happy to have done it myself – I grew up cleaning our only bathroom, you know.'

'I know, but like you say, you have Max, and Ksenia will do it in half the time.'

Sophy looked around the hallway and Mel followed her gaze. It wasn't so bad in Mel's eyes, but then Sophy had been used to the modern interior of Jeff's house that looked clean even when it wasn't. She was starting again here and the building itself was less than modern. But Mel liked that about it; it had lots of character and nooks and cupboards, which was so important with children for storage.

'Besides, you know what estate agents are like,' Mel said the words before she had time to think about them. 'I mean—'

'Don't, Mel. You don't need to say anything, let alone apologise. I feel as though it's me who should be apologising.'

'And you have, Sophy, like a hundred times already,' Mel said.

Sophy quickly rubbed her hands over her face. 'I know. I just don't know what else to do?'

'You've done enough. You've left Jeff, you've set up on your own, all in the space of a few weeks. That's some achievement, I'd say.'

'I know, but it still doesn't take away from what he did to you, when you were pregnant with Skylar as well. Or what he could go on to do to other women. And what about Max? Can I ever leave him alone with Jeff?'

Mel reached forward and put a hand on Sophy's shoulder. 'I

think you should take a deep breath and take one day at a time. I think it's highly unlikely that you'll ever have to worry about Jeff wanting to have Max by himself, didn't you say he had not taken him for a walk in his pram once?'

'Not once.' Sophy shook her head, obviously still shocked at her own confession.

'Well then, come on, I can't see him bashing your door down any time soon to take him to the park, can you?'

Sophy pulled her mouth down. 'I don't know. I hope not.'

'Well, you just tell him it's supervised visits only, and he'll soon get bored and sod off.'

'But then Max won't have a father?'

Mel raised one eyebrow at Sophy, and Sophy breathed in slowly and nodded. 'I know I know; he never was much of a father to him.'

'I mean, are you actually sure he really is the father?' Mel quipped.

Sophy groaned and nodded. 'Sadly, yes, one hundred per cent.'

'Shame. That would have solved all the problems. Never mind. You've been doing it all on your own for the last few months, you can keep doing it on your own. Right then, it's time you gave me a tour!' Mel said, and Sophy's face brightened.

'Okay, come with me.'

They found Ksenia in the kitchen, scrubbing the front of the cupboards, which were an off white.

'Kitchen, obviously.'

Sophy showed Mel through the rest of the flat: two double rooms with white walls; a bathroom with large brown tiles, a bath with a shower and screen; and a very spacious lounge, big enough to relax in and for Max to crawl around in a few months, complete with high ceilings and a fireplace. A sofa had arrived an hour ago and was against the back wall, still in its wrapping.

Mel put her arm around Sophy. 'It's perfect. I think you'll be very happy here.'

Sophy lay her head onto Mel's shoulder, then the two women heard 'Hi' and the commotion of a double buggy being positioned in the hallway. A few seconds later, a harassed-looking Aisha walked into the lounge carrying a small aloe vera plant in a green pot. 'Happy moving-in day!' She grinned as she held the plant out to Sophy.

'Oh, thank you, Aisha, it's gorgeous. Thank you, what a lovely gesture.'

'Sorry, I only brought a cleaner,' Mel said, wondering if she should have gone for the traditional moving-in gift as well.

'Oh well, that is equally a fantastic gift. You've both been so helpful, I'm not sure I would have managed without you. It's so strange. You've both been in my life just a few months, but it feels like I've known you all my life.' Sophy looked like she was going to well up, and so Mel moved in and put an arm around her. Aisha took the other side and the three women hugged silently for a few seconds.

'I find dead mouse in kitchen, where would you like it?' Ksenia's voice penetrated through the silence.

Mel let go of Sophy and looked up at the doorway to the lounge, where Ksenia was holding a very rigid dead mouse.

'Oh Christ, let's get that thing out of here.' Mel moved quickly to the doorway and escorted Ksenia to the kitchen and out of the back door, which led to a side alleyway where the bins were kept.

'Do you think we can throw it over the fence?' she asked, but before she got a response, Ksenia flung the mouse with such force it landed in the guttering of the neighbouring house.

'Yuck, filthy things.' Ksenia wiped her hands on her jeans.

'Now I clean shit off toilet.' And she walked back into the flat, leaving Mel still staring at the mouse's final resting place.

* * *

'This place is lovely, Mel. How did you know it was here?' Sophy said about the café they found themselves sitting outside later that afternoon. The babies were tucked into their prams, all miraculously asleep at the same time. The walk down had sent them all off and the fresh breeze and the gentle hum of traffic was thankfully keeping them asleep.

'I know all the best places to eat. Daz and I have friends who live around South Lambeth.'

Sophy shook her head as she cut into her panini. 'I never thought I would find myself living in South Lambeth, of all places. I know it seems really close to Clapham – and Jeff – still, but it was you two I was actually thinking of. We are still reasonably close to one another's houses and that's how I wanted it to be. You two aren't going anywhere for a while, so I had to plant myself nearest to you. I could walk to Aisha's from here, but I'd probably jump on a train to you Mel, or drive.'

'It's great, Sophy. You made a good choice, and this place is pretty metropolitan. I mean look, that bloke has a very well-groomed beard and is wearing his baby,' Mel said helpfully.

The other two girls looked across the road to where Mel was pointing and nodded enthusiastically.

'Are you trying to set me up already?' Sophy laughed.

'No,' Mel said. 'But I'm pretty sure it won't be too long until someone comes and nabs you up.'

Sophy shook her head. 'I don't think so,' she said in a tone that didn't altogether sound convincing.

'Unless you have your eye on someone already?' Mel said inquisitively.

Sophy looked her square in the eye, and for a second, she saw straight into her, and Mel knew there was someone. Sophy, who she had only known a couple of months, occasionally looked as though she were sharing a secret with herself. She would suddenly seem far away, but not in a mourning-the-loss-of-her-live-in-lover kind of way. And Mel was curious. But she didn't want to push anything or force Sophy to discuss something she wasn't yet ready to discuss yet. At least let her side of the bed at Jeff's go cold before she encouraged Sophy to move on with her life. Her so very precious life that had already been stalled by four years living with that utter creep and moron. If it weren't for the beautiful Max – who in Mel's opinion took after Sophy in every way – then she would have said the last half a decade of Sophy's life had been a complete waste of time.

'Well, we are in London, baby. Anything can happen, remember? There are hundreds of eligible suitors ready to cross paths with you.'

'Yes, and we will help you make sure he is absolutely perfect.' Aisha smiled kindly at Sophy.

Sophy looked down at her hands and into her coffee cup. And there it was again, that slight faraway look, as though she was there already. Mel was desperate to know, but she knew when to step back and allow someone space. She was just so looking forward to Sophy finally spilling all. For why shouldn't someone as beautiful and talented as Sophy not get her happy-ever-after? Mel would be there to make sure – in a subtle and not too over-powering way – that Sophy never made a colossal mistake like getting with a buffoon like Jeff ever again. But like she said, subtle.

'I know I've said it a few times, but I am so grateful I met you.

It has been like fate in so many ways,' Sophy said. 'I don't know any of my other mates who I would feel comfortable texting at three o'clock in the morning. It's so weird that we just started doing that and none of us questioned it.'

'Can I say that it is the part of the day I look forward to the most?' Aisha said. 'I mean I know I have dinner with Charley and I see my mum, and yes the twins are fun in small measures. But when I wake up in those early hazy hours, I no longer feel panicky or stressed. I know I can just message the group and there's a good possibility that one of you will be awake as well. I feel so lucky!' Aisha's voice broke at the last word and Mel, who was on her right, reached out and grabbed her hand.

'The truth is, I've been struggling,' Aisha said quietly. 'I tried so many times to say it on the chat, but it was too scary to just put it out there and not get a response for a few hours.'

'Oh, Aisha, I understand why you haven't said anything. I feel so guilty I've been wrapped up in this Jeff thing for weeks and I haven't thought about anyone else,' Sophy said.

'I'm sorry too. I think we, both me and Sophy, maybe knew that things were potentially tougher for you. And we should have reached out more, but I guess we didn't want to presume.' Mel looked at Sophy, who nodded in agreement.

'Oh, but you have helped, by being there at 3 a.m., like I said. Just knowing I had you girls there to talk to has lifted such a weight off. It has taken me a while, but I don't feel as lonely any more and that helps me through the days. I don't dread the nights now.'

'I think it's what brought us so close so quickly,' Sophy said 'Our early-morning chats. Because we are at our most raw at that time of the day, we are doing the most primal thing possible: feeding our babies, keeping them alive through the night, they have only us to rely on. So when we message, we are in fact the most authentic version of our true maternal selves.' Sophy stopped speaking and looked at Mel and Aisha who were both looking at her with their lips slightly parted, as though they felt that they should say something, but Mel knew she had nothing to top that.

'Oh my god, Sophy, that was so fucking profound! You should put that on your Instagram!' Mel said, shaking her head.

'That was really lovely, Sophy. And so true.' Aisha's eyes were glimmering with happy tears.

Sophy suddenly looked excited. 'You're right, Mel, I absolutely should do that. Truth be told, I have been struggling to connect with my content. It's all about healthy bodies and looking fit and eating really well, but sometimes, well, most of the time, I just feel tired, and I want to snuggle with Max. But I didn't want it to turn into one of those pages where I just post flat lay after flat lay of Max, you know?'

'Yeah, but I reckon you're on to something there, with the whole authentic-maternal stuff. Just make it a bit more real. Talk about what we talk about, like feeling absolutely frazzled and healing stitches, but make it light-hearted. I think mums might relate to that and get some comfort from it,' Mel said.

Sophy looked thoughtful. 'Do you think?'

Aisha nodded enthusiastically. 'Absolutely, you're a very genuine person, Sophy.'

'I don't feel like it at the moment. I feel a bit of a fraud, really.'

'So, change the content!' Mel said. 'Call it the 3 a.m. Shattered Mums' Club if you like!'

Sophy looked brighter. 'Could I? Would you mind, I mean?'

'Why would we mind? It was pretty much you're doing in the first place. I think it's the sort of content that would be much more suitable for you. Start it over, set up a new profile, send people to it and see how it goes!'

Sophy blew out a breath. 'Okay, I will!'

'Brilliant,' Aisha said.

'Hey, we're not just the 3 a.m. Shattered Mums' Club – we're Any Time of the Day Shattered Mums' Club,' Mel said triumphantly. 'And I hope we will be friends for a very long time.'

26

AISHA

Martina settled herself in the big comfy chair in the Aisha's lounge, and Aisha handed her a cup of tea. They had just fed the boys and put them down for a nap. Aisha had been preparing herself for this conversation with her mother for a long time. It had been a few weeks since she had seen Jon in the street, and she had waited until he followed through with his phone call before she decided to talk to Martina. She wasn't entirely sure if Jon was going to stay true to his word. She hadn't seen him in twenty years, and so a relative stranger in the grand scheme of things, but to Aisha's surprise and delight, she received a phone call on her mobile the following week. A conversation that hadn't cemented an instant meet-up but had paved the way for future plans. Aisha was feeling hopeful. And since Jon had come back into her life, and she had been spending more time with Mel and Sophy, she was feeling a lot better about things. Time with the boys felt a little more joyous. They had started to smile back at her regularly, and for every fifteen or so hours of work she seemed to put in during one day, whether it be night feeds, washing, cleaning, cooking or just holding and playing with the babies, she averaged out about one or two of those hours where she felt some level of contentment, and dare she say it, happiness.

Martina let out a long sigh and stretched her legs out. She was still a fit woman at just fifty, but she did occasionally complain of aching joints, but that was because she spent so much time cooking and cleaning for the cousins and helping neighbours out. She rarely sat down to properly relax.

'So, Mum, I have something to talk to you about.'

'Damn, girl, I knew there was something up with you – you been skipping round like a jumpin' bean all afternoon.'

'Is it that obvious?'

Martina nodded her head. 'Shoot.'

'Well, a few things, really. One: I heard from my father. Jon.'

'Damn sure I ain't 'bout to forget his name in a hurry, so no need to remind me,' came Martina's first response. It didn't surprise Aisha that it was one fuelled by defence.

'Right. Well, he came here, to the house.'

Martina shot forward in her chair and looked around. 'Your father! In this house?'

'No, he didn't come *in* the house, I met him in the street. He'd been working up the courage to come and knock on the door, and in the end we ended up talking on the street.'

Aisha looked at Martina, who now looked as though she had just sucked on a very bitter lemon. Aisha cleared her throat and carried on.

'I also found a letter, well, lots of letters under your bed, but I read one, from him. It explained a few things to me, and so now I know why he left.'

Aisha saw a flicker of something that looked like doubt or shame in Martina's eyes.

'I had my reasons for keeping him away.'

'I know you did. And I don't blame you, you had a lot on your plate with five kids and a depressed sister.'

'Damn right, I did. No way I could have coped trying to heal him too. He had to do that for himself.'

'Well, he says he is better now. Better than he was, anyway.'

'Well, he took his sweet ass time about it,' Martina said, and Aisha heard what she thought was melancholy in her mother's voice.

Aisha paused.

'I've agreed to see him again, and well, I want to. And maybe being with me and the boys will help him with his recovery. Because you see, I know how he feels. I haven't been feeling myself. And I know it's hard for you to acknowledge it after everything with Jon, my dad. I didn't want to burden you with how I was feeling.'

'You don't think I didn't acknowledge it cos of ya father? I said nothing cos I knew I raised you to be a strong girl who could overcome her demons. I knew you would come true and find the light like I did. I didn't want to make no big song and dance 'bout it, but I was here bringing positive energy to you and them babies. I could feel your pain. I prayed, I still pray. Every night for you and them babies.'

Aisha felt the heavy threat of tears. She swallowed and squeezed her hand to stop herself from sobbing.

'You got a good set-up here, you and your woman. You just need time, like all new mothers. Time is all it takes. There's no rush to get back to how you felt before, cos you ain't who were before. No woman can carry a child for nine months, birth that baby and say she is the same. No sirree. Uh-uh.'

Aisha put her hands over her mouth and used her fingers to catch the tears that refused to stay put.

'And you go on and cry, girl, cos those tears ain't made to stay locked up.' Aisha found Martina's words a comfort. She had never been a mother to hold and cuddle her children often. They were fed, bathed, cleaned and sent to school. There was fun, games and rules and a whole lot of eating. Aisha remembered a mostly happy childhood. But she had missed out on the unexpected cuddles that came from nowhere for no reason other than her mother needed to feel her child close to her.

Martina rocked backwards and forwards in her chair for a few moments, and then after a minute, she stood up and went to her daughter and placed her big arms around her, and in what felt like a very long-overdue moment, Aisha wept whilst her mother held her.

* * *

2.56 a.m. – Sophy: Hello. Is anyone there?

2.58 a.m. – Aisha: I'm here! How is it going in the flat?

2.58 a.m. – Mel: I'm here too! I have just put Sky down. How are you feeling? It's a week today, isn't it?

2.59 a.m. Sophy: It feels a bit strange, new sounds and all that, but I'll get used to that. What is weird is not waiting for Jeff to walk through the door any minute. I felt as though I had spent months in the house with Max, waiting for him to come home, then I would jabber rubbish to him, which he would never listen to. I feel a real sense of relief that I don't have that waiting bit any more. Does that make sense?

3.01 a.m. – Mel: Makes perfect sense to me, doll.

3.04 a.m. – Aisha: Sorry, just had to grab another twin. I'm so proud you feel that way, Sophy. It's marvellous you've been able to adapt so quickly.

3.05 a.m. – Aisha: Okay, twin sick alert. Have to go.

3.06 a.m. – Sophy: Okay, gonna try and get back to sleep.

3.06 a.m. – Mel: Oh god, that's Sky screaming again. Does she ever wanna give her mama a break!

27

SOPHY

Sophy looked up at the house, the key in her hand, and made her way to the front door. It had been exactly three weeks since she had been back to Jeff's, and she had been putting off returning to pick up the final few things from the loft that Jeff said he would have laid out in the hallway for her. Now she had the key in her hand and was about to walk into the house again, she began to feel very sick. Max was in her arms, his face red and wet. He had been fractious all the way here, she had sung 'Twinkle Twinkle Little Star' over and over just to keep his cries to a minimum, and now her throat was hoarse. It was as though Max had tuned into her anxiety and made his feelings well and truly known.

'It's going to be okay,' she said. 'We will just be a minute, and then we never have to come back to this place ever again. Well, maybe you might have to. But, anyway, just don't worry about that now.'

Sophy opened the door and stepped into the hallway. As promised, there was the pile of things Sophy had requested: a few bags of baby clothes that had been handed down to her, an old camera and tripod, and a box of old photos and letters from her school days and some paintings by local artists she had wanted to hang but Jeff had turned his nose up at.

Sophy looked up the stairs and felt a pull towards the bedroom. She crept up the stairs, wondering if maybe it was a trick, and Jeff was going to be waiting for her in the bedroom.

I knew you wouldn't be able to help yourself. She heard his voice as though he had spoken the words. But as she nudged at the door, she could see the room was empty. The bed was unmade. Sophy looked away, disgusted. Making her bed every day was the one of the most important jobs, and in all the years she had lived with Jeff, that bedroom had never looked as messy as it did now with empty glasses and cereal bowls on the bedside table. Sophy turned to the wall – her wall as she had always felt it was, with the blue spiralling wallpaper that had been the backdrop to so many of her vlogs. Max fidgeted in her arms, he was heavy at almost four months and would often try to sit forward as though he were missing the action.

Sophy took one last look around the room before she turned to leave and that was when she saw it: a tube of Elizabeth Arden Eight Hour cream on the bedside table that had been her side of the bed. One small item placed strategically as though it were claiming its space where many other items would soon follow.

Sophy felt the rush of adrenaline through her body. She was done with crying; she was now moving on to rage. How could he move on so fast? Replace the mother of his son as though four years together had meant nothing? And then Sophy remembered, the hushed phone call with the gentle tone, and she thought of Mel and how she had been treated as though it was something Jeff was acclaimed at. She remembered, she had not been replaced quickly; she had been given a get-out-of-jail-free card and saved herself from a lifetime of loveless toxicity.

* * *

When Sophy walked through into the kitchen, she was taken aback to see Niall sitting in there on the half-finished floor. Next to him, the walls of an almost-completed extension of two further downstairs rooms, the garden she had sat in time and time again now half the size.

'I can't believe you've almost finished,' Sophy said.

'Hello, stranger,' Niall said, getting to his feet and coming over to Sophy. He moved awkwardly towards her as though he might lean in and kiss or hug her hello, and for a heart-stopping second, she thought he might, and Sophy felt panic spread through her body wondering how she should react.

'How are you doing?' Niall said, his face brighter than she had ever seen it. Had he missed her? She had thought about him, she had to admit, but she overthought everything so much – Were her feelings for him real? Was he just a bit of eye candy when Jeff wasn't around? How would he fit into her life? – until eventually she had begun to dismiss the idea completely. Until now. As she stood in front of him after weeks apart, she felt her chest rising and falling, trying to keep up with her rapidly beating heart and racing thoughts.

'And how's the wee man?' Niall put his arms out, and to her surprise, Sophy found she freely handed him over to Niall, as though it was perfectly normal. Niall lifted him gently to his eye level and said, 'There he is – I missed that little face.' Then he expertly turned him outwards to face Sophy and held him in the crook of his arm.

'Wow, you're really good with babies.'

'You know I have a lot of nieces and nephews.'

'Wow, but how many?'

Niall looked up to the sky, squinted and screwed up his face. 'Like ten so far. There will be more to come, I'm sure of it.'

'That's amazing. And do you get them all presents for their birthdays and Christmas?'

'Hell no – I'm not made of bleedin' money. They get one small present each at Christmas.'

'That's lovely,' Sophy said and made a point of moving in towards Max to kiss and nuzzle him, even though he was absolutely fine in Niall's arms.

'How've you been?'

Sophy smiled and nodded. 'Not bad, considering. Bit of a mess, really.' She looked around the kitchen awkwardly.

'Ay, I didn't know too much about it except when Jeff said you weren't coming back.'

'Yeah, sorry about that. Should have said goodbye, really, but I kind of rushed out and didn't want to make a thing of it.'

'I gathered.' Max made a little gurgle and a squeak and Niall moved him up and down a little.

'It was all pretty ugly.'

'But you're all settled somewhere now?'

'Yep, got a two-bed flat a couple of miles away.' Sophy wasn't sure why she didn't say where it was she was now living. It was as if saying it might imply she wanted him to know where she was.

'Oh right. And you've settled in okay?' Sophy felt herself cringe at the momentous amount of small talk, something she was terrible at, but at which others seemed to thrive. Niall had always been good at filling uncomfortable gaps in conversations and always seemed to have something to say.

'It's a really nice flat. I was lucky to get it at the price I did. I think we'll be okay there for now.'

'And you're managing all right? Got someone putting up shelves?'

Sophy laughed and instantly felt what Niall meant. 'I don't have any shelves.'

'Got yourself a couple of nice pictures there in the hallway.'

'Oh, yes, I wanted to put them up here, but... I never did.'

'I'll put them up for ya if you like?'

Sophy laughed. 'I could probably do them myself.'

'I'm sure you could, modern woman like yourself, but I'd like to. There is actually quite an art to putting up pictures,' Niall said, a small smile playing across his lips.

'Oh, is there now?'

'It's true, I actually learned it at college. So, if you want, I can come and do it?'

Sophy looked at him and allowed herself to take him all in. His tall frame that wasn't as broad as Jeff's, his tanned arms, his rough stubble and short light brown hair. Sophy had never asked how old Niall was, but she put him about her age. Not eight years older than her, like Jeff.

Sophy thought about the wasted years, the tube of moisturiser upstairs that wasn't hers, waiting for its accomplices to come and join it. She thought of the times she had asked Jeff to make her an official part of his life yet how she had never brought up marriage, as though she knew that their relationship would not last, and that marriage would be a whole other obstacle to tackle when the inevitable happened. Then she thought of the despicable way Jeff had forced himself on Mel and how, if she had been a woman of a slighter stature, she may not have been able to fight off his advances. She worried if that had already been the case and that maybe there had been other victims. These were things she had been thinking about non-stop for weeks and she realised that now, maybe it was time to stop thinking about them and give herself a chance at happiness. Even if it were fleeting, even it was only to make herself feel better in the short term, because the reality was, men didn't just show up, fall in love with their client's girlfriends and become a new daddy to their baby.

Did they?

* * *

3.27 a.m. – Sophy: I just realised that it doesn't hurt down below any more.

3.48 a.m. – Mel: 'Vagina', Sophy, you can say 'Vagina'.

3.49 a.m. – Sophy: Okay, sorry. Yes, that word. It seems to all be feeling a lot better.

3.50 a.m. – Mel: I put it down to the fact that you're not with Jeff any more. You're a lot less stressed, so I guarantee the healing process just sped up these last few weeks.

3.51 a.m. – Sophy: Do you know what, Mel? I think you might be right.

3.52 a.m. – Mel: I know I'm right.

4.01 a.m. – Aisha: Congratulations on your vagina, Sophy! x

28

MEL

'She went down absolutely fine,' Irene said as she came back into the kitchen, having just put Sky to bed for her afternoon nap. It was a few weeks after Sophy had moved into the new flat and Mel was standing at her kitchen window, looking at Leia and her *'friend*, Mum, not my boyfriend' sitting on the grass with her. His name was Henry. He looked like a nice enough young boy – he was polite, and Leia laughed a lot when she was with him. Mel sighed and thought about what lay ahead for her with Leia, and how she worried about the choices she would make as she grew up.

'I don't know how I'm going to manage it,' Mel said to herself, but Irene joined her at the window and looked out into the garden.

'She'll be fine. She's strong and clever like her mum.' Mel looked at Irene.

'Thank you for raising a wholesome strong man in Daz.'

'Ahh, he was no bother. He was such a funny, charming little kid from such a young age. It was and still is a pleasure to be his mum.' Irene looked at Mel. 'Don't worry, you're doing a great job.'

Mel breathed in slowly and looked back out the window again.

'Am I? Sometimes I wish there was a rule book, some format to stick to so you knew your kid was going to grow up and be okay in the world without you.' Mel heard her voice break on the last word, and Irene put an arm around her waist and pulled her into her. Mel thought they must have looked a funny pair, her at almost six foot and Irene at a diddy five foot five. Mel dared not lean her weight against Irene for fear of flattening her.

'Your mum would have been so proud of all your achievements. I know you struggle without her sometimes.'

Mel nodded, and a little tear trickled down her face. She quickly wiped it away. 'How can it have been so long yet I still yearn for her?'

'Because you never stop wanting your mum, no matter how old you get. And that girl out there, she might think she's nearly an adult, but she'll be turning to you for the rest of her life for love and support and advice.'

Mel closed her eyes and sighed. 'Thanks, Irene.'

'You're welcome, dear. Are you looking forward to tonight?'

'I am. Daz can finally see me perform after all this time.'

'And your friends are coming too, aren't they?'

'Yes, they are.'

'What's that funny little name for you all?'

'We're the 3 a.m. Shattered Mums' Club.'

'Very nice, dear.'

* * *

The dress Mel had chosen for the show that evening was red silk and floor length with a plunging neckline. And she was going to absolutely rock it.

'My wife,' Daz said when he came downstairs into the lounge.

He was wearing a pale blue shirt and a beige jacket. Daz was never one for glam, and he still had a slight look of the accountant about him – more like he was about to sit and do a tax return than hit a cabaret club – but that was what Mel loved about him. Daz didn't try to be sexy, he just was in her eyes, and that, she realised, was why she still fancied him after all this time. And he wasn't fazed by the job that Mel did either. He loved seeing Mel dressed up but had never been one of those guys to ogle over other women. Once – she had been reliably informed by one of Daz's work colleagues – Daz was at one of their staff meetings, which happened to take place in a strip joint (the boss of the company was playing around with ways to 'enhance' the working day, apparently) – and the waitress, who had lost her clothes somewhere between the entrées and the main course, did so without Daz batting an eyelid and ended up going away with sound and solid tax advice rather than tips in her knickers. So, Mel knew that despite all the other acts that were set to perform tonight – a couple of them renowned for their slinky outfits and playful audience-participation act – Daz's eyes would only be on her. Which was why she could never tell Daz about the Jeff incident. It would crush him. It was merely a blip in her long career as a performer, and yes, whilst the odd man ogled and would occasionally reach out to grab her arse, she would promptly put them back in their place with a firm shove and a quick glance at the bouncer. But the fact that Mel had even for a second contemplated Jeff as a tasty piece meant she would never be able to fully let go of the guilt, and whilst what Jeff had done – or rather tried to do to her – was ghastly and deserving of having his balls stretched and strung around his neck, she knew she would never again let her professionalism slip whilst at work. Even if she had finished and was drinking at the bar. It was indeed a shame, she concluded, that there were some men who mistook a friendly, even flirtatious smile, for an indication that sex would promptly follow. But she hoped that people like her friend Sophy were raising the next generation of men to be less pretentious dickheads.

But she was trying to put all that behind her, and tonight was going to properly mark her re-entrance to the showbiz world. Irene had been here all day playing with Sky and cooking lunch whilst Mel mentally went through her set and generally geared herself up for the show. And the best part was, Aisha and Sophy were coming too. Max had slid into a routine of taking a feed at 8 p.m. then sleeping through until eleven or midnight. He would then have Sophy up half the latter part of the night, fussing and cluster feeding, but it meant that Sophy could drop Max, feed him, and come to the gig for a few hours. She would then pick him up on her way home.

Sophy arrived in sleek black faux leather trousers and a pink T-shirt. She had been wearing trainers to drive but changed into heels once she had handed a sleeping Max in his car seat over to a delighted Irene.

'Now, Mum, are you sure you'll be okay with two babies tonight?' Daz asked Irene.

'Ah yes, love. I did raise you and your brother, and you were only eleven months apart – it sometimes felt as though I had twins. I'm looking forward to it.'

'I hope they don't both wake up and cry at once,' Sophy said, a streak of worry washing over her face, and Mel quickly ushered Sophy into the waiting Uber before she could change her mind.

* * *

The crowd went wild, a proper standing ovation with foot stamping and whistles that made Mel's skin erupt into goosebumps. She waited for the applause to die down, then took one final bow and said a simple thank you and left the stage.

'Oh my god, you are amazing.' Aisha pulled Mel in for a tight squeeze when she made it back to the bar after freshening up from her set.

'Absolutely outstanding, Mel – I had actual goosebumps when you sang that last ballad.' Sophy surreptitiously wiped a tear away from her eye.

'Beautiful as always, my darling girl,' Daz said. 'And now, girls, who would like a drink?'

They all put their orders in and huddled around the table as Daz walked over to the already packed bar.

'He's such a great guy – you are so lucky,' Sophy said, watching Daz walk away.

'I know,' Mel said softly, the guilt sitting hard in her chest. Not only had she been the instigator in Jeff and Sophy splitting up, she also already had the near perfect relationship.

'It's okay – don't be sorry or anything,' Sophy said, downing her lemonade.

'Well, you know, Sophy, you're still so young, you *will* meet someone else,' Mel said, wondering if Sophy might finally open up and disclose what Mel was strongly suspecting.

'Aaaah, I dunno,' Sophy said.

'You will, for sure,' said Aisha, who was on her second glass of wine and trying to pace herself. 'You must get men checking you out on Instagram?' Aisha said.

'Oh crikey, yes, but that's not the way forward, is it?'

'Oh no, but I just meant that there are men out there who are interested.'

'Yes, I suppose, one or two.'

'One or two? Is there someone you have in the pipeline?' Mel quipped.

'No, nothing like that,' Sophy said.

'Well, like we said, we will want to meet him immediately when you do find him,' Mel said.

Sophy seemed to blush, and even in the dim lighting Mel was sure she had just seen her cheeks flush pink. She made a mental note to pursue that line of conversation another day, because if there was one thing that Sophy deserved more than anything, it was a good man that would make her happy.

Daz came back with the drinks and the women toasted Mel's performance. Robbie came over, having just done the obligatory circuit of the bar, receiving praise and adoration from the audience as though it were he who had just performed on stage. Robbie put his arms around Mel's shoulders and squeezed her tightly.

'I am so proud of my shining star!' he said and then, as quickly as he arrived, he was summoned away by a group dressed in drag that had just arrived. 'Darlings!' Robbie called as he glided over to them.

Mel looked around the room, half expecting to see Jeff make an appearance. It wouldn't have surprised her if he had. But there had been no sight of him, and Mel was thankful. She knew there was a possibility that she may see Jeff again if he ever got his shit together and started taking Max regularly, but since Sophy had left him several weeks ago now, he had seen Max twice and only for a few hours each time and both times at Wendy's house. If she had never met Sophy, Jeff would have been living in her mind forever. But he had received the ultimate loss. He had lost a beautiful family. He may not realise it yet, but one day, probably in a few years from now, Jeff Haddon would look back on his life and regret not taking better care of Sophy and Max. Mel could not say the same for his predatory ways, but one thing was for sure, she knew Max would grow up to be a hundred times the man that Jeff was.

* * *

3.01 a.m. – Aisha: Is anyone tired? I'm so tired.

3.12 a.m. – Sophy: I'm up. Have our babies officially synced waking up times?

3.12 a.m. – Aisha: We'll be syncing our periods next.

3.13 a.m. Sophy: Oh, I'm not looking forward to getting them again when the breastfeeding stops.

3.14 a.m. – Aisha: I think Skylar must be asleep.

3.15 a.m. – Sophy: I know, we never know when we'll get a bit of Mel on here.

3.15 a.m. – Aisha: Oh no, Otis has thrown up.

3.16 a.m. – Sophy: OMG, so has Max! They've synced their sick as well.

29

AISHA

'Charley, this is my, um, my dad, Jon.'

Aisha watched as Jon stepped confidently towards Charley and went in for a firm handshake, he stepped back with a bit of a swagger and looked around the lounge.

'It's a nice gaff you girls keep here,' Jon said, nodding approvingly.

'Thanks, Jon. I can't take much credit for it – it's Aisha who did all the decorating,' Charley said, giving Aisha's shoulder a squeeze.

'Ah well, she's got her mum's touch there,' Jon said. 'She loved to paint those walls at the house you all lived in.'

'I remember they were always very bright. They still are.'

'Are they now? Well, some things just stay the same, I suppose,' Jon said with a hint of melancholy in his voice. Charley and Aisha exchanged a quick look. Aisha was unsure whether she should be feeling sorry for Jon or still harbouring some resentment. Really, all she felt was nothing. Which was probably best, as that way she could start from a blank canvas.

'Shall I take your coat?' Charley said, breaking the sentimental moment in half. Jon still had his green parka zipped up to his neck.

'Oh yeah, this old thing. It's like a second skin to me.' He unzipped it and handed the coat to Charley, who went and hung it in the hallway.

Aisha and Jon were left looking at each other. Aisha put her hands in her back pockets and smiled awkwardly. This was the third time she had been with her dad since she had met him. It was all still so novel, and at times she was never quite sure what to say, or how to act around him.

'Tea smells lovely.' Jon pronounced 'lovely' *love-lee,* and with that classic Midlands tone that went up at the end. Aisha couldn't help but smile.

'What?' Jon smirked. 'You are laughing at your old dad?'

Aisha shook her head. 'I just like listening to your accent.'

'Ahh, can't beat the Brummies, eh?'

'I hope you like cottage pie – we went for something a bit neutral.'

'Keeping it old school. Like it. Hope there's some Angel Delight for afters!' Jon let out a loud laugh and shunted his neck back and forth. He could take some getting used to, Aisha thought, what with some of his mannerisms being a bit out there. She wondered if she would have felt this way if she had known him all this time?

Aisha began walking to the kitchen and motioned for Jon to follow. Charley was already there, finishing setting the table.

'Nice kitchen.' Jon nodded his head again in approval as he looked around.

'Well, this one Aisha can't take credit for. It was already here when we moved in.' Charley pulled out a chair and motioned for Jon to sit. Jon slid into the seat and laid his elbows on the table and rubbed his hands together. It was then Aisha realised he was nervous. He gave off this air of confidence and swagger, but he looked just like a little boy sat up at the table, and Aisha felt a pang in her heart.

'Are the boys sleeping?' Jon asked, rubbing at his neck – another sure sign that he was nervous.

'Yes, they have a nap about five o'clock, and then we feed them and play with them and bathe them and then get them down about eight o'clock. We get a bit of the evening together then, don't we, babes?' Charley smiled.

'Sounds like a lovely life. Lifted and laid,' Jon said.

'Well, quite. The life of a baby, hey?' Charley continued, and Aisha was so glad that she was here and that they were doing this together. Charley had a real knack for keeping conversations going, whereas ever since Aisha had left the restaurant, she would sometimes forget how to make small talk.

'We can enjoy our dinner in peace, and then you can have a cuddle with them,' Aisha said. 'If you want to that is?'

'I would love to. Think I still have the knack after all these years,' Jon said.

'It's like riding a bike, Jon,' Charley said.

'Yeah well, I fell off once, didn't I? It's taken me a while to get back in the saddle.' Jon sounded despondent again.

'But you're here now.' Charley put the cottage pie in the middle of the table and sat down opposite Jon. 'And there is only now. No point looking backwards, is there, Aisha?'

Aisha slid into the seat next to Jon and shook her head. 'No, no, not at all. We're glad to have you.'

Charley dug the serving spoon into the pie and ladled a large portion onto Jon's plate. It was fair to say he seemed like the sort of chap who would never turn down a decent plate of food and would probably be accepting second helpings as well.

Charley asked what everyone would like to drink, and Jon accepted a beer and Charley poured two glasses of red wine.

'Well, cheers, everybody. It's nice to have you—' Charley was cut off by the sound of rapping at the front door. There was only one person who knocked like that.

Charley was the one to rise, and her chair scraped on the tiled kitchen floor as she did. 'Well, I guess we'd better find out who that is.'

Aisha went to speak but didn't say anything.

'Classic timing, whoever it is!' Jon said, taking his first mouthful of food. 'Best not let it get cold,' he said into his plate.

Aisha heard the distant, high-pitched sound of Charley greeting a familiar hello. She could hear the muffled sounds of two voices coming along the hallway, and then just before they arrived at the kitchen, Aisha recognised the voice of her mother.

'Martina's here,' Charley said overenthusiastically and with an inane grin on her face. She looked at Aisha for some explanation or some sign as to what she should do next. Aisha felt a flutter of panic. This was not like Martina to just drop in at dinner time uninvited. But then Aisha cast her mind back to two days ago when she was at her mum's Brixton house and she had mentioned that Jon was coming over on Wednesday night for dinner. Martina had seemed nonchalant at the information, but now Aisha realised that this 'unplanned' visit was anything but. Aisha wasn't sure what her mother's game was, but she wasn't going to let her drive a wedge between her and her dad again. She had already lost twenty years.

'Oh wow. Martina.' Jon stood up as he almost choked on his dinner. 'How are you, girl?' He walked over to Martina and leant in for a kiss. Martina stood dead still, but turned her cheek ever so slightly to receive the kiss. As Jon stepped away, with his hands rubbing up and down his stubble, looking Martina up and down,

Aisha glimpsed something sparkly about Martina's face. Aisha inched forward to get a better look, and there it was, a smattering of light blue eye shadow across Martina's lids. As Aisha continued to look at Martina, she noticed that her mum was wearing her good jeans and a rainbow retro-style T-shirt that looked like something she would have picked up from Camden Market.

Aisha quickly pieced it all together and then almost let out a gasp as it became clear to her. Had her mother come here to claim back her man?

* * *

Charley and Aisha stood in the kitchen doing the dishes. Every now and again, they would hear Martina let out a loud yelp of laughter, followed by the deep tone of Jon's voice. Aisha silently washed the cottage-pie dish, adding some extra elbow grease whenever she heard her mother laughing, so when she came to washing the delicate wine glasses, she took with her the brute force she had used on the oven dish and cracked one clean in half.

'Shit!' Aisha said, and when she pulled her hand out of the washing-up bowl, blood was dripping down her index finger. It was the first word Aisha had said since Martina and Jon left the table after dinner, each holding a twin – who had woken halfway through dinner as if they didn't wish to miss the reunion of their estranged grandparents –and had been camped out in the lounge with bottles and nappies. Aisha's profanity rang out around the stark kitchen. Charley was at her side with a wad of kitchen roll.

'Hold that on it.' Charley moved over to a drawer where they kept everything that wasn't crockery or cutlery, and most things got thrown in there when Aisha was on one of her mad tidying sprees. Charley was back at her side with a plaster. As she stuck it over the cut, she said quietly, 'So, do you think we should go in yet?'

'I don't know,' Aisha said, grumpily.

'Oh, come on, Aisha. It's sweet. I bet they're in there now reminiscing.' Charley gave Aisha's finger a little peck. 'There you go, boo boo, all better.'

Aisha didn't smile. She was royally pissed off, but she couldn't say so, otherwise she would appear churlish. But then Jon had been here having dinner with her, and Martina had, well, she had basically barged in. Aisha hadn't had any contact with her own father for twenty years, and Martina had barely been able to bring herself to mention him over the years. Now here she was, all glammed up and laughing as though not a minute had passed.

'I mean, it's kind of romantic, wouldn't you say?' Charley put her arms around Aisha's waist and brought her closer to her. 'All these years later and they have so much to say to one another.'

Aisha dared not say that she had been thinking the exact same thing. She wanted to stay pissed off with her mother. Meeting with her father after so many years had been a shock, and Aisha was still trying to deal with that bombshell.

'I think,' Charley said, swaying her hips against Aisha's, 'that your mum never stopped loving him. Things were tough for her back then with five of you, but I don't think she ever fell out of love with him. I think she just put you lot first. Imagine how different your life would have been if Jon had stuck around? They were, what, twenty when they got together and started having kids? That's ten years younger than you, Aisha! Maybe now is their time?'

Aisha felt like the words were all coming at her too fast. She'd barely had time to get used to having a dad, and now she was supposed to get used to a mum and a dad, who were together.

'I don't know, Charley. It all feels so weird.'

'I know, I know,' Charley said soothingly, as though she were talking to one of the twins. 'There's been a lot of changes in your life recently. But maybe this could be a good thing? Two grandparents to babysit is better than one, and they are both still young enough to run around with the boys. Let's face it, we're gonna need all the help we can get,' Charley said with a nervous laugh, and Aisha couldn't help but smile.

'I know, it takes a village to raise a child, right?'

'Exactly.' Charley laid her lips softly on Aisha's and then nuzzled into her neck.

'Oh sorry, I came to get another ounce of milk for Otis – he's a hungry one, that one!' Martina scooted past Charley and Aisha to the kitchen side and poured some cooled boiled water into a fresh bottle. Aisha released herself from Charley's arms and went over to Martina's side. She reached up and took down the formula milk powder and opened the box and pushed it towards Martina.

'Thanks, Mum,' Aisha said quietly, and Martina laid her hand briefly on hers, a mere moment that said more than the two women could ever have articulated with words.

30

SOPHY

Sophy opened the door, and there, on the other side, stood Niall. Her stomach had been doing somersaults all day in anticipation of his arrival, and now it seemed to finally settle.

'O'Connor Builders at your service, ma'am.' Niall did a funny little bow with one hand, his toolkit in the other, and Sophy felt her stomach flutter. How was it possible for this man to make her feel this way just by speaking?

Sophy did her usual enthusiastic laugh and stood back to let him in.

'Ooo, this is nice,' Niall said as he walked along the hallway.

'You don't have to say that.' Sophy stopped behind him in the doorway to the lounge.

Max was sat up in his bouncing chair in the middle of the floor.

'And there's the wee man.' Niall bent down next to Max. 'Look at him sitting up now.'

'Well, with the help of his chair – he can't sit up alone just yet.'

'Ah, well, give him time. He's getting there.'

'I know.' Sophy leant on the door frame. 'I can't believe five months has gone so fast. It was literally a minute ago when I was giving birth.' Sophy realised what she'd said and then said, 'Sorry, I'm sure you didn't want to hear that.' She felt the heat rising in her cheeks. 'And I'm sorry I didn't call before, you know when you first offered. It's just been a bit hectic, what with the move and sorting things out with Jeff. Pictures were sort of the last thing on my mind. Well, not the last thing, I mean, I did think about you, I just wanted to make sure... I don't know what I'm trying to say, actually.'

Niall turned and smiled a wholesome smile, and Sophy felt another piece of her heart melt away.

He stood up and walked over to her, and stopped a mere few feet away.

'Listen, I understand. Life is full of complications. But art is important. You made a good decision to get these beauties up. Now where would madam like this one?' Niall touched the largest picture that was leaning between the wall and the sofa.

'Well, I was thinking one just above the fireplace there, and then the other three in the hallway?'

'No problem.' Niall opened his toolbox and began pulling out screws and a hammer and a power drill.

Sophy pulled Max closer to the sofa and sat down, wondering what it was exactly about a man with such an extensive toolbox that made her feel all unnecessary. Niall worked away quietly, measuring the space either side of the fireplace to get the exact central point, he took a pencil from his pocket and made a small mark on the wall before he began drilling a small hole, then putting in the Rawlplug and screw.

Then he turned around, and Sophy, who had been happily watching him all that time, looked at him.

'What?' she said.

'I'm glad this is the height of entertainment for you, but I'd be glad of a hot beverage.'

'Oh, yes. Sorry, it's just I'm not used to seeing men do manly things.'

'Oh this? This isn't that manly; I have many manlier skills up my sleeve.'

Sophy let out a giggle. 'Oh, is that right?'

Niall stood down from his small stepladder and went over to where Sophy was sitting on the sofa. Sophy felt her breath catch in her throat as Niall bent down and towards her with his eyes on hers. He put his hand out and retrieved the large picture that was leaning against the side of the sofa. Then he walked casually back to the fireplace without saying a word. Sophy watched him with her heart almost in her mouth, then she slowed it down with a few silent long, deep breaths. What was that? Their faces had been almost touching. Dear god, she couldn't deny it any longer. She had it bad for Niall O'Connor.

* * *

Sophy stood in the hallway and admired the fantastic job Niall had done.

'Oh, my goodness, I love them. Thank you. It's so nice to finally see them on the wall.'

Niall nodded. 'I like them too. And a local artist, you say?'

'Yes, I like to support local and small businesses.'

'Well, me fees are quite low, and you's no need to worry about a tip.'

Sophy looked at Niall and turned to go to the kitchen where her bag and purse were. 'Of course, I'll just—'

'Hey, Sophy.' Niall reached out and grabbed her arm and half pulled her back. Sophy felt her insides melt at the way he spoke her name. Niall still held onto her arm.

'I was joking. It's free. I'd do anything for you.' His voice quietened to almost a whisper, and Sophy dropped her arm down and found her hand slipped easily into his. Niall held it loosely, his thumb rubbing gently on her palm. Sophy hadn't known such a small action could make her stomach flutter so intensely. Niall looked at her. A moment of space and time opened up between them. Sophy could sense his hesitation, his silence questioning, 'Is this okay?' She tentatively took one step forward and placed her other hand around Niall's waist. She heard him release a breath as though he had been holding it all that time, then finally, slowly and gently, Niall pulled Sophy into his arms, leant his head down and kissed her.

31

MEL

Mel bobbed her foot on the baby bouncer as Sky clutched the teething ring. How was it possible that her baby girl had teeth already? Sky's cheeks were a soft pink, and her chin was a dribbly mess. Across the table sat Ksenia, a cup of coffee in front of her. Black, no sugar. This had become hers and Ksenia usual routine most days after she had finished her two-hour marathon stint around the house before she moved onto a client two streets away.

'What is it about cleaning that you love so much?' Mel asked.

Ksenia pulled her mouth down 'It's predictable. Mess always comes back. I will never be out of job as cleaner.'

'That is true. Mess is messy. I hate mess, but I hate to clean up.'

'I know. You like a pig – hair in sink, clothes on floor. But I do job and make it go away.'

'Until next time.'

'Yes.' Ksenia slurped her coffee loudly. 'How old is your baby now?'

'She's almost seven months.'

'You have more babies?'

'Christ no. I'm nearly forty-four.'

Ksenia took a slurp of her coffee and nearly spat it out. 'You? You look thirty, maybe thirty-five!'

'Thank you. Although I'm not sure how much longer I'll get away with looking that young.'

'Maybe it because you do no cleaning. I do cleaning and I look old.'

Mel laughed loudly. 'You don't. You look great. Anyway—' Mel stood up and took an envelope from the kitchen side '—here're your wages and a little extra. Daz, me and the kids are off on a little break, so we want you to take one too. I've paid you for the time we're away.'

'You pay me for not working?' Ksenia looked horrified.

'Yes, Ksenia – it's called holiday pay.'

Ksenia shook her head but took the envelope and stuffed it into the top of her leggings.

'Don't you carry a bag?' Mel asked.

'Yes, but no robber dare touch me down here.' Pointed to her crotch. She stood up and picked up her phone and car keys and headed for the front door.

'Thanks, Ksenia. See you in a week's time.'

* * *

'We thought you weren't coming,' Aisha said at the door. Mel was sweating in places she didn't even know she could sweat.

'I wouldn't miss this for the world.' She walked down Aisha's hallway and to the basement door. 'I take it we're down here?'

'Yep, all ready and waiting,' Aisha said.

'Brilliant. I've always wanted to do a podcast. But I never thought I would know what to do one about,' Mel said.

'Well, you don't have to worry about that now, do you?' Aisha said as Mel arrived at the bottom of the stairs and Sophy stood to greet her. 'Oh, you came,' Sophy said sweetly. Mel noticed there was a glow about Sophy, a sparkle in her eyes that hadn't been there a week ago. She kissed Sophy on the cheek.'

'You look very well, my love,' Mel said knowingly. 'And why did everyone think I wouldn't come?' Mel said. 'Hi, Charley.' She went over and gave Charley a kiss on the cheek.

'Hi, Mel, you all set?' Charley said, looking professional as she fiddled with some buttons.

'Ready as I'll ever be,' Mel said, dropping her handbag in the corner of the room.

'I can't quite believe this is happening,' Sophy said, picking Max up off the floor where she had laid him to take a flat lay.

'It was all Charley's idea,' Aisha gushed and put her arm on Charley's shoulder.

Charley kissed her full on the lips.

'Well, I just thought I'm down here with all this recording equipment and jingle music, and you girls are chatting away at 3 a.m., talking about babies and sleepless nights and all the rest of it, so I figured why not just get it on a podcast?' Charley said as she fiddled with her complex-looking mixing station.

'Oh, girls,' Sophy said 'I haven't told you the best bit! That nutritional drink company I was working with are starting a range of baby foods and have agreed to sponsor the show!'

'So that means we get paid?' Aisha asked brightly.

'Not millions, but it's a start!' Sophy said excitedly.

'And we're still happy with the name of the podcast?' Mel asked.

'The 3 a.m. Shattered Mums' Club!' Aisha and Sophy called out in unison.

'What else could it possibly be?' Sophy said grinning from ear to ear.

* * *

2.43 a.m. – Sophy: Okay. I hope you're both up, I know some of the babies are sleeping a bit better so I'm taking a chance here. You were right. There is someone I have my eye on. But it feels weird because it is so soon after Jeff and I'm a new mum and my fanny is still in tatters and I can barely stay awake to watch an entire episode of *Line of Duty* and my breasts are huge milking machines.

2.56 a.m. – Mel: OMG OMG OMG I knew it, I knew it, I knew it. When I saw you today in the basement, you were literally glowing.

2.57 a.m. – Sophy: I know, sorry for not saying something earlier. I have been trying to deny it to myself since, well, since the very day I met him, actually.

2.58 a.m. – Mel: This is epic. I need to know all the details. Who is he? Oh, hang on, I think I can guess. It's not that fit builder you were always harping on about, is it?

2.59 a.m. – Sophy: 😶

3.00 a.m. – Mel: – Christ the lord. Fiiiiiiiiit!

3.01 a.m. – Sophy: 🙂

3.01 a.m. – Mel: Okay, now's not the time to discuss this, but I suggest a play date in the park ASAP for a debrief. Aisha, are you with us?

4.19 a.m. – Aisha: Oh my goodness, sorry I'm late in tonight. Boys both slept a full five hours. I feel like a new woman! This is the best news, Sophy. I couldn't be happier. Tell us everything.

32

AISHA

Aisha finished playing *The 3 a.m. Shattered Mums' Club* podcast to Martina, who shook her head in disbelief.

'Well, my goodness, if I had spoken them words on the radio when I was your age, I don't know what people would have thought.'

'It doesn't go on the radio, Mum, it's a podcast. You listen to it on your iPhone or tablet. You can pause it or fast-forward it.'

'I know I'd be fast-forwarding all that chatter 'bout minnies.'

Aisha laughed. 'It's just a vagina, Mum – it's where we all come from.'

'I know, girl, but to keep yappin' 'bout it on the, um—' she pointed at Aisha's phone, which was sat between them on the table, a plate of ginger biscuits parked close to her elbow '—that thing.'

'It's fun. I enjoyed it. It's a bit like therapy, actually.'

'Well, so long as you happy and those blues been chased away.'

'I'm getting there, Mum. It's not always easy. But I'll get there.'

'And now you off to see that father of yours.'

'I'm meeting Jon, yes, at the park. He's staying here tonight.' Aisha eyed Martina carefully.

'Well, you make sure you make his coffee good and hot in the morning. My goodness that man moaned if his coffee was not scolding the roof of his mouth off.'

Aisha nodded. 'Hot coffee. Okay. Noted.'

Martina stood up and put her arms out to Aisha. The open invitations for hugs had become more and more recently.

'And has Jon said anything about moving back here, to you, I mean?'

'We speaking 'bout things. I'll keep you updated, girl. We taking it slowly, I think is the expression.' And Martina laughed a lovely loud laugh that made Aisha feel warm inside.

33

SOPHY

One month later

'Well, hello there, everyone, and welcome to my first vlog from my new Instagram account, The 3 a.m. Shattered Mums' Club! Thank you to each and every one of you for supporting me on ThisGirlThisBody and for following me over to this account. You can expect an array of content here, and one thing's for sure, no subject is off limits! Most of all, what I hope for you all and what I hope to help you achieve, is to form your own 3 a.m. Shattered Mums' Club, because let's face it, whoever you are, feeding your babies at those hazy hours of the morning, there is nothing wrong with reaching out. I was lucky enough to meet two wonderful women earlier this year and I can honestly say that they have altered my life, and, well, without sounding too dramatic, I don't think I can live without them. Oh, and they just happen to be here now! I've been so excited to introduce you to

the other two founding members of The 3 a.m. Shattered Mums'
Club, Mel and Aisha – come on in!'

* * *

2.25 a.m. – Sophy: Anyone out there?

2.26 a.m. – Mel: I am. I've put on *Breaking Bad*, first series, just
started. I'm sure Sky is silently reprimanding me. She's been awake for
half an hour. Bloody teeth again.

2.26 a.m. – Sophy: Oh well, you have to do what you have to do.

2.27 a.m. – Mel: Why aren't you going back to sleep? Is Niall
"sleeping over"?

2.28 a.m. – Sophy: No. You know we're not there yet. We're taking
things nice and slow. It's the best feeling ever.

2.28 a.m. – Mel: Oh god, if I could go back and have that new-rela-
tionship feeling again, I'd pay good money for it. It's the best – I wish
you could bottle it.

2.29 a.m. – Aisha: Hey, I'm here. Both twins are awake. I am feeding
two babies and texting!

2.30 a.m. – Mel: Hey, Aisha. Seriously though, Sophy, you've bagged
an absolute diamond there.

2.31 a.m. – Aisha: We're so happy for you.

2.33 a.m. – Mel: Oh my god, it looks like Sky is asleep. I should go
back to bed, but I really want to know how they're going to dispose of
this body.

2.34 a.m. – Aisha: I can't text and feed and change poopy nappies, so
see you in a bit.

2.34 a.m. – Sophy: Thanks, girls. I'm happy.

2.35 a.m. – Mel: We know – you haven't stopped grinning for a month.

236 a.m. – Sophy: Just think, if I hadn't met you lot, I would probably
still be miserable and living with Jeff.

2.37 a.m. – Mel: We're so glad you're not. Oh shit, she's awake again. Right, I'm off to walk the length and breadth of the house.

2.38 a.m. – Sophy: Best of British. We're here for you.

ACKNOWLEDGMENTS

Firstly, I'd like to thank Amanda, Nia, Emily and all the Boldwood team for taking a chance on me with this book, which is of course very different from the last six books I have written for them. I have wanted to write about my experience of new motherhood ever since my eye stopped twitching long enough to put pen to paper. But every time that happened, another baby came along. But now I am officially done with giving birth and my nights are my own again. During the lockdowns, I took the opportunity to scribble down a rough draft, which turned out not half bad. A few edits later, a conversation with my editor and the book suddenly had a life.

There is so much of me in all three of the girls: Sophy, Aisha and Mel. New motherhood is a crazy, chaotic, hormonal-fuelled ride that seems to go on forever when you're on it, and occasionally you might cry out that you would like it to stop so you can get off, but then suddenly it is over and you're seeing the world a little clearer. But those months and sometimes years when things are hazy and muddled can often be the loneliest. Especially during those night feeds when you're sort of lost in no-mammas land. Is it night? Is it day? Should I eat? I wish I'd had the support of like-minded women around me during those lonelier months and so creating these characters was still as important to me now, even though those days are behind me. I wanted to create a scenario where women who were all struggling on different levels could all connect at a time of the day that can often be the most stressful and depressing when you feel it is just you and your baby.

Thank you to every one of the hardworking team at Boldwood for helping with the production of *The 3 a.m. Shattered Mums' Club*. To Rebecca Millar and Emily Ruston for your eagle eyes and excellent editorial advice.

Thank you once again to you, the reader, for picking up this book and giving it a go. I hope you found something or someone that you could connect with.

Nina x

MORE FROM NINA MANNING

We hope you enjoyed reading *The 3 a.m. Shattered Mums' Club*. If you did, please leave a review.

If you'd like to gift a copy, this book is also available as an ebook, digital audio download and audiobook CD.

Sign up to Nina Manning's mailing list for news, competitions and updates on future books.

http://bit.ly/NinaManningNewsletter

ABOUT THE AUTHOR

Nina Manning studied psychology and was a restaurant-owner and private chef (including to members of the royal family). She is the founder and co-host of Sniffing The Pages, a book review podcast.

Visit Nina's website:
https://www.ninamanningauthor.com/

Follow Nina on social media:

twitter.com/ninamanning78
instagram.com/ninamanning_author
facebook.com/ninamanningauthor1
bookbub.com/authors/nina-manning

Boldwood

Boldwood Books is an award-winning fiction publishing company seeking out the best stories from around the world.

Find out more at www.boldwoodbooks.com

Join our reader community for brilliant books, competitions and offers!

Follow us
@BoldwoodBooks
@BookandTonic

Sign up to our weekly deals newsletter

https://bit.ly/BoldwoodBNewsletter

1985
1978
——
66

Lightning Source UK Ltd.
Milton Keynes UK
UKHW040617010323
417849UK00004B/211

9 781804 265642